Praise for *On a Summer Tide*

"Fans of Suzanne Woods Fisher will love this story of three sisters coming together on a rugged Maine island to refurbish a camp. Even as their tumultuous lives create havoc, romance blooms between one of the sisters and a handsome lumberjack/teacher. Readers will enjoy watching the island and camp take shape even as the sisters' own lives undergo a renovation of the everlasting kind. *On a Summer Tide* is an enduring tale of love and restoration."

Denise Hunter, bestselling author of *On Magnolia Lane*

"Suzanne Woods Fisher may be best known for her Amish stories, but this contemporary romance is a charmer. *On a Summer Tide* is filled with memorable characters, gorgeous Maine scenery, and plenty of family drama. I can't wait to visit Three Sisters Island again!"

Irene Hannon, bestselling author of the beloved Hope Harbor series

"Fisher creates a vibrant cast of charming, plucky characters set on redefining themselves."

Publishers Weekly

"*On a Summer Tide* by Suzanne Woods Fisher is full of surprises. . . . It was heartfelt and deep. . . . Suzanne Woods Fisher made me feel like I was there for it all."

Urban Lit Magazine

"Suzanne Woods Fisher, well known for her Amish and inspirational fiction, offers a contemporary novel of a family rebuilding their connection, adding a touch of suspense and just enough spirituality to make this a heartwarming read."

New York Journal of Books

On a Coastal Breeze

Novels by Suzanne Woods Fisher

LANCASTER COUNTY SECRETS

The Choice

The Waiting

The Search

SEASONS OF STONEY RIDGE

The Keeper

The Haven

The Lesson

THE INN AT EAGLE HILL

The Letters

The Calling

The Revealing

THE BISHOP'S FAMILY

The Imposter

The Quieting

The Devoted

THE DEACON'S FAMILY

Mending Fences

Stitches in Time

Two Steps Forward

THREE SISTERS ISLAND

On a Summer Tide

On a Coastal Breeze

On a Coastal Breeze

SUZANNE WOODS FISHER

Revell

a division of Baker Publishing Group
Grand Rapids, Michigan

© 2020 by Suzanne Woods Fisher

Published by Revell
a division of Baker Publishing Group
PO Box 6287, Grand Rapids, MI 49516-6287
www.revellbooks.com

Printed in the United States of America

Library of Congress Cataloging-in-Publication Data
Names: Fisher, Suzanne Woods, author.
Title: On a coastal breeze / Suzanne Woods Fisher.
Description: Grand Rapids, Michigan : Revell, a division of Baker Publishing
    Group, [2020] | Series: Three sisters island
Identifiers: LCCN 2019046546 | ISBN 9780800734992 (paperback)
Classification: LCC PS3606.I78 O48 2020 | DDC 813/.6—dc23
LC record available at https://lccn.loc.gov/2019046546

ISBN 978-0-8007-3864-8 (casebound)

Maddie's favorite Scripture verse is Psalm 138:8, which was taken from the Holy Bible: International Standard Version®. Copyright © 1996-forever by The ISV Foundation. ALL RIGHTS RESERVED INTERNATIONALLY. Used by permission.

Some Scripture quotations, whether quoted or paraphrased, are from the Holy Bible, New International Version®. NIV®. Copyright © 1973, 1978, 1984, 2011 by Biblica, Inc.™ Used by permission of Zondervan. All rights reserved worldwide. www.zondervan.com. The "NIV" and "New International Version" are trademarks registered in the United States Patent and Trademark Office by Biblica, Inc.™

Some Scripture quotations, whether quoted or paraphrased, are from the New King James Version®. Copyright © 1982 by Thomas Nelson. Used by permission. All rights reserved.

Some Scripture quotations, whether quoted or paraphrased, are from the Revised Standard Version of the Bible, copyright 1946, 1952 [2nd edition, 1971] National Council of the Churches of Christ in the United States of America. Used by permission. All rights reserved worldwide.

This book is a work of fiction. Names, characters, places, and incidents are the product of the author's imagination or are used fictitiously. Any resemblance to actual events, locales, or persons, living or dead, is coincidental.

Published in association with Joyce Hart of the Hartline Literary Agency, LLC.

20 21 22 23 24 25 26   7 6 5 4 3 2 1

Cast of Characters

Paul Grayson (age 60)—retired sports announcer, father of Cam, Maddie, Blaine; grandfather of Cooper

Camden Grayson (age 30)—eldest daughter of Paul, adoptive mother of Cooper, creating a self-sufficient, renewable energy program for Three Sisters Island

Madison Grayson (age 26)—middle daughter of Paul, recently certified as a marriage and family therapist; setting up a counseling practice on Three Sisters Island

Blaine Grayson (age 20)—youngest daughter of Paul, attends culinary school

Cooper Grayson (age 8)—adopted son of Camden Grayson

Rick O'Shea (age 27)—new pastor of the small church on Three Sisters Island that has been meeting in the Baggett & Taggett store for the last few years

Artie Lotosky (age 22)—college friend of Blaine

Bob Lotosky (age 50-ish)—Artie's dad, a potato farmer from Aroostook County, Maine

Peg Legg (won't reveal her age)—runs the Lunch Counter, mayor of Three Sisters Island (though it's officially too small for a mayor)

Seth Walker (age 30)—schoolteacher at Three Sisters Island

Porter and Peter Phinney (in their 20s)—sons of (formerly) prominent selectman Baxtor Phinney, serving jail time for lobster thievery

Captain Ed (ageless)—runs the Never Late Ferry between Mount Desert and Three Sisters Island

Tillie (somewhere in her 50s)—the übervolunteer church secretary

Maeve O'Shea (60s)—Rick O'Shea's awesome mother

One

JUST BEFORE MADDIE UNLOCKED THE DOOR to her office, she straightened the name plaque on the wall: MADISON GRAYSON, MARRIAGE AND FAMILY THERAPIST.

Her career was finally underway. Today was the starting day of her first real job, and she actually had clients. An engaged couple, who had made an appointment on the very day Captain Ed helped hang her shingle.

She opened the door and walked inside, smiling. The space she had rented was in the basement of an old house on First Street, just around the corner from the Lunch Counter, the hub of Three Sisters Island. Peg Legg owned and ran the diner, and advised Maddie not to rent space right on Main Street. "You won't get any customers if they think folks see them coming and going from the shrink's office."

Maddie bristled at being called a shrink, and her clients were not customers, but she was grateful for Peg's local savvy. The ways of locals were still new to her despite living on the island this past year. She doubted she'd ever truly understand them, but she hoped she could shed light on the problems in their lives. Problems, she understood.

She flipped on the light and smiled. On her desk was a bouquet of a dozen red roses, her favorite, and a little card.

Good luck today. Love, Cam and Cooper, Blaine, and Dad

This was Dad's doing. He was over-the-moon pleased that she'd completed the hours required to be fully licensed. He really needn't have worried about her. Maddie finished what she started, even if it took a little longer than expected. Blaine was the daughter he should save his worry for.

She opened a casement window to let in fresh air, for the May morning was unseasonably warm. Her gaze swept the room, looking for any pillow that needed puffing or wall frames of her diplomas that were slightly askew, but she couldn't see anything to improve. In fact, it couldn't be more perfect. It wasn't large, but she didn't need much space. Just privacy.

Cam had helped her decorate the basement and turn it into a professional office. For once, her older sister hadn't overridden Maddie's preferences. Instead of the couch and desk that Cam had picked out, as well as an accent wall of a boldly patterned wallpaper, she deferred to Maddie's choices. Comfortable upholstered swiveling armchairs instead of a couch. A palette of subdued colors for paint and fabrics—cool tones with warm pops—that invited one to relax, to linger. Not too feminine, not too masculine. Against the back wall was a tiny service kitchen with an expensive coffee machine that made single coffees. Customized coffee. Maddie wanted everything here to tell a client she respected their individuality.

She heard the stomping sounds of someone up above, someone

on the portly side, and assumed they belonged to Tillie, the church secretary, who took her volunteer job very seriously.

The spacious house had been rented to the tiny little church on Three Sisters Island, a small fellowship that had finally found a pastor who was willing to move to an island on the edge of the world for a pittance of a salary. The house would serve as his living quarters, plus his office, and it was near the building they could use on Sunday mornings—a huge upgrade from meeting in the Baggett and Taggett shop down the street. It was hard to sing worship songs about creation when a moose head on the wall was staring down at you. Accusingly.

She tried to remember what Seth had said when he recruited the new pastor. Richard Something-or-other. She squeezed her eyes shut. He was freshly out of the military. He loved Jesus and extreme sports, in that order. Oh, and he had tattoos. That's all she could remember. She'd been so distracted with starting her practice that she hadn't paid much attention. She had a lot of faith in Seth Walker's judgment. He had started the little church a few years ago when he became the island's schoolteacher, so he knew what kind of a pastor would best fit the role.

Maddie took out a blank notepad and a periwinkle blue Flair pen, then applied fresh lipstick, straightened her skirt, said a little prayer, and waited for her clients to arrive. And waited.

Outside the open casement window, she heard a commotion of excited shouts and footsteps pound down the street. Curious, she left her office and went to the street to see what was causing the fuss. She stood at the top of Main Street and shielded her eyes from the bright morning sun. Behind her came the *stomp-stomp* of Tillie's Bean boots, which stopped abruptly as she stood right beside Maddie. "Oh my word," she said. "He said he was going to parachute in today, but I didn't think he meant literally."

There, floating down from the sky, right in front of Boon Dock, was a brightly colored parachute with a man dangling underneath. "Tillie, is that our new pastor?"

"Indeed it is."

"What's his name again?"

"Richard O'Shea."

What? "Did you say O'Shea?" No! *Oh no*. She jerked her head down. "Not . . . no, it couldn't be . . ." Her mind raced back to the meeting. She'd come in late from a class and all she'd heard was the church had unanimously voted in a pastor named Richard. "Does he happen to go by the name of Ricky?"

"No."

Maddie blew out a puff of air. *Phew*. It couldn't be the same guy. No way. It couldn't possibly be the same Ricky with whom she grew up. Not a chance.

"Rick, he calls himself."

A queasy roll started up in Maddie's stomach. *No, no, no, no, no*. How could this world be so big and yet so small?

Tillie patted her on her shoulder. "I'd better get down to the dock to greet our new pastor. And you'd better see to your customers. They got confused and came upstairs to the church office. I sent them down to wait in the basement."

Maddie gasped. No! This wasn't the way the morning was supposed to go. She should be in her office, waiting to welcome her clients. And Ricky O'Shea should remain far, far away—a distant, unpleasant, suppressed-if-not-forgotten memory. Like a root canal.

⌒

After dropping her eight-year-old son, Cooper, off at school, Camden Grayson stopped at the Lunch Counter to exchange hellos with Peg Legg, the diner's owner. Peg's round, merry face lit up when she spotted Cam coming in through the door, and she enveloped her in a bear hug before hurrying to fetch her a mug of hot coffee. No matter how busy the diner was, Peg would stop and give Cam a warm welcome.

Cam not only enjoyed Peg, she admired her. Peg was the one who, last August, when the last member of the Unitarian Church at the top of Main Street passed away and the church building was donated to the town, came up with the idea of using the empty church building for the school, moving it off Camp Kicking Moose's property and into town where it belonged. That one swift action brought great relief to her dad, as a school bus full of children arriving each morning wasn't mixing well with late-season vacationing campers.

Cam sat on a red stool at the counter, sipped a mug of very mediocre coffee, and reviewed details about a new government grant she'd found, making notes in the margins. All winter and spring, she'd been toiling away on lengthy grant applications—with the hope of making Three Sisters Island run entirely by renewable energy, thereby eliminating dependency on the extremely unreliable public utility grid.

If Cam's plan worked, Three Sisters Island would become completely self-sufficient with an off-the-grid electrical system powered by water, wind, and sun. It would be an economic boost to this little island that suffered from disruptive, inconvenient brownouts and blackouts throughout the year. Summer as well as winter, with windy storms that knocked out power and canceled the Never Late Ferry—its lifeline to Mount Desert Island, and then to the mainland.

Each grant took an enormous amount of time to complete, scads of paperwork. So far, she'd had ten rejections. She needed at least three grants to cover the scope of the project she had in mind. Even three might not be enough. The rejections worried her, but Cam turned worry into action: pursuing more grants. She was determined. Partly to help the island, partly to help her dad.

Camp Kicking Moose, her dad's passion, could be a year-round destination, but that would remain a distant dream if stable energy continued to be elusive. The winters in Maine were long and dark, bitter cold, and if the island was cut off from the mainland for more than a few weeks like it had been this past winter, it became nearly unbearable. It wasn't just the lack of supplies that started to wear thin, it was the isolation that everyone felt. Peg mentioned recently that the Alcoholics Anonymous group that met early in the mornings at the Lunch Counter doubled in size during the winters.

"Cam, come on out! You gotta see this."

Cam's head popped up when she heard Peg call to her. She hadn't noticed that the Lunch Counter had emptied out. A crowd had gathered on Main Street, staring up at the sky. Cam hesitated a few seconds, reluctant to be interrupted from her work, then set her pen on the notepad and hurried outside to see what everyone was looking at. There, high above them, floating down from the sky, was a man attached to a billowing parachute.

Standing next to Cam, Peg shook her head in disbelief, fists planted on her generous hips. "I thought I'd seen everything around here. This is a new one."

Cam tented her eyes to peer at the man who dangled underneath the colorful canopy. She thought it was a man, anyway. "Who do you think it is?"

Tillie marched past them. "He's our new pastor," she said over her shoulder, as if it were the most normal thing in the world for a person to drop out of the sky.

"How about that?" Peg said, clapping with delight. "Sent to us from Above!"

～⌒～

As the Never Late Ferry chugged toward Boon Dock at Three Sisters Island, Blaine Grayson watched a skydiver come in for a landing on the small ribbon of soft sand that bordered the harbor. Whoever was under that umbrella of bright colors seemed to know what he was doing—it was a pinpoint landing. She smiled as the man gracefully bounced feet first on the sand and immediately bolted forward to run up the beach, in such a practiced way that the parachute drifted down to the ground behind him, as gently as a leaf in the wind. He seemed oblivious to the many eyes watching him. Calmly, he unbuckled the harness around his chest and set about methodically folding up the canopy.

What must it be like to skydive out of an airplane? To stand at the open door and look down? That was exactly how Blaine felt with the announcement she needed to make to her family as she finished up her first year of culinary school. She knew she would have to be prudent about the time to tell them. There was no hurry, not until Cam and Seth's wedding date was set in stone. It was her father's reaction she dreaded in particular.

As she watched the skydiver trudge up the beach toward the gathered crowd on Main Street, she thought that she could actually imagine how it would feel to jump from the plane, trusting the parachute pack to unfold at just the right moment. Everything, all of her trust, rested on that one hope. A tiny little cord of hope. Of understanding.

Two

TRYING NOT TO APPEAR AS FLUSTERED AS SHE FELT, Maddie greeted her first clients, an engaged couple named Elena Miller and Mike Nelson. She offered them coffee which, to Maddie's relief, they declined. She highly doubted she could hand them a cup of coffee without her hands shaking. *Dear God*, she prayed silently, *settle my nerves. Help me to focus on these two people and not feel distracted by . . . me! Amen, amen, amen.*

Maddie took in a deep breath and let it out with a smile, feeling herself shift determinedly into counselor mode. "So . . . Mike, Elena. What brings you to my office today?" She tried to take a guess as she took in their appearance. What was their issue? What was the presenting problem? Mike was tall and lanky, bookish, somewhere in his late twenties. Maybe he'd had a job loss? A recent death in the family? Or maybe one of them was depressed. Not Elena, she decided. Petite, with a serene, calm demeanor. Definitely not depressed.

Elena and Mike looked at each other, and she gave him the nod to start it off. "We're planning to be married, but there is something that's been worrying us." He leaned forward. "We don't fight."

"You don't fight?"

Elena, as soft spoken as she looked, tried to clarify. "We never fight."

"Do you mean . . . actually have arguments? Or do you mean you have unresolved conflicts?"

"We don't have any conflicts," Mike said.

"None?"

"None," Elena said. "We agree on everything."

"Everything?" Maddie wrote on her yellow pad of paper: *possible avoidants.* "You're planning a wedding together, right?"

"Yes," Mike said. "August fifteenth."

Maddie looked up. "And you've agreed on every detail about the wedding?"

Elena nodded.

"Everything," Mike said. "Right down to the flavor of the cake."

"Vanilla," Elena said. "We thought most everyone likes vanilla."

"Yes," Mike said. "Hard to find a reason to object to vanilla."

On the pad of paper, Maddie crossed out *possible avoidants* and wrote *circumvention.*

Oh boy. Not good. Sounded good, seemed good, but circumvention could be a sign of serious trouble to come. During her training, Maddie had shadowed a supervisor who had addressed a similar problem with a couple. Their marriage lasted about six years before it imploded into an irreparable mess. "Tell me why you think this could be a cause for concern."

Mike crossed his legs. "It started when we overheard Peg Legg say something at the Lunch Counter."

"What was that?"

"She was telling a lady with blueish-colored hair—"

"That's Nancy," Maddie interrupted. "She runs the local grocery store."

"Got it," Mike said. "Peg was telling Nancy that she had always thought she had the perfect marriage, never a single argument, until suddenly one day her husband up and left her."

"Peg said she used to be a pleaser," Elena said.

"We're both pleasers," Mike chimed in. "We bend over backwards to avoid any conflict."

Maddie wrote down *pleasers*. "So you see conflict as dangerous?"

They both nodded. "Our parents, both of them, were divorced," Mike said.

"Ugly divorces," Elena added. "We don't want that for ourselves."

"Absolutely not," Mike said.

"Sounds like you both observed a lot of conflict in the home?"

Again, they nodded.

"Okay," Maddie said. "Okay. I think I know what we need to do."

They both looked at her with hopeful eyes. "What?"

She smiled. "We're going to divorce-proof your marriage."

"Great," Elena said, clasping her hands together. "Excellent."

Relieved, Mike slapped his hands on his knees. "Lay it on us."

"You're going to learn how to argue."

At the same time, as if rehearsed, Mike and Elena leaned back in their chairs. Way back. The body language of avoidance. Maddie could tell they wanted to bolt.

Uh oh. Too soon?

Maddie knew better. During those first few sessions, as the client-therapist relationship was getting established, it was important to try to create trust, a kind of therapeutic alliance. She knew that. It was better for clients to be heard and understood than it was for them to gain any insights or make any significant changes. She *knew* all that, but enthusiasm and inexperience won out.

Again, as if Mike and Elena had set up a secret signal, they both looked at their watches and rose to their feet, making excuses for a hasty exit.

Too much, too soon.

By day, while Cooper was at school, the kitchen of Moose Manor morphed into Cam's grant-writing workstation. The big farm table was loaded with papers, books, spreadsheets, and her open laptop computer. "In here," she called out when she heard Maddie's voice at the front door. "I didn't expect you home till later."

Maddie came into the kitchen and went right to the refrigerator. "Where's Blaine? Tillie said she saw her come off the ferry." She kept her head in the fridge while she spoke. "I didn't even realize she was coming in from school today. How did I miss that vital piece of information?"

"We all did. She said she wanted to surprise everyone."

Maddie closed the fridge door and turned to Cam. "Is she upstairs? I came home because I thought she'd be here."

"She was, for about five minutes. In fact, I brought her home. Then she dropped her bags and already went to work at the Lunch Counter. And after tasting Peg's coffee this morning, I'm glad she's back at work." She slapped her palms on the tabletop. "So, how'd it go with your first customers?"

"Clients."

"Right. So how'd it go? Good first day?" She peered at her sister's distressed face. "Uh oh. Not so good? No-shows?"

19

"It was fine. They were fine. All good."

"Tell me more." She pushed a chair out and patted it. "Tell me everything."

"Nope. Private business." Maddie opened the fridge again and took out last night's leftover dinner, sniffed it, and put it back. "I'm so glad Blaine will be cooking for us again."

Cam frowned. It had been her turn to make last night's dinner. "Something's got you out of sorts."

Maddie leaned against the refrigerator. "Do you remember a boy from Needham named Ricky O'Shea?"

Cam drummed her fingers on the table. "Super good-looking. Knew it too."

"Yup. That's him."

"What about him?"

"Richard O'Shea." Her expression soured. "Our new pastor."

Cam's jaw dropped. "That's our new pastor? I saw him drop out of the sky in a parachute."

"Bingo." Maddie crossed her arms against her chest. "What kind of a person parachutes in on his first day at a new job?"

Cam opened the refrigerator and took out last night's pasta supper. She sniffed it. It smelled fine. Pretty fine. "Wow, Ricky O'Shea is a minister. That's hard to get my head around. Dad always called him a juvenile delinquent in the making. Didn't he set fire to the church?"

"He didn't actually set it on fire," Maddie said. "He was smoking in the church's bathroom and the smoke set off the fire alarm. The entire church had to be evacuated."

"Who's smoking?" Dad said, walking into the kitchen. "And smoking what?"

Maddie swung around. "Do you remember Ricky O'Shea?"

Dad stopped, glancing at the ceiling. "Oh yeah. I remember

him. He was our town's version of Eddie Haskell. How many times did he TP our house? He'd bike past and wave at me with a big innocent grin while I cleaned up the yard."

Poor Dad, Cam thought. Four sentences in a row made his voice sound as dry as toast.

"Get this," Maddie said. "He's the Richard O'Shea who is our new pastor."

Dad's eyebrows lifted in surprise. "How did *that* happen?" It came out like a whisper.

"Exactly my point," Maddie said. "Where was the vetting system?" She looked at Cam.

"Ricky applied for the job," Cam said. "Seth interviewed him and made an offer."

"But did Seth do any due diligence at all? Or was he so desperate to find a pastor that he took the only one who would agree to come to Three Sisters Island?"

"The entire church voted him in. Not just Seth." Cam pointed at Maddie. "You did too. It was a unanimous call." Though she had to admit that a lot of rules were relaxed for Richard O'Shea. He had started some online seminary classes, but he hadn't completed the degree work yet. He had zero pastorate experience but excellent recommendations from his COs in the Marines. But he was willing to come, and didn't balk at the salary and accommodations like every other candidate. Every single one. His eagerness to come to Three Sisters Island tipped the scales in his favor. But Cam didn't think it would be wise to share that insider information with Maddie. Not right now, not while she was on a rant.

"I didn't realize who he was! I had no idea Pastor Richard O'Shea was the same Ricky O'Shea who terrorized my youth." Maddie put her hands on her temples, as if she had a sudden severe headache, and slipped into a chair at the kitchen table. "I had blocked him from my memory." She covered her face with her hands. "I have to leave the island. Move far, far away. Iceland, perhaps. Or maybe New Zealand."

"A tad bit dramatic for a therapist," Cam said. "Give Ricky a chance. He's probably changed from the teenager you remember."

Maddie dropped her hands from her face. "He parachuted into Boon Dock. Everyone—the entire town—stopped what they were doing to watch him. Parachuted! Who does that? Only Ricky O'Shea. He was suspended from high school so often that the principal kept his file right on his desk. At the ready." She pounded her fists on the table. "Ricky was a wild boy and now he's a wild boy-man."

Even Dad seemed a little concerned. "Maybe he won't last. As I recall, he wasn't exactly the kind of guy who stuck with things."

"Excellent point, Dad," Cam said. "Ricky probably won't last past the summer."

Maddie brightened. "Maybe I can just avoid him."

Dad chuckled. "You work in the same building."

"And avoidance is a truly pathetic strategy from a therapist." Cam patted Maddie on the shoulder.

Maddie dropped her forehead on the table with a clunk. In a muffled voice, she asked, "How in the world did he even find out the church here was looking for a pastor?"

"Oh boy," Cam said. "She didn't tell you?"

Maddie popped her head up. "Who? What? What do you know?"

Cam lifted her shoulders in a helpless shrug, eager to stay clear of that discussion. "Better ask Blaine."

Three

IT HAD HAPPENED AGAIN. That weird dream. There was a three-in-one egg timer in the kitchen with three hourglasses of colored sand in them, signifying three different allotments of time. In Paul's dream, the longest vial of sand was just about to run out and he would wake up with a start, drenched in a cold sweat.

On this gray foggy morning, Paul poured himself a glass of orange juice and leaned against the kitchen counter. Cam had taken Cooper to school, Blaine was already at work at the Lunch Counter, and Maddie was buttering a piece of toast, seated at the large farm table in the center of the big kitchen.

He cast a glance at her, his sensitive middle daughter. Maddie, the resident therapist. "What would you say about a customer who had recurring dreams?"

"Client," Maddie said. "I would say that he is suppressing something and his subconscious is trying to get his attention." She looked at him with a smug smile. "So what's your dream about, Dad?"

He pointed to the egg timer. "That."

"The egg timer? Oh. That's easy peasy."

"What's easy peasy?"

"Analyzing the meaning of the dream. Psychology 101."

"What is it?"

"What do you think it could be?"

"Can't you just tell me?"

"Better if you figure it out."

He scowled. Whenever she put on her therapist hat, conversations became frustrating. Too hard. "Well, it's an egg timer. So I'm guessing it's about the egg. Do I want to be considered as soft-boiled? Medium? Hard?"

"The egg?" She looked at him as if it were an absurd conclusion. "Interesting. What else, Dad?"

He stared at the egg timer and suddenly it dawned on him. "Oh. Oh, oh, oh. Time is passing."

"Yup. More than just passing. It's running out." She tipped her head. "Profound dream. We're going to have to spend some time on this, Dad."

"Nope. Nope. All good."

"You shouldn't ignore stuff like this." She poured the rest of her coffee down the sink drain. "Speaking of time, I'd better get going. A *client* is due soon." At the doorjamb she stopped and turned. "We'll dissect this dream later." And then she was gone.

In the quiet of the kitchen, Paul picked up the egg timer and turned it over, watching the sand run through the hourglass. Time was running out.

He hated knowing that.

In his late fifties, he had felt reenergized, ready for the next stage of life. He'd made radical life-changing decisions. Sold the family home. Bought a dilapidated old camp on an island in Maine. Pushed forward to get it ready for the summer season by opening day. Provided small grants to locals to help them paint their exterior storefronts, and saw how it improved their businesses. Decision after decision after decision. Made. Checked off. No regrets, even when he'd made mistakes. No overthinking. Full steam ahead.

And then, this last winter, Paul turned sixty. He worried his best years were behind him.

Ever since, he'd become cautious, unable to make decisions about Camp Kicking Moose. So many pieces of the camp's development sat in the pending pile: Should he consider getting solar panels on the roof of Moose Manor before he tackled the interior of the house? And that kitchen. It was long overdue for a major remodel. He was afraid of making mistakes because he'd made so many already in his life and feared he wouldn't have time to clean up the mistakes anymore.

But time was running out.

⁓

Midafternoon, when Maddie knew that the Lunch Counter would be empty, she slipped inside and sat on a red stool, waiting for Blaine to appear. She heard her talking with Peg in the back storeroom. Cinnamon scented the air, so Maddie leaned over the counter to peek at a coffee cake baking through the lit oven door. Not a moment later, the timer binged and Blaine hurried in from the back to check on her cake, so focused that she barely waved to Maddie to acknowledge her.

Peg appeared at the storeroom door, a puzzled look on her face. "Where are you going? Oh good grief. I can't even hear that kitchen timer, and to your ears, it's like Pavlov's dogs." She smiled broadly when she saw Maddie. "Hey there, honey. What can I get you?"

"Just an iced tea, Peg. I came in to see Blaine." She kept her eyes on her little sister, who was absorbed with poking a toothpick into the cake to check if it was done.

Peg poured a glass of tea over ice and handed it to Maddie. "If you two have some talking to do, I'm going back to the storeroom and try to figure out that new system Blaine created."

Blaine put the cake back into the oven and reset the timer for five more minutes.

"It smells good in here. All cinnamon-y."

Blaine pinched her face. "Does it? I can't smell it."

"Welcome home, little sister." She put her hand in the air to high-five her. "You've grown since I've seen you last."

"You saw me last month."

"Your hair is longer."

"I just got it cut."

Maddie heard some exasperated sounds floating in from the storeroom. "Peg seemed bothered."

"She's upset because I just organized the pantry and she can't find anything."

"Already? What's your new system?"

"Alphabetized. Everything. How hard could it be to find things when they're alphabetized? It's impossible for Peg. She says she can only work in chaos."

"Speaking of chaos . . ."

"Uh oh." Blaine pulled the oven mitts off her hands. "What's wrong with Cooper?" She reached over and took a sip of Maddie's iced tea. "I told Cam that she needs to hurry up and get married. Give that boy some permanence."

Maddie didn't disagree, but that wasn't why she was here. "I'm not here because of Cooper's chaos. I'm here because of you."

"Me?" Blaine's face was a picture of innocence.

"Did you have something to do with bringing Ricky O'Shea to the island as our new pastor?"

Blaine whirled around, bent over, and peered through the oven door. "Gotta check on my cake."

"I can wait." Maddie had no more clients for the day. Or the week.

Blaine busied herself with the cake. Checking it again for doneness, taking it out and putting it on a cooling rack, turning off the oven, taking off her oven mitts and hanging them on the hook next to the oven. All very precise, slow movements. When she ran out of things to do, she glanced guiltily at Maddie. "We needed a pastor. Rick needed a job."

"How did you know that?"

"We're Facebook friends. He had posted that he was out of the Marines and looking to be a pastor in a small, off-the-beaten-path location. A perfect fit."

"Blaine, you never told me that you connected Rick to Seth."

She lifted her chin in the air defensively. "That's because I knew you would freak out."

"I'm not freaking out. I'm wondering why you felt you needed to hide the truth."

"I never lied to you about him. I just never . . ."

"Bothered to tell me the truth." Maddie swirled her drink so that the only sound in the Lunch Counter was the clinking of ice cubes. "Why?"

"I thought you'd put the kibosh on it. Three Sisters Island has needed a pastor for a long time, and I couldn't handle one more summer of Captain Ed's weird fishing sermons."

"You really think I'd interfere with the church finding a pastor?"

"I think you would've voted against Ricky, and we agreed it had to be a unanimous decision." She crossed her arms against her chest. "Admit it, Maddie. You've always been"—she wiggled her shoulders—"twitchy about Rick."

"We had a lot of history together. Most of it was not very good."

"Come on, Maddie," she said, rolling her eyes. "Don't you think it's time to let go of the port-a-potty incident?"

Maddie could feel herself stiffen and tried to not let her discomfort show.

"You're the one who's always telling me that true relationships require a lot of letting go."

She jerked her head up. "Ricky O'Shea and I don't have a relationship. We have history."

"Maybe you could."

"Whoa." She set the glass of iced tea down so that it sloshed. "Hold it right there."

"I don't mean"—Blaine made air quotes while dropping her voice an octave and leaning forward to draw out the word—"a relationship." She leaned back again. "A friendship, that's all. Like Artie and me."

"Not-the-boyfriend Artie?" Maddie couldn't resist.

Blaine didn't bite on the bait. "You of all people, a certifiable counselor—"

"Certified."

"—should be able to allow a few mistakes for a guy on his path to manhood. Can't you try to get to know Rick for who he is now?"

That smarted, because Blaine was right. Stalling, Maddie took a few sips of the iced tea. "I still think you could've been honest with me."

Blaine made a rocking motion with her hand. "Maybe. Maybe not. I think you would've derailed his coming. And we need him here. If for no other reason than to get Cam and Seth married."

Maddie swallowed the last of the iced tea and rose to her feet. "When the time is right, they'll get married."

Blaine looked at her, shocked. "Seriously? You're not eager for them to hurry up and get married?"

"I'm eager for them to get married, but not to hurry. Why do you feel a sense of urgency?"

"Cooper!" she said, throwing her arms up in the air.

"Cooper's doing well." When Blaine gave her a skeptical look, she amended her remark. "Cooper's doing better." He still had a lot of quirky anxiety issues. Last weekend he lost another tooth and it sent him into a tailspin. He was convinced he had no replacement tooth. Losing things was hard for Cooper, but then, he'd lost a lot in his young life.

"I think he'll do better still when he has a mom and a dad under the same roof."

"True, but that day will come. Remember, he doesn't know yet that Seth is his biological father. For a child with Cooper's anxieties, research has shown that slow revelations of important events are best."

Blaine waved her hands dismissively. "Research, schmee-search. That boy needs his mom and his dad together. Under one roof. Period." She snapped her fingers. "Simple."

Maddie walked toward the door. "Spoken from someone who has been home for less than twenty-four hours." And spoken from someone who thought she knew best for everybody. Including bringing Ricky O'Shea, the one person in the world Maddie would rather forget, right onto the island.

That last part, Maddie didn't say out loud.

———— C✳⊃ ————

MADDIE, AGE 9

The cross-country runs were always the same. The Grayson family gathered near the runners' start line. The fake gun would go off and Cam and Libby would disappear with the crowd of junior high runners, their birdlike legs pumping like pistons, up and over the hill, not to be seen until they returned to the finish line an hour or so later. Mom and Dad would clap and clap as if Cam and Libby had just summited Mount. Everest. Ridiculous.

All they did was run around town. Besides, Libby always won, and then Cam would be in a bad mood all afternoon. In this one area, Libby outshone Cam. That cross-the-finish-line moment made the stupid cross-country runs worthwhile for Maddie.

If she could have chosen an older sister, Maddie would have preferred Libby, their across-the-street neighbor, over Cam. Libby was much nicer than Cam, and far more interested in Maddie and Blaine. Dad liked to tease that Cam thought she was an only child, and that her two little sisters happened to rent rooms in the house. A tease with truth in it.

On this stifling hot afternoon in June, as soon as the runners disappeared, Maddie tugged on her mom's sleeve. "I have to go to the bathroom."

"What?" Mom frowned. "Why didn't you go at home?"

"I forgot. And I can't wait."

Mom gave a quick scan of the park and pointed to a port-a-potty. "You'll have to go in there." She looked through her purse for a small package of tissues and handed it to Maddie.

Oh no. Not a port-a-potty. Maddie's science class had just finished a segment on germs. Looking through a microscope at what a germ actually looked like—tiny little worm-like molecules—had deeply disturbed her. Germs were everywhere!

But she really, really had to go to the bathroom. She took one tissue out of the package and used it to open the door, but before she stepped inside the dark, smelly space, she took several deep gulps of air. Then she held her breath, went inside, and latched the door, did her business quickly and efficiently, not touching anything. Not anything. And then she heard a click.

She turned the handle, but it wouldn't open. She took out more tissues, tried the handle again. And again. Latched tight. She had to let her breath out before she passed out, gagging from the odor. She shouted, over and over, but no one came. Once Mom got talking to the other parents, she probably wouldn't even think twice about Maddie. She might die here, in this stinking, germ-laden port-a-potty. Hours passed, or possibly minutes, before Mom finally noticed she hadn't returned and came to rescue her.

"What happened to you?" Mom said.

Maddie heaved in gulps of fresh air, trying to clean out her lungs. "Someone locked the door."

"Oh Maddie. The latch was probably just jammed."

"No! Mom, it was locked! I heard someone outside."

"You can't lock it from the outside."

Maddie tried to explain, but Mom wasn't listening. Her attention was on the cross-country runners who had finally returned and were cresting the hill, heading downhill toward the finish line. Libby was out in front, long legs striding like a graceful gazelle. Cam was yards and yards behind her, arms pumping, trying so hard to keep up. Libby crossed the line first, barely winded. Cam's face was bright red, and she fell on the ground, gasping for breath. So dramatic.

Blaine, the self-appointed town crier, ran to Cam and Libby to report Maddie's port-a-potty crisis. Normally, Cam would've been cranky because she lost the race, but not today. The port-a-potty story made her laugh so hard, she had tears running down her face. Libby, so much nicer, gave Maddie a sympathetic hug. Maddie vowed to never set foot in another port-a-potty.

As they walked to the car, they had to pass the port-a-potty. Hiding behind it was the horrible Ricky O'Shea. He held up the stick he'd used to latch the door shut and flashed a smug grin. No one else saw him, only Maddie. She shouted his name and pointed to the port-a-potty, but by the time her family stopped and turned, he had disappeared. That kind of scenario took place again and again and again. Ricky did something terrible to Maddie, she would get upset, he would disappear.

It became their dance.

Four

THERE WERE DAYS, LIKE TODAY, when Paul Grayson couldn't believe his eyes. Camp Kicking Moose, the very place where he'd spent his college summers, where he'd met Corinna, his future wife, and where he'd proposed to her, had been transformed.

His gaze took in the three-storied Moose Manor, now a subtle charcoal-gray color with crisp white trim and a cranberry-red front door. All evidence of the Pepto-Bismol pink that someone with appalling taste had once painted it was covered up. Man oh man, a coat of paint could work wonders. Three coats, as he recalled.

There was still work to be done on the interior of Moose Manor—a complete gut job, if his daughters had any say in it—but from the outside, the old dinosaur looked pretty great. Cared for, loved. Lilac bushes in full bloom lined the skirt of the house. The expansive grass lawn looked like green velvet. A duck family—mom, dad, and three ducklings—waddled across the far end of the lawn and disappeared behind a cabin. One came back to stare at him for a long moment, then scurried away to join its family. Paul wasn't one to notice such moments of nature, but this island changed a man. Slowed him down. Made him pay attention to small things.

His gaze took in the wide covered porch that lined the entire front of the house. A cold buffet breakfast for campers would be served on that porch each morning, even on rainy days, and the system worked out well last summer. It would have to do for this summer too. Down the road, he had plans to restore full dining service in the large sunroom. Paul was waiting for Blaine to graduate from culinary school for that next stage of development for Camp Kicking Moose. He hadn't promised the chef's job to her, but that was his intention. First, he wanted to see her graduate, to make sure she was truly committed.

He unlocked the boathouse and opened the doors wide, breathing in the musty air. The last time he'd been in here was early September, just after Labor Day, when he'd brought in the last of the canoes and kayaks for the season. He walked down the aisle, unlatched the trunk that held the life preservers, and opened it a little cautiously. Last year, as he'd opened it, out jumped the biggest rat he'd ever seen. The camp's resident coon cat had slipped in behind Paul and saw it too. It shot through Paul's legs and suddenly the quiet boathouse turned into a flurry of squeals and fur and then . . . silence again. Paul had left quickly, his lunch threatening to turn upside down.

Happily, on this beautiful May day, the trunk was void of rodents. It pleased him to see the condition of the life preservers. He ran a hand along the gleaming wood of the canoes that hung from the ceiling. Artie Lotosky and his dad were the ones to thank for that. Artie's dad had inspected, cleaned, and dried each piece of equipment that was stored in this old boathouse. Paul wished his daughter Blaine felt for Artie what it seemed obvious that Artie felt for Blaine. Paul already considered him like the son he'd never had. Here Artie was in medical school, all the way on the other side of the country, yet he had made time to come out in late May and then again in early September to help Paul open and close Camp Kicking Moose.

Of his three daughters, Paul worried most about Blaine, his youngest. Cam wasn't hard to read, Maddie told them *everything* that was on her mind—which was sometimes terrifying for him. How could she find so much to worry about? Blaine . . . she was a mystery. Emotional, sensitive, easily disappointed . . . and lately, she seemed strangely distant. He wondered if it had something to do with culinary school.

There were times when Paul thought that arranged marriages— arranged by the fathers, that was—should be brought back into vogue. Artie would be his pick for Blaine, hands down. The young man was reliable and trustworthy, smart as a whip, had a solid faith, and adored his daughter. When Paul pointed out those fine qualities to Blaine, she said he made Artie sound like a dog. That was ridiculous, Paul told her . . . but if he *were* to compare people to dogs, Artie would be a cross of a loyal golden retriever and a hardworking Labrador retriever. The perfect dog. The perfect man for Blaine. She, on the other hand, would be a fussy French poodle.

He wondered what Artie's dad might think of an arranged marriage. Bob Lotosky, pronounced *Bahb* with that drawn-out Maine *a*, was a true Mainer, a potato farmer from southern Aroostook County, whose son was the first college graduate in the family and was now on the path to becoming a medical doctor. Would *Bahb* really want a creative, indecisive, artistic, impossible-to-please wife for his boy? Probably not.

As Paul pulled the canoe oars down from the racks and stacked them on the ground, he pondered more comparisons of people and dogs. Cam could be likened to a German shepherd—loyal to a fault, task oriented, undeterred toward a goal. While other dogs might be thinking about naps and mealtimes, a German shepherd's brain was probably working out a formula for nuclear physics. That would be Cam.

Now Maddie, she would be one of those small lap dogs that stood at the window and barked to alert the world that pedestrians were walking down the road. Paul didn't know the names of those little dog breeds; he thought of them only as Chicken Little dogs.

He checked himself. If his daughters were to hear his thoughts right now, they would be furious. Oh boy, he would never hear the end of it.

Thankfully, the girls would never know what errant thoughts were running through their dear old dad's mind as he opened up the boathouse for the season. Paul's voice remained a coarse, scratchy whisper due to a case of laryngitis that came and never left, and despite losing his career as a radio man, he had found some gifts in this imposed near silence. The best gift of all . . . he had finally learned to keep most of his thoughts to himself. Not all bad when a man had three daughters. Not so bad at all.

Day Three. So far, Maddie had successfully avoided Ricky O'Shea, though it had taken quite some effort. He had moved into the house rented for the church office, directly above her basement office, and was in and out all through the day. She'd already developed a sixth sense for his unique sounds. Such a booming voice! Such a bold and confident stride up the wooden steps to the church's front door. So different from Tillie's heavy-footed lumbering. How could a man have so much self-confidence? Maddie had struggled with confidence for as long as she could remember. Not so for Ricky.

Maddie vividly remembered how, on the first day of kindergarten, Ricky had refused to take part in resting time when the fresh-out-of-college teacher, Miss Apfelbaum, asked the class to lie down on mats. "No more naps," he had said, with a lisp because his front teeth were missing. His refusal empowered all the boys to join in on the napping strike. Wide-eyed, Maddie had watched the stand-off between the very young, very inexperienced, very timid Miss Apfelbaum and the little boys, led by Ricky. "Naps are for babies," he said, his hands on his hips.

Miss Apfelbaum was waffling, so Maddie, who loved naps and felt sorry for her teacher, tried to help. "Naps are good for you," she said—which was not a popular position to take among the kindergartners. Starting with Ricky, they threw their crayons at Maddie. Miss Apfelbaum backed down. No naps for the kindergartners, all year. Instantly, Ricky had established himself as the pack leader, a leading role which lasted through senior year of high school.

She was finishing up for the day when she heard a door slam from above, rattling the window in her little basement office. She froze. That was Ricky's customary slam. She heard his footsteps pound down the porch steps and waited to hear the front gate squeak. From what information she could piece together, he took most of his meals at the Lunch Counter. That was another unfortunate discovery, as she loved going to the diner, especially now that Blaine had returned to do the cooking. No longer. Cam's comment that avoidance was a pathetic strategy kept needling her, but she couldn't overcome her dread of seeing Ricky. The last time she'd seen him, she'd embarrassed herself beyond belief. It still haunted her.

She waited, and waited. Had she missed hearing the squeak of the gate as he reached the sidewalk? She glanced at her watch, tapped her foot. She needed to meet Blaine soon or she'd miss her ride home. They carpooled to town as often as they could because gas was so costly. She put her ear to the door. No sound. Slowly, she opened the door a crack and peered out. No sign of Ricky. She opened the door a little more and poked her head out. And there he was. *Waiting*.

"Hello there, Maddie Grayson."

Ricky! She shut the door, mortified, fully aware that she was acting as if she were still in junior high.

Through the door came Ricky's deep voice. "It's kind of silly to keep avoiding me. Three Sisters Island isn't that big."

That, she couldn't deny.

"We're going to have to see each other sometime. Why not now?"

Slowly, she opened the door, defeated. "Ricky O'Shea," she said in a flat voice. Maddie studied his appearance. Even with his thick hair now close-cropped, he looked pretty much the same as she remembered—though a little older, with sun-squint lines fanning from the corners of his eyes. Dark eyes, with thick brown eyebrows. More powerfully built, with bigger, broader shoulders. Unapologetically masculine. Oozing confidence, strength, fearlessness. The best-looking boy in town, that's what her mother used to call him. Mom was right then, and she was right now. Ricky O'Shea was a gorgeous man.

But Maddie was older and wiser, and determined to remain immune to Ricky O'Shea.

"So, Madison Grayson." A grin dawned slow across his face. "You haven't changed a bit from the last time I saw you."

Maddie winced inwardly. Senior Prom. Of course, that night would be the first thing he brought up. Of course, he'd reference it, right out of the starting gate. As their eyes met, she felt her cheeks grow warm. "Ricky—"

"It's Rick now. Or Pastor Rick." He lifted one shoulder in a casual shrug. "Whichever you'd prefer."

Or neither.

"So how are you, Maddie?"

Frazzled. Trying hard not to show it. "Fine." Her voice was unemotional.

"You look fine. Better than fine."

For a long moment, she considered him, trying hard to discern his motives. Unfortunately, despite knowing all the right things to do and say, she just couldn't quite get them to the surface. Instead, what blurted out was, "Why? Why here, of all places?"

"What, me? Being here? Why not here? It's a lovely island. A great opportunity for an extremely inexperienced but enthusiastic pastor."

"And what is *that* about? As I recall, your mother dragged you to church."

"Funny, that. Life has a way of taking a person in a full circle."

No kidding. His lip curved up a little on one side. Ricky looked at her squarely, kindly, with sincere admiration in his dark brown eyes, in a way that made her thoughts dash in different directions and then vanish. *Pull it together, Maddie!* Was he messing with her? Probably. She couldn't get past that feeling of waiting for a shoe to drop when she least expected it from him. "Cam said she doesn't think you'll last the summer."

His dark brows lifted, eyes danced with amusement. "Really? Well, I'm flattered she'd even be talking about me."

Boom. Same old Ricky. A knack for turning an insult into a compliment.

"Shall we go?" He held out his arm, as if he were an escort to a grand ball.

"Go where? I'm meeting my sister and heading to Camp Kicking Moose."

38

"As am I. Blaine invited me to supper tonight."

Without telling anyone. A coil of anger started to heat up inside Maddie's stomach. She'd told Blaine how she felt about Ricky the other day, yet her sister went ahead and invited him to the house for dinner. Like he was a normal pastor, new to town.

"Maddie, you keep looking at me as if you've just seen my face on one of those FBI WANTED posters in the post office."

Yes! That's exactly how she felt. Suspicious, wary, waiting for something terrible to happen. Because something awful *always* did happen when Ricky O'Shea came around.

In a flash of memory, Maddie was swept back to the beginning of her sophomore year in high school. She had finally made the lone piccolo spot in the high school marching band after getting passed over the year before. That very day, Ricky tried out for the band with the tuba—he was given the spot only because there was no other tuba player. Maddie was sure he'd never even played a tuba before that tryout day—somehow he finagled his position on the field to be right behind hers. He blasted at her as they marched all around the football field, drowning out her sweet little piccolo notes. She'd had a ringing in her ears that lasted all through football season. And then Ricky promptly quit marching band. Bored with it, he told everyone.

"I haven't seen you for nearly a decade. Lots has happened in our lives. Can't we start fresh? Friends?" He grinned. "You don't even have to call me Pastor Rick."

Seriously? Was he going to brush off the night of Senior Prom, like it was nothing? It was the most *humiliating* night of her life. Something snapped shut inside of her. *Pretend it never happened*, she thought. *It never happened.* "I just remembered that I have some important work to get done tonight," she said crisply. She forced a smile, meeting his eyes. "Enjoy your time at Camp

Kicking Moose." And she closed the door—gently—on his handsome face.

⌒

On Friday morning, Blaine and Peg stood outside of the Lunch Counter, peering at the sidewalk sign that trumpeted the daily specials. "I'm trying to drum up business, since you're home for the summer and I can temporarily retire as chief cook."

Blaine's stomach tightened. She wasn't planning to be here beyond Cam and Seth's wedding . . . whenever that event actually took place. She'd been pressing Cam for a date but was getting nowhere. Cam said she had to wrap up the grant applications, then she could focus on the wedding. So frustrating! "I like the idea of the sidewalk sign," Blaine said, "but I think it could use a little finesse."

Peg had scrawled *Tomato Soup and Grilled Cheese $5* in a sideways, downward slant. Below it: *Duck. Freshly shot by Captain Ed. $10.*

In a skillful, swirling font, Blaine imagined writing *Fire-Roasted Tomato Soup with Three-Cheese Grilled Sandwich on Ciabatta Bread $10. Sugar Cane Lacquered Duck Breast over a bed of Farro, Cherry Tomatoes, and Arugula Salad $20.*

"Honey, you do whatever you want to do with it." Peg handed her the chalk and went inside.

Oh, how Blaine loved that phrase. Peg had such confidence in her! It was like she'd handed her the keys to the kingdom. Her favorite thing in the world was to experiment with new flavors, combinations of unusual textures. She could taste the idea of a recipe before she made it. She flirted with breakfast dishes, lunch dishes, dinner entrées, and other types of desserts. But at her heart, she was a pastry chef. Sweets of all kinds, that was her true love.

Blaine couldn't imagine her family having the kind of rock-solid confidence in her that Peg did. Maddie, possibly. Dad, maybe. Cam, definitely not. She wiped down Peg's scrawl and sat cross-legged on the sidewalk to start again.

She'd brought up menu suggestions to Cam for the food at the wedding reception, but her sister waved it off. Too busy, too distracted with the grant work or . . . or maybe she didn't think Blaine had the chops to prepare the food.

If that was true—and the more she thought about it, the more she decided that probably was the *very* reason Cam clammed up and wouldn't discuss wedding plans—that *really* smarted. In February, when Cam had called to tell her that she and Seth were getting married, she had asked if Blaine was planning to be home for the summer. Blaine had mistakenly assumed she had asked because she wanted her to handle the reception. And of course that meant the cake!

Cam wouldn't ask someone else to bake the wedding cake, would she? Blaine huffed in indignation. That would be just like her sister. Cam still thought of Blaine as a ten-year-old playing in the kitchen, adding water to a dusty store-bought cake mix. One time, just one time, Blaine had left cracked shells in the batter and Cam had never let her forget.

Blaine brushed back a lock of hair. Why did she always do this? It was like she sat on the top of a slide of self-doubt and willingly went down. Her friends considered her to be fiercely creative, fiercely independent. Bold and determined. But when she came home to her family, she regressed to a needy little sister. She annoyed *herself*.

Well, if that was how Cam still viewed her, then that was her problem. If Cam didn't want to see the sketches Blaine had made of her wedding cake this spring, or hear about the flavors—almond vanilla cake with a thin coating of tart raspberry jam and sweet buttercream icing between each layer, a combination of flavors she had experimented with nine times to get just right—well, that was her loss.

Blaine finished the chalkboard sign, leaned back to make sure it looked as good as she thought it did, and rose to her feet. She heard the cheery toot of the Never Late Ferry as it came into Boon Dock, and lifted a hand to shield her eyes to see who might be coming to Three Sisters Island. It was too early for summer visitors. Her attention swept over the dock, then zeroed in on one familiar person who was jogging down the dock. What . . . was that him? It was! Artie.

With a whoop, she dropped the chalk and sprinted down Main Street to Boon Dock. Artie opened his arms and caught her, spinning her around in the air once, then twice more. Carefully, he set her back on her feet. She took a step back, set her palms on his shoulders. "You didn't tell me you were coming."

"Yeah, I did. I left a voicemail."

"Voicemail doesn't work on Three Sisters Island."

"Ah, you're right. I forgot. Next time I'll send a pigeon."

She grinned. She hadn't seen him since last September, when he and his dad came to Camp Kicking Moose to help close it up for the winter. "Dad came with me. He's still on the ferry. He and Captain Ed were having a heated debate about which potatoes go in lobster chowder. Captain Ed should know better than to question an Aroostook County potato farmer about potatoes."

She tilted her head, peering at him closely. "You look tired."

"That's because I am tired. I'm a first-year med student. I haven't slept in months."

"Your hair's gotten long."

"Yours has gotten shorter."

"You've lost weight."

"Remember . . . first-year med student. No sleep. No food. Walking zombie."

She frowned. "This is where you're supposed to say, 'Why, Blaine. I do believe you've lost weight too.'"

"But you haven't."

She thumped his upper arm. So she'd added a few pounds this year. Maybe more than a few. "I'm in culinary school. We have to taste what we create."

"I think you look great."

"Really? Cooper's first words to me were asking exactly how many pounds I'd gained."

"I wouldn't change a thing about you. Not a single thing."

He gazed at her with such a sweet caring look in his eyes that she felt warm and loved and happy and grounded. Artie had a way of emotionally steadying her. He was the best friend a girl could have, and she would never, ever jeopardize their friendship. She knew her dad and sisters wanted her to fall in love with Artie, but they didn't understand. Friendship was better than a broken love relationship. Besides, Artie wasn't her type. He was wry and faithful and as constant as time. Her type? Exciting, dramatic, unpredictable. Short-lived, which she preferred. Like a flame that flared up brightly, then extinguished. "I missed you."

"I missed you too."

She stepped back and set her hands on her hips. "So, how have you been? Really been?" They'd kept in regular contact with each other through phone calls, texts, and FaceTime, but they lived on opposite coasts, and the time change was a pain. "Dating anyone?"

"Nope. No time." He glanced back at the ferry. "No sign of Dad yet." He turned back to her but avoided her eyes. "What about you?"

"I was dating this guy in a baking class, but we broke up over Valentine's Day. He criticized my chocolate."

"Oh, dumb move." Artie made a chopping movement against his throat. "Out with him."

Dear, wonderful Artie. He understood her so well. She linked her arm through his, and they walked in the direction of the ferry to find Artie's dad. As they walked, she caught him up on her family. Cam and Seth planned to get married this summer, though they had yet to set a date. There was a new pastor in town, someone from their hometown, and get this . . . he dropped in on a parachute. Oh, and Maddie had just opened up her shrink business.

"I'm pretty sure Maddie doesn't want you to describe her life's calling as a shrink business."

"Probably not."

"What she's doing is important work, you know."

"I do." And she did. She knew better than to disregard a life's calling. Hadn't she just been quietly blaming Cam for being so dismissive about her culinary skills? She would try to treat Maddie's therapy work with more respect. But as far as she knew, Maddie had no customers. After all, this was an island. Who would go to a shrink when you saw that same shrink at the diner each day? *Not me*, she thought. "There's your dad."

Off the ferry walked Artie's dad. Bob Lotosky came up to them and stood shoulder to shoulder with his son, nodding a hello to Blaine. Artie was a spitting image of his dad, a younger version, though much warmer. More like his mom, she gathered, though she only thought that because of how Artie talked about her. He was only a boy when his mother died. His dad raised Artie and his sisters on his own.

"Welcome to the island, Mr. Lotosky," Blaine said. "My dad will be so pleased you've come back to help."

"Ayup. The seed potatoes are in, so there's not much else that can be done until potato recess."

Potato recess meant school was closed. All hands, young or old, were needed on deck to harvest the potatoes. "Maybe I could try talking my dad into coming to help you out in September."

"Your dad?" Artie pondered that suggestion, looking doubtful. "Kind of hard to imagine him as a farmer."

Blaine shrugged. "I never thought he'd be running a summer camp on an island."

"Thanks but no thanks," Mr. Lotosky said. "No interest in talking an amateur through the potato harvest."

Blaine looked up at Artie, confused. Was potato harvesting that difficult? A lone dimple sank in his cheek. He leaned over to whisper, "Potatoes are everything to my dad."

"Besides, I'm only partially here to help your dad wake up that sleepy old camp for the summer." Mr. Lotosky hooked his thumbs around his belt loops. "I've got something else on my mind this year." He looked at the Lunch Counter. "I'll see you both later."

Blaine watched him head over to the diner. "What's all that about?"

"I think he's come courting."

"What? Who?"

Artie nodded toward the Lunch Counter. "Who else?"

"NO WAY! Peg?" She let out a puff of air. "Whoa."

And suddenly she felt a slight clutch in her gut. In the back of her mind, she'd held a distant hope that her dad and Peg might end up together. She really had no reason to think there was anything stirring between them. Once Peg had said that her dad's scratchy voice was sexy, and he had seemed so pleased. But nothing, as far as she knew, had come from it. Maybe Blaine wanted Peg to become an official part of the Grayson family for her own sake.

"Something wrong?"

She shook her head. "No. All good. You must be starving. Let's go in and get you something to eat." She grinned. "Name your sandwich. I'll make it."

"Tuna fish?"

"Except that. Peg bought a tuna from Captain Ed and it smells funny."

"Skip the tuna. Okay, then, surprise me."

Oh, now that was her second favorite phrase. That, she loved. Such confidence it instilled in her! It occurred to her, just now, that Peg and Artie were much alike.

"I'll let you try a slice of the wedding cake I'm working on for Cam. It's based on my secret cake batter. A genoise sponge. The best you'll ever taste. Flavorful, moist, buttery, ultra-soft."

"Well, good to see your chef-esteem is still high."

"It is. And my sisters still don't appreciate me as they should."

"Cam, you mean. Maddie does."

"True."

"Is this cake sturdy enough for fondant? Or would it be better to use buttercream icing?"

She nearly gasped, so overwhelmed by a sweep of gratitude . . . just because he'd known the right questions to ask. That he cared. "Still deciding."

Artie held the Lunch Counter's door open so she could pass first. "Artie Lotosky, prepare yourself. I'm going to make you the best sandwich you've ever eaten. A banh mi."

"A bunny? I'm not sure how I feel about eating bunnies. I used to have a pet bunny named Harvey."

She jabbed him in the ribs with her elbow as she passed and he let out an *oof*, like he'd been mortally wounded.

Man, she had missed him.

Five

ON SUNDAY MORNING, Maddie fought an inner battle. She wanted to skip church but knew she shouldn't, she couldn't. It had taken a long time to get her family to attend church regularly; at long last, it was a regular part of the Graysons' routine. She had to go. She blew out a puff of air. She would go. She wasn't going to let Ricky O'Shea take church away from her. And she couldn't deny that a big part of her was interested in what kind of sermon he'd preach.

There weren't many churchgoers on Three Sisters Island, but those who went were friendly and welcoming—an encouraging sign for Seth Walker. He was the one who had started the church when he first arrived to teach school at Three Sisters Island. He'd been looking for a pastor for the last two years to serve the growing church. When the school was moved to the Unitarian Church last August, it was Seth who quickly negotiated with the town (aka Peg the mayor) to rent the space on Sunday mornings. The church stood at the top of Main Street, its steeple the highest point on the island—such a common sight throughout all of New England. It was a beautiful structure that dated back to 1859, built and owned by locals, but was missing a congregation.

That's how island living worked—nothing went to waste, everything could be repurposed.

Just as the parishioners voted in the new pastor, Edward Williams's rickety old house on First Street came on the rental market, and Seth grabbed it for a place for the new pastor to live and have an office. The Unitarian Church had only a small sanctuary, filled with children from Monday through Friday. Seth talked Maddie into renting the basement for her practice, and he gathered a couple of guys to paint the house and clean up the yard to make it more appealing for the new pastor. Tillie, whose daughter and grandson had relocated to the mainland after a particularly brutal winter, needed something to do and volunteered to direct the project. She created an office for the new pastor out of the kitchen, and set her desk in front of it, in the formal dining room.

And so, Maddie thought, *here we are today*. A significant day. The first for Rick O'Shea to lead the worship service. Standing by the kitchen sink, sipping her coffee, she squeezed her eyes shut with a defeated sigh. She needed to be there.

Cooper hollered from the open door at Moose Manor, calling to everyone to come. "Hurry up, everyone! Grandpa's getting the van. Artie and his dad are already outside."

Blaine and Cam jumped up from the kitchen table and set their coffee cups on the counter. Blaine grabbed her purse and vanished. At the kitchen doorjamb, Cam turned to Maddie. "Coming?"

She took a last sip of coffee. "I guess so."

"Give the guy a chance. He's all grown up now."

Something happened during Blaine's dinner this week that Maddie had purposely avoided. Her entire family had joined the

Ricky O'Shea Fan Club, even her dad. It was kindergarten, all over again. "You've gone to the dark side."

"Try," Cam said with a laugh, "to be a little bit mature about this, Maddie."

Her sister was right. She was being immature. They were no longer teenagers. People changed. She had changed, hadn't she? For heaven's sake, she was a qualified therapist now, helping her clients (well, still only Mike and Elena, who hadn't made a second appointment yet, but it was a start) overcome their difficulties. She was living the life she'd always dreamed of. Maybe it wasn't New York City like she had originally planned, but one thing her dad had promised as he persuaded her to set up a practice on Three Sisters Island: where there were people, there were problems. Maybe not the same problems, but problems all the same.

She hoped he was right. It still worried her to start a practice on an island with a population of scarcely more than one hundred people. Summer provided more opportunities with vacationers . . . but summer didn't last long. She took in a deep breath, reminding herself that she had promised her dad a year's effort. If nothing else, a year of private practice would be good on her résumé. Just a year.

Maddie's dad drove everyone to town in the new old van he'd bought for Camp Kicking Moose this past winter. They made quite a crowd: Maddie, Blaine, Cam and Cooper, Dad, plus Artie and his dad, who were here for the weekend, working hard alongside the family to get the camp ready for the season. There was a buzz of excitement in the van that was palpable, even to Maddie, who was both dreading Ricky's sermon and eager to hear it. In a way, that summed up her permanent feelings about Ricky.

Enough, Madison Grayson. Enough of the old insecurities. That was then and this is now. It's time to grow up, to see yourself as grown up, and to let Ricky O'Shea—Rick—grow up too.

They arrived at church in plenty of time but not a moment too soon. The lawn in front of the church was full of people. Seth had been watching for the Moose Manor van and strode over, beaming. He helped Cam down, gave her a peck on the cheek, and high-fived Cooper. "I tried to save seats up front for you, but people had already staked out their spots. About halfway on the right, I put some reserved cards on a pew. Hope they're still there." He gazed around the milling crowd that packed the yard. "A lot of folks came over from Mount Desert Island this morning to hear the new pastor. Pretty exciting, isn't it?"

Hold it, Seth, Maddie thought to herself. *Hold on. This is just week one. The new guy hasn't even delivered a sermon yet. Let's see how many people come next week, and the week after that.*

Enough, Maddie. Stop being so sour.

They made their way to the front door of the church, and Maddie realized why there was a bottleneck at the entrance. Ricky stood at the door, greeting each person. Maddie sized him up from a distance. Had he always been so handsome? Yup. It was half the reason she had such conflicted feelings about him since school days. She felt her body react to him the same way it had when she was sixteen years old. Heart racing, skin flushing with excitement. In his khakis, starched blue button-down shirt, polished loafers, he looked like a man who was completely comfortable with himself. And he was. He always had been.

One by one, at the door, each person received Rick's full attention. He listened carefully to them, deeply attentive. As she waited in line, Maddie set aside her feelings about Rick and wondered what he might be feeling this morning. His first sermon delivered to his first church. That must be a pretty overwhelming moment in a person's life.

And yet he didn't seem at all nervous. As her family moved

toward the door, his eyes took them all in. "Well, well, some familiar faces in the crowd. A welcome sight. Good morning, Graysons." He shook their hands, including Cooper's, and then came Maddie. As he reached for her hand, his dark brown eyes met Maddie's with intense steadiness. She dipped her chin to avoid his gaze, but he wouldn't let go of her hand until she looked up at him. "Maddie," he said with sincerity, "I hope you wish me well on this momentous morning."

Did she? No, she didn't. She had even entertained a hope that he might embarrass himself during this momentous morning. She'd gone so far as to imagine scenes of mortification for him. In one, he forgot to bring sermon notes and stumbled and bumbled through a talk that made no sense. In another, the wind blew the pages of his Bible and he couldn't find where he'd been. And then he would slink away from Three Sisters Island, never to return.

A little smile came into his eyes, as if he could read her mind. In that moment, her stomach tightened with conviction. What kind of a person was she? Truly vindictive. He was waiting for her to respond, but more people stood in line behind her, pressing in, and she tugged her hand loose from his and scooted through the door.

Avoidance. It was becoming her way of life.

~◯~

Tillie stood at the back of the church, wearing bright green Crocs—her version of church shoes—directing traffic. Maddie skirted around her and wiggled through the crowded center aisle to where Seth had saved a pew for her family. "Scoot over and make some room," she told her sisters.

Cam wiggled over. "Ricky was a cute boy," she whispered as Maddie slipped into the pew. "Pastor Rick is a gorgeous hunk."

Blaine leaned over and chimed in. "No kidding." She sighed. "He's ridiculously handsome. Too bad he's way too old for me."

Maddie rolled her eyes. Rick's full-blown handsomeness had not escaped her sisters' notice, nor the notice of every other woman. She had seen it out front: the double takes, the arched eyebrows, the way women eyed him with interest, the way they fluttered around him.

Well, Rick's attractiveness wasn't up for debate. That didn't mean, however, that Maddie had to be affected by his good looks. She stiffened her back. No longer. More than eight years had passed and today heralded a new day. A new beginning—for her, for Rick, for the church. She imagined a clean ocean breeze sweeping through her mind, emptying it of cobwebby critical thoughts. Yes, she did wish well for Rick O'Shea on this momentous morning. As long as he kept his distance from her.

Dad leaned over and whispered, "If this island had a fire department, we'd be in trouble." The church was completely full, every pew, and people kept coming through the doors.

"Pretty cool," Blaine said. "Who would've ever thought our little church would already be outgrowing its space?"

"Seth did," Cam said, her eyes fixed on him as he tuned his guitar in front of the church. "He had a vision for the church from the start."

Sweet. Maddie was still amazed that Cam and Seth had found each other on this remote island, had fallen in love, and were planning to be married, as they couldn't be more different. Seth was an outdoorsman; Cam, a city girl. Even more surprising to her was how Seth had spurred Cam's faith to grow, and as it grew, she was changing. She was still Cam—bossy, determined—but there was a softer side to her now. More reflective. And eight-year-old Cooper, her adopted son, had gone from a highly anxious child to a . . . well, a less anxious one. Maddie's rambling thoughts continued in that vein until suddenly the room grew quiet, and Seth began to play the guitar for the opening hymn.

~⌒~

Maddie's imagined scenarios of mortification for Ricky's first sermon could not have been further from the mark.

"Most everyone knows the story of Jonah and the whale," Rick started out. "We know it as a children's tale of a big fish and a reluctant prophet."

Pretty smart, even Maddie had to admit, to launch the first sermon as one about Jonah. Rick was preaching to an island church full of fishermen. She could read the body language around her. Eyes were riveted on Rick, old and young and every age in between.

Rick opened his Bible to the book of Jonah, though he never looked at it because he quoted the text from memory. He also had no sermon notes. Those, too, seemed to be memorized or so much a part of him that he had no need to check his notes. Never once did he falter. Not a single stumble.

"Instead of going to Nineveh like God had asked him to do, Jonah jumped on a merchant ship, filled with goods to transport, heading in the opposite direction." He glanced around those in the pews. "This ship was filled with good, skilled sailors. Men just like the men of Three Sisters Island. They had a job to do and they took their work very seriously."

Maddie noticed the room had become utterly silent. Not a cough, not a wiggle. They were hanging on to Rick's every word.

Rick's gaze swept the small sanctuary. "The ship set out to sea. Jonah went down below deck to rest. Or maybe to hide." His voice dropped to a near whisper. "But you can't hide from God. A storm blew in. A fierce one. The worst storm these experienced sailors had ever faced."

Captain Ed, sitting up front, leaned forward in his pew and slapped his hands on his knees. "A real nor'easter!"

"Go on," Oliver Moore called out from the other side of the room. "What happened next?"

Peg turned around to shush him.

"The storm raged," Rick said, "threatening to break the ship in two. The sailors threw the valuable cargo overboard."

"To lighten the load!" shouted Oliver. "Keep the mast from splitting!"

Peg shushed him again.

"Exactly right. To keep the ship in one piece." Rick didn't seem to mind the interactive turn the sermon had taken. "But the storm kept up, and the sailors—these toughened, experienced, hardy men—"

All at once, Maddie saw every man in the church sit up straight in their pews, spines as stiff as pokers, as if Rick were talking right to them.

"—they were terrified. They woke Jonah up and told him to come up and pray to his god, certain they were all going to die."

"What did Jonah do?" This time, it wasn't Oliver Moore who interrupted the sermon, but Peg!

"Jonah confessed that he was running from God. He knew he was the reason for the storm. The sailors knew he was the reason. He told them to throw him overboard, and the storm would stop."

"No, he didn't!" Peg was wide-eyed.

"He did." Rick turned in a half circle. "Those good men, those hardy sailors, that fine captain, none of them wanted to cast him overboard." He tapped his chest with his fist. "They were an admirable lot."

The fishermen in the pews nodded their heads, murmuring approval, as if Rick were describing them.

"Jonah insisted on it," Rick said. "And do you know what happened?"

"What?" Peg asked. "Don't stop!"

"Keep going!" Oliver shouted.

Tillie jumped to her feet and glared at Peg and Oliver. "That's enough out of you two." She turned back to Rick and lifted a palm in the air, queen-like. "Carry on."

Rick waited until Tillie sat down, then snapped his fingers. "They threw him overboard—and the wind stopped." He snapped his fingers again. "The sea ceased from its raging."

"Nawwww," Captain Ed said. "Just like that?"

"Just like that," Rick said.

Maddie glanced down at her open Bible. Verse 15: "The sea ceased from its raging." *What?* Did Rick have the entire passage memorized?

Rick continued. "And how do you think those sailors felt?"

"Relieved!" "Overjoyed!" "Hungry!"

Tillie rose to her feet, turned to face the pews, and planted her fists on her hips. "All of you, now, hush up so our new pastor can finish his sermon."

"Thank you, Tillie," Rick said kindly, "but I don't mind the interruptions. In fact, I encourage them. Helps to know folks aren't nodding off."

Hardly. They were riveted to his every word.

Tillie slowly settled into her seat, but only after sweeping the congregation with a stern look of warning.

"Scripture says they were seized by a greater fear than when they thought they would drown. Why?"

On an easel behind Rick was a flip chart. He picked up a pen and wrote a number one, then:

Even the wind and sea obey God.

"Next lesson. Who was to blame for that terrible storm?"

"Jonah!" Cooper piped up. Cam beamed.

"Exactly!" Rick said. "But those sailors, they were caught in the storm too, weren't they? So what's the takeaway for you, and for me? For all of us?"

Silence.

Rick set the pen on the easel. "I want you to think of storms as a metaphor for problems."

Captain Ed let out a loud breath of air, as if he just now caught Rick's meaning.

After number 2, Rick wrote:

Some storms are caused by others, yet hurt us.

"Perhaps the most important lesson of all. Where was God in this storm?"

Again, silence.

"God was in that ship, even if the sailors or Jonah did not feel him or see him." After number 3, he wrote:

God is present.

Then he rested the pen on the easel and turned around. "God is never absent. There is no place you can go that God is not there. He is in the midst of every storm of your life, bringing all things— all things—to his purposes." He let that settle in for a stay, then said, "Let us pray."

Everyone's chins tucked to their chests in a prayer, all but Maddie. She was watching Rick as he prayed aloud. He had just delivered an outstanding sermon, well-crafted to his audience, entirely biblical. Good grief. She should have known he would knock it out of the park. That was a classic Ricky move.

In that moment, Maddie's stomach tightened with tingles of forgotten longing. For Ricky O'Shea. Oh, for heaven's sake.

And suddenly he opened his eyes and looked right at her, catching her staring at him. She jerked her chin down, heat infusing her cheeks.

Six

IT WAS AMAZING HOW MUCH COULD GET DONE in forty-eight hours. With help from Artie and his dad, the Grayson family spruced up Camp Kicking Moose for Memorial Day weekend, the official start of the summer season. Lawns were mowed, gardens weeded, trees trimmed, gutters cleaned, cabins swept free of cobwebs and dead moths, windows washed, lightbulbs replaced, indoor rugs and outdoor furniture hauled out from the carriage house and put into place for the summer.

Late on Sunday afternoon, Blaine and Artie carried paint cans and brushes as they inspected the exterior of each cabin, looking for trim that needed a touch-up. Blaine had yet to find the right time to tell her dad about her plans. As Artie stopped to scrape the sill on Never Enough Thyme's back window, she decided to practice her story on him first. Artie and his dad were heading out in a few hours, and she wasn't sure when she would see him next. "Artie, I need to float a plan by you. Listen and tell me what I need to change so that my dad doesn't freak out."

Artie brushed off the flecks of paint from the sill. "Shoot." Half listening, he dipped the paintbrush in the can.

"I'm going to take a break from culinary school."

His head jerked up. "Oh wow. I feel for your dad."

Blaine frowned. "Artie, you're supposed to help me. I need to find a way to break this to Dad gently but firmly. Pretend you're him."

"Are you crazy?"

"Now you're sounding a little too much like him. If you whisper in a shocked tone, you could practically be him."

Artie set the brush in the can and turned to face her. "Why would you throw this opportunity away?"

"I'm not throwing it away. I'm taking a pause. I finished the spring semester. I haven't wasted any tuition money. I'm just going to take time off."

"And do what?"

She focused on painting a stripe of white down the window's edge. "Travel. Around the world. Try new cuisines. Find my own voice. Food voice, that is. They talk a lot about that in culinary school. Finding your food voice."

"Why can't you finish culinary school first?"

"Okay, now that's good. That's the kind of thing Dad will ask. Keep going."

"I'm serious. Why can't you finish school? Travel afterwards?"

"Because . . . I'm losing my creative spark in that school." She thumped her chest. "My very soul. They're turning me into a robot. Artie, it's so intense. They make you feel as if there's one way to do things and it's their way. There's no room for experimenting or taking creative license."

"That's because they're teaching you foundational skills."

She sighed. "I've already got plenty of skills. Look at how successful the Lunch Counter is when I come back each summer."

"There's a big difference between a good grilled cheese sandwich and being qualified as a true chef."

She rolled her eyes. Everybody seemed to be an expert about the culinary world. "I need to find out who I am first. What kind of cooking do I want to do? Once I find out, then culinary school will be meaningful."

"How are you planning to pay for this year?"

She glanced down at her feet. "I'm still figuring that out. I've had friends who've traveled to Europe. They stay at youth hostels, buy food at grocery stores."

"I thought your point was to eat your way around the world."

"Well, yeah . . ."

"That'll take money. A lot of it, especially in the big cities. Paris, Milan. Unless you're talking street food in Third World countries."

Street food? What did that mean? She rolled it around and found she liked the sound of it. "Yes, street food." Third World countries . . . that she hadn't given much thought to. She should go to Third World countries. Definitely.

"Depending on the countries, you'll take a chance at getting sick. You'll need to plan for that too. I had a friend who got deathly ill in Morocco after eating street food."

"Man, Artie." Miffed, she scowled at him. "When did you turn into such a killjoy?"

"Killjoy? I'm trying to talk some sense into you, Blaine. You're treating culinary school like it's optional. What kind of doctor would I be if I felt I could bypass training?"

"Hold it. You can't compare cooking and baking to cutting someone open to take out an appendix." She waved her hands. "No comparison." Sheesh, Artie seemed almost angry with her. She almost wished she hadn't told him her plan. On the other hand, this was good practice. Dad would definitely be angry.

Artie picked up the brush and skimmed the extra paint off it before carefully painting the windowsill. Not a single drop of paint fell on the ground, or anywhere else. He would be a very good doctor one day, she realized. Incredible attention to detail. He glanced at her. "Any chance this whole bail-on-culinary-school has something to do with a guy?"

Blaine froze. She hadn't expected that question from Artie, but she should have. Of course, it would come up. Her sisters would certainly sniff it out.

The question was . . . how to explain *that* guy?

On Monday morning, Paul opened the windows in each cabin to air them out. They still smelled musty to him after the long winter. Later this week, before the start of Memorial Day weekend, Maddie said she would put fresh linens on the beds. Blaine was in charge of providing coffee supplies for battery-operated coffeemakers. That was a golden find—a source for battery-operated equipment. Coffee in the cabins would keep campers in their cabins a little longer in the morning. Too many mornings last summer, Paul woke to early riser campers who boldly knocked on Moose Manor's front door to demand hot coffee.

The Graysons did the best they could to provide breakfast, starting service at 7:00 a.m. Before she left for work at the diner each morning, Blaine set up a cold buffet on the porch of Moose Manor—granola, yogurt, orange juice, cereal, milk, berries. At nine o'clock, Cam and Paul took in the breakfast food and provided the makings for the campers to create their own brown-bag lunches: sandwich bread, peanut butter, jams and jellies and honey, apples, fresh-baked cookies, bottled iced teas and sodas. Maddie was in charge of shopping for breakfast and lunch supplies.

The campers were on their own for dinner. It worked out pretty well last summer—many ferried over to Mount Desert Island for

supper, or picnicked, or made do. Cam had said that if expectations were clearly spelled out, people didn't complain. It was only if
they didn't know what to expect . . . that's when they complained.
As usual, Cam was right.

"Dad?"

Paul spun around to find Blaine standing at the open door of
the Sea La Vie cabin. "Hey there. What are you doing home in
the middle of the day?"

"Power went out. Peg closed up."

Hands on his hips, he gave the interior of the cabin a final once-
over. "Looks pretty good in here, I think. The cabins are ready for
you girls to add your magic touch. We have a waiting list through
summer's end, though if it's like last year, there's a lot of movement. Next year, I'm going to have people put a deposit down when
they make a reservation, so there's less chance of cancelations."
Too much. Too long a phrase. He needed to keep to short sentences
if he wanted a steady, less-gravelly sounding voice.

"Make it nonrefundable."

He grinned. Good thinking. She was learning a lot. "Today's
mail brought the tuition bill for culinary school." Still too much.
He sounded raspy.

"Hold off on that." She took a step into the cabin, hands clasped
behind her back. "About this summer. Dad, as soon as Seth and
Cam get married, I'm planning to take off."

"Take off?" It came out like a squeak.

"I'm going to do a little traveling."

Hmmm. "Make sure Peg's okay with you being gone a week or
two." She counted heavily on Blaine's help at the Lunch Counter.

"Not a week or two. The whole summer." She dropped her
eyes. "The fall too."

Oh no. "Blaine, what's going on?"

"Dad, I need to find my culinary voice."

"Your *what*?" It was barely audible.

"I want to travel and try new cuisines."

"You want to vacation and eat?"

"No. Yes but no. I want to learn, Dad. About different kinds of foods, by traveling to their origins."

"Origins?"

"Regions."

"Regions?"

"Um, well, countries."

Whoa, whoa, whoa. He stood motionless, trying to keep his cool. "So let me get this straight," he whispered. "You are planning to travel to Europe—"

"Around the world, actually."

"—and eat your way through."

"That's not how I would frame it."

He lifted his palms in the air. "Frame away."

"I would like to explore regional cuisine in a variety of places. To attend some classes that would give me skills I can't get at the culinary school I've been attending."

Stay calm, stay calm, stay calm. Inside, Paul felt himself start to boil. He should've known, should've expected something like this from Blaine. She'd hardly called this last month. He had assumed, blissfully unaware, that she was busy with finals. Nope. She was busy planning her latest exit. He rubbed the tips of his fingers together. "How?"

"Can I afford this, you mean?" She moved forward into the cabin, nonchalantly looking over the décor. "I thought, maybe, I could use the tuition for the semester." She spun around with a hopeful look. "Consider it a hands-on education. An investment in your daughter."

"Nope."

"I'll pay you back. Every cent. With interest."

He shook his head. "That tuition money is set aside for you to finish culinary school. To graduate."

"Fine." She frowned, then jutted her chin out stubbornly. "I'll figure something out on my own then." She went to the door. "I'm still going to go, Dad. Right after the wedding." She turned and disappeared from his view.

He went to the cabin's threshold and watched her stride toward Moose Manor.

He shook his head like a dog after a swim. *That girl!* Blaine never finished anything. Every opportunity she was given, she took, excelled in, then lost interest and moved on to something else.

And Camp Kicking Moose! He was counting on Blaine's help with breakfasts at Moose Manor for the summer. Peg counted on her at the Lunch Counter. It amazed him that his daughter would disregard Peg's confidence in her. He was angry, so angry.

This was a rare moment when Paul was actually grateful he had no voice. At least he'd said nothing he regretted.

~⌒⊃

Maddie stopped in at the Lunch Counter to get a cup of coffee to go. It was a foggy Tuesday, a clammy cold that seeped into your bones. Coffee sounded good. Especially Blaine's dark roast coffee.

Nancy, the town's grocer, stood in front of the old-style register to pay for a coffee and muffin to go, chatting with Peg as she waited for change. Blaine was nowhere in sight. Maddie stood behind Nancy, hoping her presence would hint that she should take her coffee and muffin and go.

"Listen to that chatter," Nancy said.

There was a buzz in the small diner, a background hum of conversation.

Peg beamed. "Been like this since Sunday. It's all they're talking about in here. That boy's sermon. I'll bet you a free blueberry muffin that church'll be doubled in size next Sunday."

Near Maddie were two old fishermen sitting on the red stools at the counter. One was Oliver Moore, who had blurted out commentary during Rick's sermon. He was telling his friend all about Jonah and the sailors. Much of it was incorrect, but nevertheless, the sermon was on his mind. "You'd better come next week," Oliver told his friend. "He's talking about fishing."

As Maddie kept waiting for Nancy to finish her conversation with Peg, she became acutely aware of how many times she heard someone in the Lunch Counter mention the name Pastor Rick. It was like she felt a little zing each time someone said it. Like someone turned up the volume knob on "Pastor Rick!" then down again.

"Maddie, what do you think? I think Danny DeVito. Nancy wants Justin Timberlake."

Maddie snapped to attention, suddenly aware that Peg had been talking to her. "What do you mean?"

"Who would you cast in the role of Jonah? Danny or Justin?"

"I . . . uh . . . you mean, for a movie?" Seriously? These two women were talking about Rick's sermon as if it were a movie?

"Speaking of movies," Nancy said, giving Maddie a nudge with her elbow, "don't you think our new pastor looks like a young Tommy Lee Jones?"

"Ooooh . . ." Peg's pigtails, tucked behind her yellow headband, bounced up and down. "I can see the resemblance, Nancy. A young Tommy Lee, though. He hasn't aged well."

"A young George Clooney." Oh no. Did Maddie just say that out loud?

"SO SPOT-ON!" Peg said.

"My oh my, isn't he handsome?" Nancy asked. "And such a nice young man." She pocketed her change and turned around. "If I were you, Maddie Grayson, I'd get in line and try to stake my claim on that boy."

"He's not my type," Maddie said crisply.

Nancy looked her up and down. "No, I suppose not," she said, as if Maddie had asked for dating advice. "Fellas like that preacher don't drop out of the sky too often."

Ironic choice of phrase, Maddie thought. Very punny.

"Nancy," Peg said with a warning tone, "you're going to scare this girl into leaving the island."

"All I'm saying is that there's plenty of men on this island but not many a gal would want to snuggle up with on a cold winter night."

Peg nodded in agreement. "You know what we say around here . . . the odds are good but the goods are odd."

At that moment, Rick walked down Main Street toward Boon Dock. The three women watched him through the large picture window. Nancy sighed, patting the hair on the back of her neck. "If I were only twenty years younger."

"More like fifty," Peg murmured, handing Maddie a to-go coffee cup.

Maddie gave her a few dollars. "Keep the change, Peg." She couldn't take another minute of this rambling conversation.

Slowly, she walked up Main Street, sipping the coffee, mindful—but just barely—of how good it tasted now that Blaine had returned to Three Sisters Island. More on her mind was her discomfort over Rick's success. It shouldn't bother her that Rick had made such a splash, but it did. It felt like middle school all over again. He could do nothing wrong. She was the wet blanket nobody liked.

What was this all about? She didn't want to be a person who couldn't get past middle-school jealousies.

Argh. Was she jealous? She wasn't normally a jealous person, but something about Ricky O'Shea brought out a weirdness in her. She wasn't herself. Or maybe she was.

"Watch out!"

In the next instant, someone yanked Maddie off the sidewalk as a boy on a bicycle rounded the corner and barely missed hitting her. Shaken, she looked up to discover that Rick was the one who had pulled her from the path of the bicycle. "You!"

"No. *You.* Not sure what was so preoccupying, but you were heading straight into a run-in with that bicycle." He looked down the sidewalk at the boy, speeding away.

Coffee had spilled all over Maddie's white blouse, and she tried to brush off drips. *Shoot!* She had a new client this morning and no time to run back to Moose Manor. "Well, I guess I should thank you for yanking me so hard that my coffee spilled." She started back to the office, and he jumped in stride with her, as if invited.

"No thanks necessary. So, Maddie, what did you think?"

"Of what?"

"Of Sunday. The service."

"It was . . ." She glanced at him. "Well, lots of people seemed to have enjoyed it."

He shrugged off the praise. "I'd like your thoughts, Maddie." His eyes twinkled gaily, as though he'd paid her a great compliment, or as though there was a secret understanding between them. He touched her arm. "Tell me the truth. What'd you think?"

"It was fine."

"Just fine?"

"Better than fine." She tried to swallow down reluctant admiration. "Why does it matter what I think?"

"You and I . . . we're a team."

She stopped. "Oh no. We are *not* a team."

"Sure we are. Why, just yesterday, I met someone over in Bar Harbor and referred her to you. I'm hoping she'll set up an appointment with you for counseling."

Ah, so *that's* who had called for an appointment today. "Thank you for the referral." She held her chin at a strong angle. "But we are *not* a team. My practice is entirely separate from the church. I am merely renting space. Soon, I will need to move to larger quarters." Where did that come from? She loved her little basement office. Besides, she could barely afford the rent. Clients were few and far between. But they were coming. The couple who worried about agreeing with each other too much called yesterday to say they checked with their insurance company and were happy to discover that insurance would pay for the sessions. They made another appointment, and she had hung up the phone and danced a little jig. Her first repeat business.

"Our work overlaps. We're both in the business of helping people."

That was hard to argue against. She lifted her eyes to look at him. In this morning light, Rick did kind of resemble a young Tommy Lee Jones. Or a young Dennis Quaid? Actually, Rick was even better looking. *Maddie! Do not go down that path again. You know better.* She broke eye contact before she said something stupid.

"So what was on your mind just now that you nearly got creamed by a bicycle?"

"My mind?" Right, as if she would admit out loud that she was thinking of him, of feeling jealous of him. Of being annoyed with herself for her pettiness over him. "I'm working on some therapy to divorce-proof a couple."

He gave her a look of surprise, then his brows knitted together. "Brilliant! Maddie, you're way ahead of everybody else. You always were. Instead of focusing on divorce recovery, you're focusing on divorce-proofing."

Stop! she wanted to shout. *Stop being nice to me, to everyone.* At the front door of the house that served as the church office, she spotted Tillie waiting for Rick with a handful of pink phone messages in her hands. Maddie took the opportunity to veer to the left toward the basement, lifting her hand in a wave. "Looks like you've got a busy day ahead."

She resisted the urge to look at him. If she looked at him, she'd be powerless to stop herself from wanting him. No thank you. She'd been down that road before.

$$\sim\!\!\circ$$

Two days in a row, right around noon, the power on the island went out and stayed off for hours. Peg always closed the Lunch Counter during outages. Her philosophy was "Why fight it? Take a nap." So Blaine hung up her apron and went home, arriving to find Cam at the big kitchen table, papers spread out everywhere. Blaine's eyes went straight to Cam's big leather messenger bag on the table, and she set it on the floor.

"Why'd you do that?" Cam said, glancing at her with a frown.

"Germs." In one of Blaine's culinary classes, an instructor had shown slides of bacteria from a purse. They were warned to never allow patrons to put their purses on top of tables. Food and flatware, those were the only objects that belonged on a tabletop.

Blaine opened the fridge and took out a can of seltzer water. "Are you working on the wedding?"

Cam lifted her head, puzzled. "Wedding?" She looked back to her open computer. "I'm working on a presentation for the town hall meeting. The first stage of developing a plan for alternative energy for the island."

Blaine popped the lid on her can and sat down at the table, facing Cam. "What about the wedding?"

"What about it?"

"Cam, I came back for your wedding this summer, but I do have other plans. I can't just hang around, waiting for you to choose a date."

Cam looked at her in complete confusion. "What other plans?"

Blaine took a sip from the can. "I have a life, you know."

"I'm not asking anything of you. Other than to be here for the wedding."

Not asking anything of you. In other words, no plan to ask Blaine to bake a wedding cake. "And just when is this wedding?" Her voice had an edge to it.

Cam stretched, then picked up her pencil. "We had to wait to set a date until we had a pastor on the island."

"Pastor's here." Blaine made a check sign in the air. "You know, most brides are actually excited to set a date."

Cam scratched something out on her pad of paper. "I am excited."

"Most brides start planning their wedding the moment they get engaged."

Cam let out a puff of air. "Just because I'm not like most brides doesn't mean I'm not excited to marry Seth. I am."

"Then prove it. Set a date."

She put a palm down on her papers. "First things first. I need to focus on this project."

"Good grief, Cam. You're turning right back into the Type A person you've always been."

Cam glanced up, surprised. "What is *that* supposed to mean?"

"First things first?" Blaine scoffed. "Seth wants to marry you. Cooper needs Seth. And all you can think about is business. That's your only priority. Not your family."

"It's not just business, Blaine," Cam said, eyes narrowed. "I'm trying to help everyone on this island. Take Peg's Lunch Counter, for one. You of all people know how frustrating it is when the electricity goes off and on. Just yesterday, you came home fuming. Your stones were ruined."

"Scones."

"You said they were rocks."

"They'd been baked to the point of hard as rocks. But they were *scones*."

"And Cooper does have time with Seth. He and Seth spend every day together at school. Cooper's doing great. No anxiety issues. Or . . ." Cam hesitated. "Less of them."

"But Cooper still doesn't know that Seth is his biological dad."

"Not yet. Maddie's the one who told us to handle that carefully, to maybe wait until after we're married, so it doesn't create anxiety for him. You know how he has a tendency to focus on one thing to the point that he becomes . . ."

"Fixated."

"For now, Cooper and Seth are building their relationship. Creating a solid foundation."

"So what about Seth?"

"What about him?"

"He wants to marry you, Cam. That means you live together." She pointed to the ceiling. "One roof."

Cam frowned. "I'm well aware."

"Shouldn't first things first mean that the people you love come first?"

Cam didn't have an answer to that. After a long silence, she said, "You know what I think? I think you're using my wedding as a decoy. Maddie calls it a deflection tool."

"What?"

"I think you've got something else on your mind besides my wedding."

"What's that supposed to mean?"

Cam leaned back in her chair. "You've been acting odd since you came home."

In the middle of a swallow, Blaine coughed. "Odd?" She wiped her mouth. "Odd, how?"

"Nervous. Jumpy as a flea on a dog."

Blaine stared at her. Her first thought was that she was shocked Cam had even noticed her, that she'd been paying attention to her at all. Her second thought was that Cam was right. She couldn't be still. Even now, under the table, her legs were crossed, one foot was tapping in the air.

"Blainey," Cam said, spoken softer now. "Is something wrong?"

Eyes on the can of seltzer water, Blaine hesitated. She needed to talk to someone, but Cam had never been the sister she confided in. The very last person she would ever share a problem with. The very last! Cam would do one of two things—deny it as a problem or immediately try to fix it.

What was weighing heavily on Blaine's mind this summer was not something that could be denied nor fixed.

She got up from the table and threw the seltzer can in the recycle bin. "I'm going to need the kitchen tonight. I invited Pastor Rick for supper. I want to make something special." She scratched a mosquito bite on her arm with the tips of her fingers. "Assuming the power comes back on."

"Fine. If you don't want to talk to me, then talk to someone." Cam flicked a look at her and said no more.

Seven

IT WAS MIDAFTERNOON. Maddie sat inside her office, waiting for her client to arrive. A new one, the referral from Bar Harbor to whom Rick had alluded. A woman had called to say that she was having consistent trouble with her daughter-in-law and needed some advice.

In-law problems. She could almost hear her sisters' cackle: How are *you* supposed to give advice to a mother-in-law when you aren't even married?

She squeezed her eyes shut as a ripple of disquiet spread through her, and her stomach clenched tightly. *Stop it, Maddie. Those old insecurities!* They just kept finding her, creeping up on her, trying to spook her.

This whole area of self-doubt . . . she'd been working on it very intentionally over the last year, after her wedding was called off to college boyfriend Tre. Without his big personality calling all the shots, she became aware that her lack of confidence—always wobbly—had virtually collapsed sometime during their unhealthy relationship. She couldn't even find an internship to get her hours in for certification of her degree, and it wasn't because she didn't have opportunities. The reason was that she kept bombing the interviews. Too meek, too waffling, too docile. Mild as a sheep. One interviewer finally asked her, "Do you have any opinions at all?"

At home, Maddie had plenty of opinions. But home was one thing, out in the professional world was another.

In that lightbulb moment, Maddie sensed the Lord was telling her, *Time to get serious about working on this. You've got this self-worth thing all mixed up.* It wasn't like a voice, but she sensed it all the same.

And so she set to work to better understand God's perspective on her, and in that light, how she should view herself. Maddie knew the best thing she could do was to pray about her lack of experience and allow the Lord to turn her perceived weakness into a strength. She knew she had nothing to offer today's client without God's guidance and wisdom. And that was her strength. That was her rock of confidence. Not what she thought of herself. Not what others thought of her. Only what God thought of her.

She glanced at the clock. Ten minutes until the client was due to arrive. She took out her Bible and read a favorite verse that always gave her a boost of healthy, whole confidence—the right kind. "The Lord will complete what his purpose is for me. Lord, your gracious love is eternal; do not abandon your personal work in me."

Together she prayed, *we can do this, Lord. Fill my mind and mouth with your wisdom, healing, and hope.*

She heard a knock on her office door and snapped her Bible closed. She blew out a puff of air. "Okay. Let's go."

Maddie opened the door to a striking sixtysomething woman. She was well-dressed and had a slender figure, long French-manicured fingernails, and expensive Italian leather shoes. Maddie knew the brand because Cam liked the same shoes. This was definitely not a typical female local, the majority of whom dressed in Birkenstock sandals over white socks, baggy T-shirts, and saggy well-worn jeans.

"Are you Madison Grayson?"

"I am. Come in. You must be . . ."

"Elizabeth Turner. I live over in Bar Harbor. I met your handsome pastor a few days ago, and when I explained my . . . situation . . . he suggested I come have a chat with you."

Maddie tried not to visibly stiffen. Rick was not *her* handsome pastor. But she did appreciate his referral. "I'm glad you called, Elizabeth."

"I didn't want to see a family therapist on Mount Desert Island. People talk, you know. Everybody knows everybody's business. There are no secrets on an island." Her mouth puckered in disapproval so tightly it all but disappeared.

That, Maddie understood. "Can I get you some coffee?"

Elizabeth looked around the room and her prim mouth relaxed slightly. "No, I'd rather just get to the point. The ferry's captain told me to return to the ferry in an hour or so."

Or so was more accurate. "Captain Ed won't leave without you." Maddie pointed to a chair and sat across from it. "Please sit. Tell me what's on your mind."

Elizabeth sat down and crossed her ankles, launching into her story as if she'd practiced it: She'd been widowed early in her marriage and raised a son alone. They'd had a very nice relationship, even after her son had married. Elizabeth had relocated from Portland to Bar Harbor to be closer to her son and daughter-in-law.

All was going well, she said, until her daughter-in-law had a baby. "All I want to do is to spend time with my granddaughter, but my daughter-in-law acts as if I'm incompetent. As if I can't be trusted. She's practically barred me from their household."

She paused. "When I was a new mother, I would've loved this kind of help. I was all on my own, a widow, without anyone to step alongside me."

As she listened to Elizabeth, Maddie's automatic response was to express sorrow for her, to take sides against this unreasonable daughter-in-law who had crowded out this nice woman from her family's life. Her only son. Her only grandchild. Maddie suppressed that initial empathetic response because she now knew it was so often wrong. Her lips tipped downward. "How old is your granddaughter?"

"Sophie is eight years old." Elizabeth took a tissue and dabbed her eyes. "I've waited a very long time to be a grandmother. I became a mother in my midthirties, and then my son took forever to marry, and then they both were older and it took a while for Vivienne to get pregnant. So here I am, in the last quarter of my life, finally having the grandchild I have dreamed about for years . . . and I'm banned!"

"What kinds of things have you been banned from?"

"Only areas that helped them. I would pick Sophie up from school and volunteer at events. I teach her Sunday school class. And last week, I signed up to lead Sophie's Brownie troop. That's what set off Vivienne's latest snit. But she didn't want to lead the troop, and no one else was willing to do it, you see. This generation of mothers . . . they're all too busy for their children."

Red flag, red flag. Maddie felt a hitch in her gut. "Elizabeth, did you ask your daughter-in-law first about those things?"

"What things?"

"Well, for example, volunteering at a school event."

"Why should I? She doesn't do any volunteer work. She works full-time. More than full-time." She squeezed her lips together. "I'm only stepping into her absences. She should be grateful." She

76

crossed her hands on her lap, giving the distinct impression that she was in the right.

"But your daughter-in-law, she's not grateful."

"Not at all. And last weekend, after the Brownie troop debacle, we exchanged some rather unpleasant words. She said I am no longer welcome in their lives. That I need to respect their boundaries." She teared up. "Boundaries! From my own son and granddaughter." She blew her nose. "I don't know what to do. Maybe I should just move back to Portland."

That, Maddie could tell, was the last thing this woman wanted to do. She let Elizabeth compose herself, then said, "It's not hopeless. But I think the key here is going to be your daughter-in-law."

Elizabeth's head snapped up. Her shoulders straightened. "What? She's the one who's being so awful!"

"But she's the key, isn't she?"

"She holds power, yes."

"That's one way of saying it. I have a feeling she may say you have quite a bit of power too."

"How's that?"

Should Maddie say what she was thinking? The work of therapy was to ask the right questions until something happened that led a client to a better understanding of themselves . . . eventually to their own self-awareness. She could say what she was thinking in such a way that Elizabeth could pick up on it. "There's something grandparents do that we call the End Zone Run. To get to the grandchildren, the grandparents bypass the parents."

"Bypassing! I'm only trying to help. To have a relationship with my granddaughter. I never had grandparents."

"Of course, and that's a good thing to want a relationship with Sophie. But in doing so, I think you might have gotten caught up in the End Zone Run."

"Or maybe my daughter-in-law has gotten caught up in being self-centered and cruel." Elizabeth cocked one eyebrow and thought a moment, then leaned forward. "She's French, you know," as if that explained everything.

"But you're here and she's not, so that tells me that you're the one willing to make a change. Could I give you a few things to work on this week? To see if you can reestablish a relationship?"

She hesitated. "I really don't think this will work."

"Elizabeth, at this point, do you have anything more to lose by trying?"

She let out a breath. "I suppose not."

Maddie picked up her pen and wrote a few things on her pad of paper. "Okay. First thing, you're going to apologize."

"What?! Me?" Elizabeth squeezed her lips together in disapproval.

"Yes. You're going to tell your daughter-in-law just what you told me. That you didn't have any grandparents, that you were on your own as a mother, that you wished you'd had family as you raised your son. And because of that, you might have overstepped your boundaries."

Elizabeth's thinly arched eyebrows raised in skepticism. "Me?" She thumped her hand against her chest. "Overstepped?"

"And you're going to tell her that you'd like another chance to do it right."

Now her eyebrows furrowed. "I thought I was doing it right."

"Your heart is definitely in the right place." Maddie leaned back in her chair. "Elizabeth, if you are willing to try, I think you can gain back your family."

Elizabeth Turner did not look at all convinced by Maddie's advice as she gathered her things and prepared to leave. In fact, she asked just how long Maddie had been working as a therapist, and

Maddie kind of hedged with a vague "Quite some time" response—but Elizabeth did make another appointment for one week from today. And she offered a tight smile as she turned to leave.

Well, Maddie thought. *It could be the start of something.* Through the basement window, she watched Elizabeth walk toward Main Street and offered up a prayer for her.

A gentle rain was falling. Cam had been working on a grant on her computer at the Lunch Counter when the power went out. Her computer battery had been perilously low to begin with, which was why she'd gone to the Lunch Counter in the first place. She sighed and shut down her computer. Like it or not, the workday was over. When Peg closed up the diner, Cam walked up to the school. The kids were outside for recess, even in the rain. Standing under her big umbrella, she watched Cooper play tetherball with Quinn, his friend with pink hair. Seth noticed she was standing by the fence and joined her under her umbrella.

"Where's Dory?" she asked.

"Inside. Remember? She doesn't like rain."

She held the umbrella up high so it would shelter him. "I'm not sure Dory understands what it means to be a Labrador retriever. They're supposed to love water."

He grinned. "Not Dory. And don't even mention thunderstorms around her. Pathetic." He reached out to tuck a lock of hair behind her ear. "What's up?" he said in a gentle tone. "You look frustrated."

"I am. I can't even get a grant for energy written up because the power keeps going off." Sometimes she felt almost angry with this island. It seemed to be intent on sabotaging her efforts to help it move into the twenty-first century.

Cam had planned to start the first phase of the energy project this summer. Not a chance! Not after a long winter, when the island virtually shut down, isolated from the mainland. Not after a rainy spring, when she kept missing deadlines for grant applications because the power went out with storms. This summer, she felt fortunate whenever she made the tiniest bit of headway. It was ridiculous, how slow this was going. In the business world, time was money. Things got done. Not here. This island was driving her crazy. "I think I'm going to head over to Bar Harbor and work in the library. Someplace where the power stays on."

"If you can wait until school gets out today, Cooper and I will join you."

"Are you sure? Blaine's cooking a big dinner at Moose Manor. She's invited Pastor Rick."

"Cooper and I were planning to take Lola to a gathering of goshawks. A couple of bird lovers are meeting up on Cadillac Mountain this afternoon to let their birds take flight. Cooper talked your dad into coming. Peg too."

She peered around the edge of her umbrella. "But it's raining."

"No matter. I've got all the right gear for rain. I learned that lesson the hard way. After the first winter here, I bought whatever equipment I needed to be able to get outside. That's the way you learn to live here. There's no point in fighting the island, Cam. Instead, just don't let those frustrating parts stop you."

Cam did let those things stop her. The weather stopped her. So did the lack of consistent electricity. Not Seth. He figured out ways to get around those frustrations. She smiled, remembering how just last week during yet another power outage, he'd brought every candle he could find out to her at Moose Manor so she could edit a hard copy of a grant application. He smiled back at her and she stood on her tiptoes to kiss him. How she loved this gentle man. Seth challenged her to be a better version of herself.

Cooper ran up to them and Cam pushed his wet hair off his forehead. "I just beat Quinn in tetherball."

Seth high-fived him. "You're turning into the school's tetherball champion."

Cooper's glasses were dotted with raindrops, but there was no mistaking the beam of his smile.

⁓◦

Maddie looked in the mirror and combed her hair, twisting it tight and neat on her head, then tried to turn it into a messy bun the way Blaine had showed her. She studied her face in the small mirror. Looking back at her was a curvy brunette of average height, average weight, average attractiveness.

Average, average, average. Boring, boring, boring. She was a mess.

She pulled out the hair elastic and started again.

Come on, Maddie. Stop that accusing spiral. You know that isn't how the Lord thinks, or talks, or considers you. God was a giver of encouragement and affirmation, not belittling jabs. Those were the enemy's work.

She looked herself right in the eyes and gave herself a pep talk: "Think of how far you've come this year. You aren't the same woman you used to be. You aren't crippled with fear like you used to be. You aren't sinking in self-doubts. You aren't fearful of sneak panic attacks." The woman looking back at her was no weakling. She stood in the Wonder Woman pose—hands on her hips, legs spread a foot apart. Did it help her confidence like all the self-help books promised? She wasn't sure.

A short ringlet escaped her bun and she tucked it behind her ear, thinking of the shaving lather that was left on Rick's chin this morning. She'd bumped into him at the Lunch Counter when she went in for morning coffee—something that was becoming a regular event. Bumping into Rick, that was. Every morning lately, he seemed to arrive whenever she was there. It was strange, because her timing varied. Then Blaine had invited him for dinner tonight, and he was due to arrive at Moose Manor any minute now. She didn't know why Blaine had to keep inviting Rick to dinner. Big, lavish dinners too. She never stopped cooking lately. It was like she was in overdrive, constantly planning or doing, wanting the family to get on the same page as her.

Tonight shouldn't be a big deal to Maddie. Really. It wasn't a big deal. Blaine was cooking, Maddie had no responsibilities. Dad and Cam and Seth and Cooper would do plenty of talking. All Maddie had to do was to be hospitable to the new pastor. That's all.

She pulled out her elastic, brushed her hair hard, and tried to twist it into a bun again. It wasn't just a new pastor coming to dinner. This was Rick O'Shea. And he continued to be extremely nice to her—referring more clients to her, seeking out her opinion about ideas for the church, buying coffee for her when they both happened to end up at the register of the Lunch Counter—but that only made her suspicious. When would the other shoe drop?

She heard a car pull up the gravel driveway and gave up trying to create a messy bun. She shook out her hair and applied another coat of lip gloss. Down the stairs she went, heart drumming so loudly she could hear it herself, and in came Blaine and Rick. He stood at the open door with two big brown paper grocery bags in his arms, watching her come down the last few steps with an appreciative look on his face. Another wave of nervousness rippled through her. "Where's everyone else?"

Blaine dropped her purse on the hall table and headed toward the kitchen. "They're heading over to Bar Harbor."

"What? Why?"

Blaine had already disappeared into the kitchen. Maddie avoided Rick's eyes.

"Your hair's pretty, down like that," he said. "In fact, you look . . . lovely."

Flustered by his compliment, her hand went up to the back of her neck. "Um, uh. What's going on in Bar Harbor?"

"Not exactly sure, but it had something to do with a bird."

"Seth's bird?"

A pair of creases appeared between his dark eyebrows. "I think so." Rick was still watching her. "They went over to Bar Harbor to meet up with other bird lovers." He shifted the bags, which looked pretty heavy. "Cam's going to the library to work on a grant." He shifted the bags again. "Wanted to be clear, just in case you were thinking of avoiding me by heading to town. No one's there."

She squared her chin and looked him dead in the eye. "I had no such intention." Total fib.

He looked back at her directly, eyes crinkling in amusement. "You never could tell a lie," he said, as he walked around her toward the kitchen.

Good grief. Could he read her mind? Or was she that obvious? It had been on the tip of her tongue to excuse herself and hurry to town.

Blaine called to her and she joined them in the kitchen. "I'm making something special. A new recipe I've been thinking about." She took the grocery bags from Rick and handed him a bottle of Chardonnay and two glasses, plus an opener. "I'll need help in about thirty minutes. But I have to get one thing in the oven first, and I'd prefer if the kitchen were all mine." Before Maddie could object, Blaine pushed her away. "Your cheeks are suspiciously rosy," she whispered.

"What?"

Blaine winked at her. "Go. Take Pastor Rick to the front porch and watch the sunset on this beautiful day. Leave me in peace."

Maddie gave her an arched-eyebrow look and headed through the kitchen door. Tonight, the peachy pink sky was showing dusk off. The front of Moose Manor faced west. She gestured to the porch swing for Rick to sit in and she plopped down in a chair. "If you're very quiet, and listen carefully, you can hear the surf hitting the rocks."

"Which way is the ocean?"

She pointed toward the trees, beyond the carriage house that used to serve as the schoolhouse. "Boon Dock is that way." She stuck her thumb in the other direction. "The Atlantic is on the other side of the island. Open seas. Seth calls it the frantic Atlantic."

He tipped his head, opening the bottle of wine with practiced ease, and popped the cork. "I don't think I could ever grow weary of the sound of breaking surf." He poured a glass for her, one for him, and they clinked glasses. "How do you like living on an island?"

"Took a while at first, but I like it quite a bit."

"You're settling down?"

"I suppose so. For now." She took a sip of wine, wondering how long she would stay on Three Sisters Island. "What about you? It's one thing to visit an island, another thing altogether to live on it." She glanced at him. "Any regrets?"

"None so far." He took in a deep breath and looked out over the large grass lawn that surrounded Moose Manor. "I think of wilderness as an ungroomed masterpiece of nature."

Swallowing, she practically choked. "Don't let my dad hear you describe this front lawn as wilderness. He's declared war on the wilderness. Currently, there's a family of ducks that won't leave. Dad is trying to train the coon cat to go after them."

"Big changes at Camp Kicking Moose?"

"Huge ones. Dad has slaved over this property." She snapped her gaze back to him. "You should've seen it this time last year." She set down her wine glass and pointed to the roofs of the cabins, barely visible from the porch. "Those cabins were a disaster." And she looked behind her at the exterior siding of Moose Manor. "This old house was a disaster too. The previous owners painted it bubblegum pink."

Rick grinned. "Tell me more."

"Dad and Cam have big plans. Cam, really. She's the one with the vision. She thinks Camp Kicking Moose could be a year-round destination spot."

"Even in winter? What would people do?"

"Cross-country ski on the old carriage roads, for one thing."

"I wouldn't think an island gets enough snow."

"Fifty-nine inches this last winter."

His eyebrows lifted appreciatively. "I think I'll order a better down jacket than the one I have." He moved one ankle over his knee. "The camp's so far from town and there's only one main artery on this island. If you get that much snow, isn't it a problem?"

"Everything's a problem on Three Sisters Island in the winter. Everything. That's why Cam's so fired up to get this renewable energy program up and going."

"As a pastor, I like the excitement that's brewing on this island. It's one of the reasons I came here. People, like your sister Cam, are looking to the future. Trying to get ready for it."

So what's the other reason you came here? It was on the tip of her tongue to ask, but she wasn't really sure she wanted to hear the answer.

Since Maddie didn't ask that question, she ran out of things to say and so, it seemed, had Rick. But it wasn't a comfortable silence between them. The air felt thick with unsaid words, a sharp contrast to the serenely setting sun. A queer mixture of feelings came over her: familiarity, longing, caution.

After a prolonged silence, she could feel his attention on her. "Maddie, we really should talk about—"

She jumped from her chair. "I'd better go see if Blaine needs help."

He sat, motionless, giving her a terse nod.

"You stay put and enjoy the sunset." Why did she say that? He hadn't budged.

Stupid, stupid, stupid. She was only piling on more weirdness between them. It was all her doing. She felt annoyed with herself and supremely bothered that he was behaving as the more mature one. Willing to face hard things head-on, while she was doing all she could to avoid them. Avoid him.

Unbelievable. Ricky O'Shea and mature were two words she never would have imagined could be in the same sentence.

But it was true. She was acting like she was still in high school and he was behaving like a grown man. A gentleman. A healthy individual.

She, on the other hand, could not stop remembering how things had been left between them on the night of Senior Prom. *Mortifying.*

***

MADDIE, AGE 18

Maddie's date for Senior Prom was her best friend's older brother, Chipper, who currently attended the local junior college. Chipper had been a varsity tight end on the high school football team and should have—could have—had an athletic scholarship

for college . . . but for his poor GPA and even worse test scores. He
was model-gorgeous, somewhere in the league of Fabio, with long
flowing hair, a chiseled jaw, piercing eyes, and a body of sculpted
muscles. He'd started modeling for a Boston ad agency. During
high school, Maddie had been his science lab partner. While she
wasn't entirely immune to his good looks, he was as dumb as
a box of rocks. He had nothing to say, because nothing was on
his mind other than catching a football. And catching a view of
himself in a mirror.

As Senior Prom approached and Maddie still didn't have a date,
her friend Lacey suggested she ask Chipper. "No way," Maddie
said. "Why would a college guy come back for Senior Prom?"

"Because Chipper owes you, Maddie. Big time. If it weren't for
you, he wouldn't have even graduated from high school."

Maddie thought about it for a few days, then finally broke down
and asked Chipper to come. Lacey must have prepped him, because
he instantly said yes. If nothing else, in her beautiful periwinkle
blue dress, with gorgeous Chipper on her arm, she'd have good
photographs to show her children one day.

Maddie, Lacey, and a few other friends spent the day of Senior
Prom primping for the ball: nails, toes, updo hairstyles. That was
the best part of a dance—the primping with her friends. But it
was expensive too. This one day cost her a full month of babysit-
ting Blaine. Worth every penny. When she heard Chipper's voice
downstairs, she appraised herself in the mirror one last time. Even
to her own eyes, she liked what she saw. She'd never thought of
herself as attractive, not sandwiched between two striking sisters.
She'd always felt like a common daisy between a bold sunflower
(Cam) and an exotic orchid (Blaine). Tonight, she looked—even
better, she *felt*—beautiful.

Just like in the movies, Chipper's eyes lit up when he saw her come down the stairs. He couldn't take his gorgeous eyes off Maddie, even throughout the stern lecture her father gave him on behaving like a gentleman.

Wasted words.

The ball was held at a local hotel. After the pictures were taken, before the band started to play, Maddie went into the ladies' room to touch up her makeup. When she returned, Chipper was nowhere to be seen. Lacey said she thought he had probably gone outside for fresh air.

He had gone out for fresh air, plus to drink beer and who knew what else with his former football buddies—but Maddie didn't realize all that at first. When he finally reappeared, she was dancing with a boy from her English class in the middle of the dance floor. Chipper made his way through the crowd of dancing couples to pull Maddie by the hand.

"Sorry, little dude," he said to her surprised partner. "Tonight she's all mine."

Maddie didn't mind the abrupt interruption. The room was hot and the music was loud and the boy from her English class kept stepping on the hem of her dress. Out on the patio, she noticed a few couples making out in shadowy corners and worried that was what Chipper had on his mind, but he stopped in the center, turning to her, swaying to the music. He was a good dancer, and she joined in, moving to the beat. Then came a slow dance, and that was when she smelled the beer on his breath. He pulled her toward him with a jerk, his big sweaty hands against her back, then moved slowly down. She swatted his hands away, but he kept squeezing her bottom. The harder she pushed him away, the tighter he held her, kissing her clumsily. She started to panic, squirm, elbow him, but he had her firmly in his arms, tight against his huge chest, covering her mouth with his.

And then someone grabbed him from behind, hard. Chipper released Maddie suddenly, swirling around. Ricky O'Shea, a foot smaller than big Chipper but faster, quicker, and not drunk. Chipper swung to punch him, but Ricky ducked. Chipper went flying into the hedge, stumbled to his feet, then slipped to the ground like a rag doll, chin on his chest.

Ricky had been poised like a boxer, readying for a fight, then slowly dropped his arms to his sides. "Well, I'll be," he said in a tone of wonder.

"Is he dead?" Maddie said. "Did you kill him?"

"Nope. Just passed out." Maddie and Ricky looked at each other and burst out laughing. "Let's get out of here."

"What about your date?"

Ricky spun around and pointed to the corner, to a couple making out. "I think she's in good hands." He put out a hand for Maddie to hold on to as she stepped over Chipper's tree-trunk-like legs.

"I can't just leave him here."

"Someone will find him." He tugged her hand, but she didn't budge. "Maddie," he said with a sigh, "do you always have to be so responsible?"

"I do." But she was ready to go. This ball was a bummer. "Let me just tell his sister." She went inside and found Lacey, whispering to her about the condition her brother was in out on the patio.

Lacey didn't seem terribly surprised, and not at all troubled. "Just go," she told Maddie. "I'll take care of him." She grabbed Maddie's arm. "I'm sorry."

Maddie wasn't at all sorry. She was leaving the ball with Ricky O'Shea, the last person she would have ever imagined. She never left anything early. She'd always been the type who stayed to the very end of events. At weddings, she wouldn't let her parents leave until the bride threw her bouquet and drove away with her groom.

And here she was, in Mrs. O'Shea's minivan, riding shotgun to Ricky. She realized he had someplace in mind, weaving through Needham to get to Interstate 95, then south on Highway 3. "Um, where are we going?"

"To Chatham."

Her eyes went wide. "Cape Cod? Tonight?"

"Yup. To the lighthouse." He glanced at her. "Okay with you?"

She tried to keep her smile contained, modest, oh-so-cool. Inside, she was turning cartwheels. Ecstatic. Giddy with this turn of events. "Okay with me."

Eight

MEMORIAL DAY WEEKEND HAD COME AND GONE. The second summer of Camp Kicking Moose was underway. There were a few kinks to work out, a few minor mishaps—a mouse in one cabin, a midnight encounter with a skunk as one camper got lost finding his cabin in the dark. That very camper was miffed when he woke at noon and discovered breakfast was no longer available. And then there was a brown duck that kept wandering around the cabins—but those kinds of things were to be expected. Overall, the first full week of camp was going pretty well.

On a warm June day, besides being hungry, Paul stopped by the Lunch Counter to check on Blaine. He grinned when he caught sight of Peg's lime-green polka-dot headband. A different color or pattern each day. The headband framed a round, cheery face. Cute too. Such an awareness startled him, because he hadn't given Peg's appearance any consideration. But it suddenly occurred to him that Peg Legg was cute. Very cute. Happy cute. She was always happy.

She waved to him from behind the cash register. "Sit on down at the counter and tell me what's going on out at Moose Manor."

He swung a leg over one red stool, sat down, and leaned on his elbows. "Week one. So far, no complaints."

"Your voice sounds a little better."

"Think so?" He thought so too. Peg noticed things about him that his own daughters failed to observe.

"I sure do. Less of a kicking-up-gravel sound." She placed a glass of iced tea in front of him. "You still seeing that speech therapist in Bar Harbor?"

"Not for the summer. She's got kids at home." Peg was the one who had found the speech therapist for Paul. He continued to faithfully do his exercises and worked to keep sentences short, to the point, so his vocal cords could rest. Never use more words than necessary, she had warned him. He looked around. "Blaine?"

"She's gone for the day. Not sure where she went, but she had something on her mind."

It figured. Elusive, that girl.

He was just about to ask Peg if she had sensed Blaine's restlessness this summer—far more than usual—when the overhead bells on the door tinkled. Paul could tell by the expression on Peg's face that she was pleased to see whoever had just come in.

"Pastor Rick! Come sit down next to Paul Grayson and I'll get you a glass of iced tea. On the house."

Peg hadn't offered free iced tea to Paul. Pastor privileges, he supposed.

Rick gave him a gentle pat on the back and shook his hand before claiming a stool. "How are you doing, Paul? You don't mind if I call you Paul, do you? Or do you prefer Mr. Grayson?" He genuinely seemed to want to know.

Paul hesitated before answering, gathering his thoughts. Rick O'Shea had clearly evolved from the awful little kid who'd TP'd and egged the Grayson house on a regular basis, but that didn't mean Paul viewed him as his pastor. Not yet, anyway. Rick continued to wait for his response, as if he had all the time in the world. "Paul's fine." Okay, if this kid wanted to play pastor, Paul would give him a chance. "Turned sixty. Can't make a decision anymore."

Rick took a sip of iced tea, as if he, too, were weighing his words carefully. "In the last two years, seems like you've made a boatload of big decisions."

Paul nodded. There was a lot of truth in that. He'd sold a house, bought an old camp on a remote island in Maine, fixed it up, started a summer business. Put that way, he had done a lot of decision making. He sat up a little straighter.

"Have any of them been wrong decisions?" Rick asked. "Really bad, I mean. The kind that aren't easy to recover from."

Sipping from his glass, Paul pondered that question for a long moment. Peg was coming in and out of the storeroom, and he waited until she had left again. "Not bad ones. But not easy ones."

"Maybe you've needed a little breather from heavy decision making. Take the pressure off yourself for a while. Let your batteries recharge. Maybe that's what's going on with turning sixty—a time to reflect and recharge. When you're ready, start slow. One step at a time." Rick finished the iced tea and rose to his feet. "You've made a lot of good choices in the last few years, Paul. You'll survive if you botch a few up here and there." He took a few dollars out of his wallet and left them on the counter for Peg. "She's always trying to comp me, but I won't let her. She's got a business to run." He gave Paul another gentle pat on the shoulder and left the diner.

A time to reflect . . . and recharge. Paul liked that. It was much more encouraging than the thoughts he'd been having about turning sixty. Grim thoughts. He heard Peg's voice laughing from the storeroom. Sounded like she was on the phone with someone. She was always laughing, a tonic to be around.

He thought about asking Peg if she'd like to go on a hike with him to the lighthouse sometime. Sunday after church, maybe. He'd get Blaine to pack a picnic.

The thought cheered him up considerably. Asking Peg to go on a hike . . . *that* was a decision. A step. He'd thought about it before, once or twice, but never got around to it. Start small, Rick had said. He turned to see Rick right outside the Lunch Counter's large plate glass window, talking to Nancy. That boy impressed him. Not a boy, a man. Rick O'Shea was a grown man.

Peg returned from the storeroom, still chuckling. Before he could open his mouth to ask her about a hike, she said, "That was Bob Lotosky on the phone. Coming in this weekend, he says. Potatoes are growing nicely and told him to take some time off." She chuckled, like Bob Lotosky had made a clever potato joke.

Paul frowned, staring down at the ice in the bottom of his glass. So much for asking Peg on a hike this weekend.

He chided himself. Bob Lotosky was a good guy who'd given up his own time to help Camp Kicking Moose. Paul appreciated him, respected him, though he also couldn't deny that Bob had a way of making him feel a little inept as a handyman. Bob seemed to know how to fix anything and everything. Part of a farmer's life, Paul figured. He, on the other hand, faced a steep learning curve of do-it-yourself repairs.

"Can I get you something to eat? Blaine's chicken salad is gone. So is her tuna salad. But I can whip you up something."

Uh oh. Last time Peg had whipped something up for him, he ended up with a stomachache. If Blaine wasn't doing the cooking, he wasn't interested. Peg was a wonderful person and a terrible cook. "Thanks, but I'll just have the iced tea."

"Be sure to tell Blaine that Artie's dad is coming in." Peg's smile faded. "I wish that girl could see what a gem she has in Artie."

"You and me both," Paul said, shifting off his stool. He left a couple of dollars by the empty glass. "See you later, Peg Legg."

She spun around, hands on her hips. "Call me that one more time and I'll slip arsenic in your iced tea."

He grinned, leaving the Lunch Counter with a lighter heart. That happened a lot to him there. He'd come into town feeling a little discombobulated and leave feeling all put back together. There was something about Peg that made folks feel as if everything was going to turn out okay.

"Paul," Peg called out. "Don't forget to tell Blaine about Bob's visit."

"Right," he said, his smile fading.

⁓

The very next morning, Blaine stood behind the counter at the Lunch Counter and evaluated her most recent attempt at making peppermint ice cream.

Better. Though still not quite right. Something was lacking. Its finish was bland. Not complex nor interesting enough. Yet.

How to fix it? What to fix?

Nothing was quite right. Nothing. She couldn't make it better. She couldn't fix anything. Instead, she just kept ruining what she had. She leaned her fists against the counter, chin dropped on her chest.

"Honey, what's wrong?"

Blaine lifted her head to realize that Peg had come in from her storeroom and stood by the refrigerator, watching her. "This . . . peppermint ice cream. I just can't get a strong enough flavor."

"Let me have a taste."

Blaine scooped out a spoonful and handed it to her. Peg tasted it, then coughed, spitting it out. "Not strong *enough*? Honey, it's practically toothpaste."

"Are you serious?" She sniffed the bowl. "I can barely smell the mint."

"No kidding? I can smell it way back in my storeroom." Peg tipped her head curiously. "You coming down with a cold? Allergies?"

Slowly, Blaine shook her head. "Yesterday, a customer said the roasted tomato soup was too salty. I told him he'd obviously never tasted soup that wasn't out of a can before."

"Hmm," Peg said.

"What's that? What does that *hmm* mean?"

"Two days ago, someone complained that the chili was so spicy it blew their brains out."

Blaine gasped. She had noticed that no one had finished their chili that day. "Overseasoning." A culinary sin. She leaned back against the counter. "Why didn't you tell me?"

"I didn't know it was a trend."

"Peg, what's wrong with me?"

"You're overseasoning."

"I realize that. But why? To me, my food tastes bland."

"Maybe your fancy culinary school has altered your taste buds."

"My palate? You think it's been ruined?"

"Not ruined. Just fancified. The locals . . . they like down-to-earth fare." Peg patted her shoulder. "Just stick to your recipes. Don't go all Emeril Lagassé on the food." She grinned. "No more BAMs!" She headed back to the storeroom, snapping her fingers in the air as she went. "Simple solution."

Blaine would definitely stick to the recipes, though she hated cooking like that. Still, it was a simple solution for the Lunch Counter. But the solution to her palate problem was not so simple.

Maddie was watering her one little houseplant in her office when the door opened and Blaine walked in. "Blaine! You can't just walk right in."

"Why not? No one's here." She looked around the room. "You moved things around."

"Yeah. Cam set the room up in a way that would work great for a magazine shoot, but not really helpful when you're trying to listen carefully to someone. I brought the chairs in closer together and took away the huge coffee table." She pointed to a small side table. "That's for the tissues."

Blaine gave a wry smile. "I suppose weeping and wailing from your customers is part of the counselor gig."

"Clients, not customers. And so far, only a few tears." She sat down on a chair. "What are you doing here?"

"The lights went out at the Lunch Counter, so Peg closed up until the electricity comes back on. She doesn't want me opening and closing the refrigerator. And I can't cook without power."

Maddie tried a light switch. "Still not on."

Blaine plopped onto a chair. "Cam is determined to fix the island's energy dilemma."

"More power to her." She smiled smugly. "Get it? Pun?"

"Bad one." Blaine shifted in the chair as if it wasn't comfortable. "Did you hear the Phinney brothers are getting released from jail? Wiggled out of serving their full sentence and heading back into town. Peg says she won't serve them at the Lunch Counter. Says that lobster thieves don't get served on her watch." She gave the thumbs-up signal.

"I've heard the news. A few days ago, I received a call from their probation officer. Get this . . . they have to get therapy. Part of their early release program."

"Good. They need therapy." Then Blaine's eyes widened. "Oh

no. Don't tell me. You have to be their therapist?" She coughed a laugh, but not in a mocking way. "Poor Maddie."

Maddie nodded. "Poor me." Then she pointed to her sister. "I shouldn't have told you they're coming for therapy. Forget I said that."

"Forgotten."

Good. Frankly, Maddie had blotted that phone call from the probation officer from her mind. Knowing the Phinney brothers, highly skilled at slipping out of responsibilities, they wouldn't follow through. "We haven't really had much time alone since you came back. How's culinary school?"

"It's fine," Blaine said nonchalantly, but she seemed out of sorts.

"Is it everything you hoped it to be?"

Blaine snapped her head up, looked at her with eyes wide, then her face pinched together like a prune and she burst into tears.

Nine

MADDIE HELD THE BOX OF TISSUES while her sister pulled one after the other, sobbing. She had no idea what had caused such a meltdown and felt a tweak of guilt over having no clue that Blaine was in this much turmoil. Just the other day, Cam had said something to her about Blaine, that she radiated restlessness. Maddie had noticed, too, but had been so preoccupied with Rick O'Shea that she didn't think much about it. Obviously, Cam—who had remarkably poor intuition about people—was right. Something was very, very wrong.

When Blaine's tears finally seemed spent, Maddie shifted out of sister mode and into counselor mode. "I brought up culinary school, and it triggered a strong response out of you."

Blaine's eyes welled up with tears. She dabbed them away, but she seemed to have some control. "I hate to cry. Once it starts, I can't stop. And then I'm all red and puffy eyed for the rest of the day."

"I'm a fan of crying. It's good for you. It's a release . . . of emotions, of toxins, of all the stuff you've got bottled up." She leaned forward and put a hand on her sister's knee. "So what have you got bottled up?"

"Nothing. I just can't go back to culinary school."

"Can't go? Won't go?"

Blaine shrugged. "Does it matter?"

Maddie was paying close attention to Blaine's behavior. Fidgeting in her chair, twirling her hair, looking around the room. Maddie tried to meet her eyes, but they were darting from the window to the diploma on the wall to the pillow she pulled onto her lap. One leg was crossed over the other, and she was rapidly tapping her foot in the air. What wasn't getting said was just as important as what was getting said. "Does it matter that you don't want to go back to culinary school?" Maddie repeated. "You tell me."

One breath. Two, three, four. "There was an instructor who singled me out for some extra projects. He really liked my work and he said I was the most talented student he'd ever had. Ever. He even submitted a wedding cake I'd baked for special recognition."

"Go on."

"I appreciated what he did for me . . . and he made me feel very special . . . and he's very highly thought of—like a culinary genius . . . plus he has that kind of tortured poet vibe going on." This all came out as one long sentence. "But I didn't . . ."

Maddie knew what she didn't want to say. She waited, but when Blaine didn't offer the words, she did. "You didn't think that meant you owed him something in return."

Another round of tears started, but Blaine choked the words out. "We were in the kitchen at the school one afternoon, alone, and suddenly he was behind me, touching me . . ."

"What did you do?"

"I pushed him off me and told him I would tell the supervisor.

He said that I was the one who had been coming after him, giving him signals. He said he had proof with my email." She shuddered. "I'd written one email to him, thanking him for all he'd done for me, asking if there was anything I could do to repay him." She let out a big puff of air. "I meant . . . babysit his kids. Not . . ." She shook her head. "I should have offered to babysit his kids. Spelled it out. Not left it open-ended like I did."

"So he's married."

"Yes. To another instructor." Blaine's hands clenched together, balling her tissue. "She's such a sweet woman. Everyone loves her."

Maddie noticed that Blaine intentionally did not offer up any identifying names. That raised a red flag. "So if you said anything to the supervisor, you think you're hurting her too."

"I don't just think it. I know it. She adores him. They have two little kids. I'm totally trapped. Plus . . ."

"Plus what?"

"He said I was the best student he'd ever had. Me!"

"Blaine, I don't mean to take anything away from your talent, but has it occurred to you that he has probably said the same thing to other students?"

"What?" Blaine's mouth dropped open and she rocketed up out of the chair. "Just once—just once!—it would be nice if someone in our family appreciated my culinary skills as extraordinary."

"We do appreciate your skills. They are extraordinary! Maybe we don't tell you as much as we should, but we all know you are gifted. But what you've described is a classic scenario of a predator."

"Oh Maddie . . . don't go all Sigmund Freud on me."

"He is a predator, Blaine. A wolf. He knows exactly how to woo a young girl into his lair. Make her beholden to him. And then he goes in for what he's really after."

Blaine tucked her chin, twisting the tissue in her hands. "So you're saying, I'm not the first."

"Not the first. And definitely not the last if you don't do anything about it."

She lifted her chin defiantly. "I told you. I can't! I won't hurt his wife. I refuse to."

"You're not the one who's hurting her. He is."

Blaine shook her head. "I'm partly at fault."

"Your fault . . . because . . . you believed him to be an honorable instructor? Worthy of your admiration? Your appreciation?"

"Don't make more of this than it is," Blaine said with a scowl. "I'm going to learn my lesson and move on."

"Move on . . . how?"

"As soon as Cam and Seth get married, I'm out of here. I'm going to travel through Europe. Discover my culinary voice."

"Travel is good," Maddie said. "Running away is not so good."

Click! The lamp turned on, filling the room with light. Blaine, already uncomfortable, used the return of electricity as an excuse to bolt. "I'd better get back to work." She grabbed one more tissue from the box and strode to the door, then turned back. "This stays confidential, right? That's what this office is all about, isn't it?"

Maddie swiveled her chair to face her sister. "Absolutely."

"And you won't bring it up again?"

"Not unless you do."

"Thanks, Maddie." She waved a tissue and opened the door.

"Blaine! Wait. You're not powerless in this. You might feel as if you are, but you're not."

Blaine gave a slight nod to indicate that she heard her but kept going.

Maddie went to the door and closed it. Through the window, she watched her little sister walk to the sidewalk and down the street, chin tucked low. She looked so sad, so full of shame and guilt. Blaine was taking partial blame for some reason, but whether or not that was true, a certain amount of blame belonged to the rest of their family. It was probably true that they hadn't given Blaine enough affirmation of her gifts and abilities, enough so that she didn't need to seek it from elsewhere. Maddie should have realized how vulnerable Blaine might be this year, her first time living away from home. It wasn't a complete surprise that she was susceptible to someone in authority. Someone handsome, charming, persuasive, manipulative.

Flooded with empathy, Maddie switched from counselor mode back to sister mode.

She wanted to strangle that instructor.

MADDIE, AGE 6

Saving her baby sister from getting too close to the open oven door was one of Maddie's earliest memories. It was Thanksgiving Day. Blaine was eighteen months old and Maddie had just turned six. Her mother had pulled the roasted turkey out of the oven and lifted it up on the counter. Before her mother could set the turkey down, Blaine toddled right toward the open low door, oblivious to danger.

Maddie saw the baby heading toward the oven and tackled her before she could touch the hot open door. They both tumbled on the floor and Blaine, frightened, started screaming.

"What on earth is going on?" Mom said, peering down at them.

Still holding tight to her baby sister, Maddie looked at the oven. "Close the door!"

"Oh my goodness." Mom spun around and shut the oven door,

then scooped up Blaine, who continued her scream rant. "Quiet down, now. Maddie wasn't trying to hurt you. She was protecting you."

When Blaine finally stopped her screaming, Mom marched into the other room, turned off the television, and plunked the baby in Cam's arms. Maddie had followed close on her heels, eager to see the drama unfold.

"Hey!" Cam was outraged. "It's my favorite show!"

Mom glared at her. "You were supposed to be watching the baby."

"It's Maddie's turn," Cam said.

"Cam, I asked you to watch the baby while I got dinner ready."

"But, Mom, I watched her all morning. Libby and I want to watch our show. And where's Dad, anyway?"

"He said he'd be home by four."

"It's already five. I say we skip it and eat in front of the TV. If Dad doesn't care about Thanksgiving Day, why should we?"

Mom stared directly at Cam for a very long time. Her jaw flexed, and even Maddie knew Cam had scored a direct hit. Her sister had a way of doing that. Cam was spot-on. Dad always put work ahead of family. Always.

Then came a fired-up indignation. Maddie loved that look best on her mother. She planted her hands on her hips and stood with that wide-legged stance of a seaman. "Camden Grayson, in this house, we do not skip an opportunity to give thanks to God for a meal. Any meal. Especially so on Thanksgiving Day. So watch your baby sister while I carve the turkey." As Cam opened her mouth to object, her mother pointed to her in that way she had. "Not one more word."

Not twenty minutes later, Dad arrived, tossing out apologies for being late on a holiday. Mom brushed them aside as she stirred the gravy, but she was steaming mad. Cam wasn't speaking to anyone because she was mad at Mom. Libby kept her eyes on her dinner plate. Dad tried to be excessively cheerful and complimentary about the meal, trying to make up for his lateness. Then he gave up too.

Someone had to do something.

Maddie rose to her feet. "I have an announcement."

All eyes looked to her, except for the baby, who was mashing her peas in her high chair. "I think Blaine doesn't see well. I think she needs glasses." Then she sat down.

Her parents turned to each other. "She does seem to bump into things quite a bit," Mom said. "More than the other girls did."

"Come to think of it," Dad said, "just the other day, she couldn't see an airplane in the sky. It was low flying, right above us. I tried to point it out to her. She was looking for the sound but couldn't zoom in on the plane."

"I thought she was just super clumsy," Cam said. "Poor blind baby." She patted Blaine's sticky hair. "Don't you worry. We'll get you a guide dog."

Later, long after Maddie had gone to bed, she listened to the pleasant hum of her parents' conversation in the kitchen as they cleaned up dishes. In a way she couldn't entirely understand until she was much older, she knew she had played a role in turning things around.

On Monday, the pediatrician agreed with Maddie's observation and sent Blaine to a pediatric ophthalmologist. She came home fitted with special bendable toddler glasses. Maddie thought she looked cute, like she was wearing swim goggles.

As her mother gave the doctor's report at dinner that night, she looked directly at Maddie. A gentleness flowed into her eyes and hung there a moment. "Early intervention is key, the doctor said.

Most likely, Blaine will grow out of her farsightedness. He said that we all need to be sure to thank you, Maddie, for being such an observant and insightful big sister."

That night, Maddie was given a double scoop of ice cream, and Dad let her stay up late to play Chutes and Ladders with him and only him. (He lost.)

Ten

WHEN CAM FIRST ARRIVED ON THREE SISTERS ISLAND, she was surprised at how the locals had adapted to such limited, unreliable electricity delivered from a faulty, antiquated underground cable in need of repair . . . and a very low priority to Maine's utility company. Washing machines and dishwashers couldn't be run on the same day, for example. Some locals had diesel generators and propane tanks, but those were costly alternatives. Besides, during winter, the island was frequently cut off from the mainland and its oil deliveries.

Hopefully, with what Cam planned to present to the island to-night at the town meeting, there could be a way to make Three Sisters Island self-powered. She'd triple-checked her PowerPoint display, her ducks were in order, and she was ready to present the sustainable energy plan.

As she packed up the kitchen table, she felt a familiar inner hum of excitement. When she had worked for the start-up renewable energy company in Boston, she used to make these types of pre-sentations to C-suites: CEOs, COOs, CFOs. She loved presenting projects, answering complicated questions, surprising the C-suite with her intelligence and communication skills.

She knew she looked young and inexperienced, so she always took care to make her appearance reflect her competence. It was her uniform: wild curly hair was tightly held back into a bun, clothing was severe and plain, glasses instead of contacts. Anything to make herself look like she should be taken seriously. After all, she should be.

Cam paused. What should she wear tonight? She glanced down at her baggy T-shirt and jeans. Wow. How much had changed in the last year. She ran a hand over her hair, loose and hanging past her shoulders. She should have thought to go over to Bar Harbor to get it cut and styled straight. She used to have such expensive hair.

"Don't you dare."

She whirled around to see Seth at the doorjamb. She smiled. "Don't I dare *what*?" But she knew.

"Don't you dare cut your hair." He stretched his arms out and she took a few steps to sink into them, hugging him tight, pressing the side of her face against his chest for a long moment.

She breathed him in, loving the way he smelled—like the outdoors. Like balsam fir trees and salty ocean air. She lifted her face to smile at him. "I didn't hear you come in."

"I don't think you could've heard a stampede of cattle coming in. You were concentrating pretty heavily." He glanced at the stack on the table. "Ready for tonight?"

She wiggled out of his embrace. "Almost. I was just trying to decide what to wear. Somehow, a stern navy-blue suit doesn't seem right for this crowd." She stepped back and pulled on her baggy T-shirt. "But this doesn't either."

"Something in between."

"Good idea."

He grabbed her hands in his. "After tonight, we start working on *our* plans. Right?"

"Right. Absolutely. This is just . . . so important, Seth. If I can get the community to support this plan, it could bring such prosperity to this island. Instead of just limping along like everyone's been doing."

"I'm fully supportive of this. You know that. I haven't nagged you about setting a wedding date. But . . ."

"But what?"

"What about you and me? And Cooper? If the town rallies behind you, seems you're going to be even busier than you've been."

She glanced at the clock. "Such worry! You sound like Maddie." She gave him a quick kiss on the lips and darted around him. "I'd better get ready."

As she dashed up the stairs, she heard him call out, "Cam, you never really answered my question!"

At the top of the stairs, she shot back, "One thing at a time, Seth. You're always telling Cooper that very thing." She turned, heading to her room, as Blaine came down the hall. "Blaine, we're leaving in twenty minutes."

"Leaving for where?"

She lifted her hands in the air. "The village meeting! It's tonight."

"Why do I have to go?"

"Because I need your support. Don't give me that eye roll. Dad and Cooper and Maddie are already there, setting up chairs. You're coming with Seth and me."

Blaine gave her an exaggerated huff, but Cam paid her no heed.

~⌒~

Blaine went down the stairs and into the kitchen. Seth was staring out the window over the sink. "Hey, Seth. What's up?"

He spun around. "Just waiting for your sister."

"Welcome to the club." She sat on the chair. "Seth, when is this wedding going to happen?"

He folded his arms against his chest. "Sometime this summer."

"But when? I came back this summer to help with the wedding . . . but there doesn't seem to be a wedding on the calendar."

"One thing at a time, Blaine. You know your sister. If something is worth doing, it's worth overdoing."

She frowned. Normally, she admired Seth's Zen-likeness, but not when it came to this wedding. If he didn't push Cam, it wasn't going to happen anytime soon. Seth was the only one Cam listened to. "All I'm asking for is a date. A stake in the ground."

He smiled. "To be honest, that sounds pretty good to me too. But tonight . . . let's just support Cam's energy plan and worry about weddings another day."

"Tomorrow, then."

"Deal." He grinned.

"Deal." She lifted her hand for a high-five and slapped his palm. She heard a door shut and Cam's light footsteps come down the stairs. "Let's go show our support."

⁓

Three Sisters Island was about eight miles long and three miles wide. It sat below and to the right of Mount Desert Island, jutting into the Atlantic Ocean. Cam looked over the room of locals in the Baggett and Taggett store, waiting for the village meeting to get started. She was pleased with how many had turned out. The store was crowded, with a row of people standing along the counters. She hadn't been in this store since the church had moved out. She hadn't missed it at all, not with those stuffed moose heads on the walls. Not after Blaine had pointed out how the mooses' eyes followed you around the room.

At seven o'clock sharp, Peg, as mayor, stood in front of the room and clapped her hands to get everyone's attention. "Folks, thanks for coming out. We've got a few things to discuss tonight, starting off with Cam's idea to help us all get power to our homes on a regular basis."

"It's plenty regular!" Oliver Moore shouted. "Regularly out!"

Peg pointed to him. "You are so right, Oliver. That's why we need to all zip our lips and listen to this little gal." She patted Cam on the shoulder. "You go right ahead, honey."

Cam smiled. She loved it when Peg called her honey. She pressed the clicker in her hand and started the presentation with a short video, an aerial view of Three Sisters Island, taken by a drone. Instantly, the room grew silent. They probably hadn't seen such a view of their island. Seated up front, Seth gave her a thumbs-up. He had helped her find a guy with a drone who shot the footage.

The video zeroed in on the lighthouse, and the crashing waves against the sea, and faded out. Just the effect Cam had hoped for.

"This beautiful island," she said, "has all that it needs to create our own energy. We don't have to be dependent on importing electricity."

"Secession!" Oliver Moore shouted. "At last. Captain Ed's been calling for it for years."

The room started buzzing with side conversations, loud ones, so much so that Peg stood up. Everyone immediately quieted down.

"I think we can all agree that the island needs sustainable energy."

"Get the state of Maine to fix that cable!" Oliver shouted.

Cam was ready for that. "It's not up to the state. The cable was put there by the public utility company, and they've determined it's too costly to repair. Also, the risk of repair is too high for human safety. Today's safety standards are far stricter than in the old days." She paused, expecting another interruption. But the group returned her gaze with curious attentiveness. So far, so good.

"There are so many benefits of living off the grid," Cam continued. "We'll be living green, keeping this island pristine. We'll all benefit from the plan I'm proposing tonight." Cam used a laser to point to the waves against the rocks. "Near the lighthouse, we can create a windfarm."

"A windfarm?" A man named Euclid piped up. "That'll make for some interesting plowing."

The room burst into laughter. Peg waited until the wave of laughter settled down. "Next person who interrupts this little gal will get tossed out."

"Thank you, Peg," Cam said. "A windfarm is an area of land with a group of energy-producing windmills. So the plan I'm proposing would have three windmills out by the lighthouse. Over here"—she clicked a slide forward and pointed the laser to another part of the island—"the plan is to harness the power of water, called a hydro, because windmills can't do it all."

"Why not?" This time Peg was the one who interrupted.

"They have a capacity factor." Silence. Cam looked out at a sea of blank faces. She had tried so hard to keep this portion simple and clear, but it wasn't simple enough. In her most patient voice, she said, "The capacity factor is the amount of time the windmill generates usable power. That's why we're also using solar panels, so the sun will charge the battery. We can take power for the island off the battery. We'll have a control center inside the lighthouse, which belongs to Camp Kicking Moose. Paul Grayson, the owner, has graciously given over the site for using it as a control center."

"The lighthouse?" From the side, Blaine spoke up. "Not the lighthouse! It's supposed to be a bed-and-breakfast someday!"

"Can't," Cam said. "Sorry, Blaine. We need it used as the control center. It's ideal for that." She clicked forward on some slides. "The water comes down here, in there"—she pointed the laser at the slide—"and there's a turbine—a wheel that's pushed by the fast-moving water—that flies around to produce continuous power. And voilà! That's how electricity will be created. Eventually, if this all works, I'm hoping we'll be able to produce more electricity than we can use."

Baxtor Phinney, the former mayor who still considered himself as mayor, rose to his feet. "Who's paying for all this?" Money was always the topic he involved himself in.

"A combination of things. I've been applying for some government grants." Cam dropped her voice a notch or two. "And then we may need to raise money for remaining costs."

Baxtor heard. "What kind of remaining costs?"

"Well, I suspect we'll need help from an engineer for a year or two, until we learn how to manage it." Cam looked around the room.

"This island is just fine the way it is." Baxtor turned to face the crowd. "Do we want our way of life to be ruined?" His grim-looking wife sat next to him, nodding. "We don't need strangers to tell us what to do."

Peg frowned at him. "Camden Grayson is not a stranger." She pointed. "Sit down, Baxtor."

"Let her talk, Phinney!" shouted an old lobsterman from the back row.

Cam clicked to the next slide. "If I can get some grant money, then we might be able to avoid passing on any costs to residents."

Baxtor Phinney remained standing, his fists on his hips. "But if you can't?"

"I'll keep you all informed. There won't be any surprises."

"And if you can't get those grants?" he repeated.

Cam felt her stomach tighten. Baxtor hit a sore spot. Her greatest fear had been that she wouldn't get a single grant approved for this project, and so far, that fear was coming true. "Then we might need to add a small percentage tax to goods purchased on the island. Just until we start creating more electricity than we need."

"Hold it just one minute," Euclid said. "This is supposed to save us money. Sounds like it's costing us."

"At first, it might cost a little," Cam said. "It's an investment. It's an investment in our island."

"Our island?" Baxtor said with scorn, crossing his arms over his chest. "Let me remind you that your father bought Camp Kicking Moose, not the entire island. You Graysons have barely lived here a year."

Cam sighed. Summer people were one thing, but new residents to small towns were not warmly welcomed. Peg said it took generations before they stopped calling you an outlander behind your back.

"What are the chances that additional electricity that gets generated could be sold back to the mainland?" Seth said, trying to be helpful.

"So glad you brought that up." Relieved, Cam gave him a grateful smile. "If that happens, and I hope it will, you'll all be receiving tax credits."

Another round of side conversations started to hum. These sounded more positive, she thought.

Rick O'Shea stood.

Euclid pointed to him. In a loud voice, he said, "Who's that fella who looks like GI Joe?"

Cam cringed. Euclid was always a day late and a dollar short, but she had to admit that Rick did project a military presence. He stood with legs slightly apart, his back stiff and straight. He was clean-shaven, hair cropped close to his skull, shirt tucked into his pants. All that was missing was a uniform. She thought his GI Joe look suited him, especially with his rugged features, but she could only imagine what these old bearded fishermen would think about it. Even Blaine had put money on Rick growing his hair before the first month passed.

Rick didn't seem at all offended by Euclid's bluntness. "I'm the new pastor at Three Sisters Island. My name is Rick O'Shea." He lifted a hand in the air, like a pause on the conversation. "On a side note, you're all invited to come to church on Sunday morning. Ten a.m." He dropped his hand. "But aside from giving the church a quick commercial, I wanted to say that I can already tell what a warm, tight-knit community you have here. I couldn't be any more pleased to be here."

"Get back to us after your first winter!" Oliver Moore shouted. Chuckles and elbow jabbing rippled through the room.

Rick didn't miss a beat. "What Cam Grayson is trying to do with her plans for renewable energy . . . it's for the common good. This plan will benefit every single person on this island. But it's going to require the cooperation of everyone. Seems to me, that's what Three Sisters Island has going for it that a lot of other places don't. You all care about each other. Already, I've heard dozens of stories of how you help each other, especially through those long hard winters. I can tell that this is an island that wants the best for its residents. It's a remarkable thing . . . to have a community come together the way you people do, helping each other through thick and thin . . . and it's the most important part of this venture of renewable energy. Cam's done the hard part for us all, the heavy lifting. She's asking everyone to do the easy part, because it's already woven into the fabric of your life here. If people work together, anything is possible." He sat down.

The room was silent. Cam could sense a shift in her direction and she grabbed the moment. "I can't do this without you, each one of you. But if we work together, anything is possible." That line was so good, in fact, that she was already thinking it could be a slogan for the island's renewable energy initiative.

Peg wisely jumped in. "Cam, I think it's fair to say that we're all supportive of you pursuing this grant money. Thanks for all you're doing for our island. We're all counting on you." She thumped her gavel in sound agreement, grinning at Cam, pigtails bouncing as her head nodded. "You go, girl."

⁓◦

Elena and Mike returned for a therapy session with Maddie on healthy conflict. Once she saw that the word *arguing* had a negative connotation for them, she changed the term. Mike told her once the word made him feel as if he'd gotten tangled in a ball of yarn, without a start or end. Maddie was impressed with his description—it said so much about the conflicts he'd observed as a vulnerable child in his parents' marriage. Unhealthy, unresolved, complicated.

"Conflict doesn't have to be a bad thing," Maddie said. "In fact, it can be a very good thing. Differences can be refining. The thing is, most people handle conflicts so badly. Avoiding, personalizing, attacking, stuffing. The trick in a good marriage is to see conflict in a different way. Because a good relationship does not mean it is conflict-free. It doesn't mean you do all you can to avoid conflict."

Elena raised her hand. "So what does it mean to see conflict in a different way?"

Maddie smiled. "You don't have to raise your hand. It means that conflict is viewed as a means to growth. Because it can lead to growing closer together if conflict can be resolved peacefully, respectfully, and productively."

Mike and Elena relaxed, ever so slightly.

"From what you've described about yourselves, my hunch is that when you have experienced some kind of conflict—a differing opinion, or a misunderstanding—your tactics are to withdraw. Grow quiet. Shut down."

"Yes!" Mike said. "Elena did that on the way over here."

Elena dipped her chin. It was plain to see that she did not like the turn this conversation had taken.

"I asked if you'd like to stop at the Lunch Counter after our session, and you said it didn't matter. But I think maybe it did."

Maddie turned to Elena. "Did it?"

"Well, yesterday I had told him that it'd be nice to picnic down on the beach afterward."

"Ohhh." Mike slapped his forehead. "I forgot."

"It's fine. No big deal."

But Maddie could see that it was a bigger deal than Elena was admitting, even to herself. "Elena, why do you think Mike forgot you had suggested a picnic?"

Elena shifted in her chair, looked away. To Maddie, she seemed extremely uncomfortable. "It doesn't matter. It was just something silly I had suggested."

"Does he forget about those things a lot?"

Mike's eyebrows shot up. "Do I?"

Elena's foot tapped restlessly. "This really isn't necessary."

"But it is," Mike said, and Maddie was proud of him. "Elena, do I forget things that are important to you?"

Several beats of silence. "Yes," she said in a low tone. And then, "But it's probably my fault. I'm not clear enough."

"I'm not purposely trying to forget," Mike said. "I can be a little dense. My mom shouted a lot, and sometimes that's the only way I pay attention. I don't want you to feel like I don't listen to you. I know that's how you felt when you were growing up, like no one listened. I am so sorry."

Elena's foot stopped its tapping.

Maddie had to bite on her lip to stop herself from cheering. Mike had just displayed an important step toward great relationships: a sincere apology.

"Honey, can we work on this?"

"How? I don't want to turn into a shouter."

"I don't want you to, either. I love your gentle nature. But I would like you to work on being more direct and I'll do my best to become a better listener."

As they left her office, hand in hand, Maddie couldn't have felt more pleased. She knew it had nothing to do with her skill as a therapist, because she used very little of it. Avoidance was one of the biggest problems in people's lives, hard to recognize and hard to overcome. Elena and Mike were willing to address their tendency toward it. Those two . . . they were going to do just fine.

It occurred to Maddie she was avoiding Rick O'Shea. He'd done a noble thing last night, coming alongside Cam at the meeting to help sway everyone toward Cam's vision. She knew she should be more forgiving, more open-minded. She should. But she couldn't.

MADDIE, AGE 10

Dad had given Blaine a puppy for her fifth birthday, a golden retriever named Winslow. He hadn't cleared the gift with Mom before giving a puppy to Blaine, so there was a lot of tension in the house that summer. Mostly because Dad was on the road with the baseball team and Mom was left to train a puppy she had never wanted. Especially a big, strong, energetic puppy that frightened Blaine. Mom's solution was to make Cam and Maddie walk the puppy around the block several times a day to tire him out.

On a hot and humid afternoon in late August, it was Maddie's turn to walk Winslow. She'd gotten halfway around the block and was crossing a street when Winslow stopped. He refused to budge. The harder Maddie tried to get him going, the more he resisted. All he did was lie down and lick his big stupid paws. Suddenly a swarm of boys on bicycles turned onto the road. She knew them all from school as they parted around her and zoomed past without a word. On their way to swim at the neighborhood pool, with towels hung around their necks, in swimsuits and flip-flops. No helmets, she noticed.

And then one rider peeled off from the pack and turned around. She frowned as he pedaled back toward her. Ricky O'Shea. He circled in the road near where Winslow had parked himself. "Something wrong with your puppy's foot?"

She hesitated, especially because the pack of friends had realized he had left them and stopped on their bikes, yelling at him to hurry up. Maddie had a firm policy of ignoring all boys, especially Ricky O'Shea, but she was also in a jam. Stuck in the middle of a street with a big stubborn puppy. "He was fine one minute. Then suddenly not fine."

Ricky jumped off his bike and let it drop to the ground. He bent down to take hold of the paw Winslow was licking, ran a finger over the pads, then stopped. He pulled a thorn from the pad and held it up to her. "He should be fine now." He stroked Winslow's head tenderly. "I always wanted a dog, but my mom says she's allergic." Then he hopped on his bike and pedaled off to catch up with his friends. Winslow sat up and wagged his tail.

Maddie felt annoyed. At herself for missing such an obvious problem in Winslow's paw. At Ricky for revealing a tender side. It was the first time he'd ever been nice to her. First time. It made it harder to dislike him.

Eleven

CAM HAD JUST FINISHED PACKING HER OVERNIGHT BAG when she heard a sound and looked up. Cooper stood at the door with a stricken look. "Where are you going?"

"Hi, Coops. Come on in." She patted her bed. She'd been waiting to tell him that she was leaving on another quick trip. "I'm just going overnight to Augusta. You know where that is on the map. I'm going to see if my grant got approved." She pinched her two fingers together. "I'm *this* close to nailing it down."

Obviously, from the sour look on his face, Cooper couldn't have cared less about the grant. "I want to go with you."

"Another time."

"It's the state capital. I should go."

"This trip is all business. It's my job right now, and you've got a job too. You've got school to go to. You need to stay here with Grandpa and Seth and Maddie and Blaine."

"And Dory. You always forget Seth's dog. Dory's part of our family too."

It was spoken in a tone she hadn't heard from Cooper before. Almost . . . teenager-ish. "And Dory too." She reached out and pulled him close to her. "I'll be back tomorrow night in time to tuck you in to bed. Okay?"

But he wiggled out of her embrace and bolted out the door.

"Cooper!" she yelled. "We're leaving for school in five minutes." She waited to hear a response in return, but nothing came. She let out a sigh of exasperation.

Cam was the only one who was sorry the school had been moved to town instead of remaining in the carriage house on the property of Camp Kicking Moose as it had for the past three years, ever since the school building was hit by lightning and burned down. But when the camp reopened last summer, the school started to impinge on the vacationing guests. Campers in late August complained about the clunky sputtering of the school bus and boisterous noise of the children arriving in the morning. It was Peg's first action as the newly voted-in selectwoman.

"Paul Grayson's trying to run a business out there," she told everyone at the first village meeting she presided over. "Let's get that school back to town where it belongs."

Seth was the one who brought up the idea of the town renting the empty Unitarian Church. It had a large fenced-in yard for the children to play in, and the sanctuary was just the right size to suffice as a one-room schoolhouse. Not too big, not too small. Things were meant to be used, he said, even buildings. Such a landmark structure on Three Sisters Island shouldn't remain vacant, purposeless, decaying. Peg clapped her hands to approve the motion, until Seth reminded her that she had a gavel.

On this June morning, Cooper hopped out of the car as soon as Cam parked down near Boon Dock. He went flying up Main Street to the school and dropped his backpack by the gate. By the time Cam reached the church, he was already deep in a tetherball game with Quinn, his pink-haired friend. He loved that game, and unlike most every other sport, wasn't too bad at it. Dory barked, bounding toward her. When Seth realized Cam was standing at the open gate, he walked over to her and opened his arms to envelop her in a hug.

"Still on a high from the other night?" he said, pulling back, giving her that crooked grin that made her legs feel like Jell-O.

"Still floating," she said. "But I'm coming back to earth with a thud. I'm heading over to the mainland today. Would you mind taking Cooper home? He's a little out of sorts."

"Count on it. What's going on in Bar Harbor?" He released her, stepping back with a big grin on his face, eyes lit with happiness. "Let me guess. Wedding dress shopping? Invitations?"

Uh, nope. She bit her lip. "Not Bar Harbor, actually. Augusta. I'm going to hand-deliver a government grant. I thought it might lift its chances if I take it myself."

The lighthearted look slipped right off Seth's face. "Cam, we agreed. After you presented the plans for the project to the town, then we'd get to work on wedding plans."

"And we will! I just want to talk to a few people. See if I can get this grant approved."

He tipped his head. "Maybe Blaine's right."

"What do you mean? Right about what?"

"She warned me. She said she doubted you would ever set a wedding date this summer. That you'll always come up with a reason to postpone it."

Cam faced that with a smirk. "You're taking advice from a twenty-year-old girl who has a new boyfriend every month."

"She said you seek significance out of work and that will always trump your relationships."

"That is just . . . ," Cam huffed, "just ridiculous."

"Is it? Then let's set the date. Right now."

"Seth, slow down a minute. The village meeting took place just two days ago. I'd like a little breathing room after working so hard on it. I can't just jump from one huge project to another."

"A project?" He sounded insulted. "Sheesh, Cam. Am I a project? Is Cooper?"

"No, no. Of course not. But a wedding . . . now that's a project. A wedding requires a lot of planning and decision making and thoughts and effort and—"

Seth held up his palms to stop her ramble, midstream. "Doesn't have to be. It's really just about you and me and Cooper. And a pastor, which we now have."

"It's more than that. Like . . . finding a time when your family is free to come to Maine. And then there's the reception." She scratched her forehead. *Oh my goodness. The reception.* She hadn't even given a thought to it yet.

"Cam, it doesn't have to be a big huge deal." He looked down at Boon Dock. "It could be a very small deal. Down at the beach." He took a step closer to her, eyes softening. "It could be this weekend."

"This weekend?" She tilted her head. "*This* weekend? Seth, your mother would be furious. She'd blame me, and that's not the way I want to start out married life." She reached out and tugged on his hand. "Our wedding doesn't have to be a big huge deal, but it doesn't have to be a spur-of-the-moment thing, either. Something in between, maybe?"

He looked down at their hands. "I suppose."

"Let's talk about it this weekend. We'll set aside time and focus just on wedding plans. And we can involve Cooper, too, so he knows he's part of this."

"Fine. But I want us to get married sooner rather than later."

"You sound like Blaine."

"She wants us to get married so she can get on with her life. I

123

want us to get married because I want to wake up every day next to you." He leaned over to kiss her.

Cam smiled through the kiss. "I want that too." She heard the familiar engine sound of Captain Ed's car-toting barge start up, and she gasped. If she missed that, her entire day unraveled. "I gotta go. Thanks for getting Cooper home!" She pecked him on the lips and hurried out the church gate and down Main Street. Her mind was already turning to the grants and the people she wanted to contact today, so much so that she barely noticed Peg sweeping the sidewalk outside the Lunch Counter.

"Hey, Cam. Cam! Camden Grayson! Hold your horses!"

Cam stopped abruptly. Peg pointed back up to the school at the top of the hill. Cooper was waving to her from the gate, Dory standing loyally beside him. Shoot! She forgot to say goodbye to Cooper. Maddie was the one who had figured out that each time she forgot to let him know she was leaving, he ended up having stomachaches at school. She waved her arms frantically and blew kisses to him. Seth stood beside him, a disapproving look on his face that Cam could read even one hundred yards away. He lifted his palms in the air, his way of saying, "What is *wrong* with you?"

Peg was frowning at her too. "You didn't even hear that little boy call your name?"

Cam blew out a puff of breath. "I didn't. I'm catching the ferry." She gave Peg a shrug. "Those grants. Takes a lot of work to get this energy project going."

Peg lifted her eyebrows, then returned to her sweeping. "Better be careful, Cam. To be happy at home is the ultimate result of all ambition."

"Socrates?"

"Can't remember who said it, but I've always liked it."

The barge horn beckoned and Cam lifted an arm in a wave to Peg, rushing to get her car on board.

⁓

The little church had doubled in size in the last month. More accurately, attendance had doubled. Maddie didn't even recognize a fair number of people. Seth said they'd come all the way from Mount Desert Island to hear the new preacher, that Pastor Rick seemed to be making a splash.

Maddie lifted a hand, palm up. "But how did they know?"

Seth shrugged, grinning. "No secrets on an island." Odd, how that phrase kept returning to Maddie.

On this Sunday morning, Rick stood in the front of the room with an open Bible, but like last week, he didn't look down as he quoted the verses. "And the Lord appointed a great fish to swallow up Jonah. And Jonah was in the belly of the fish three days and three nights." He gazed around the room. "Sounds pretty hard to believe, doesn't it? But there are some accounts of individuals who had been swallowed by large fish and survived."

"No way!" shouted Oliver Moore. "Not possible!"

Tillie, seated in front of him, batted a hand to shush him.

"You might be thinking that it's not such a bad thing, to be swallowed whole and hang out in a fish belly for three days." He pointed to some little boys in the back row. "Sounds exciting? Better than a ride on a Ferris wheel?"

Three of the boys nodded enthusiastically.

"Not quite so fun. First of all, it's completely, utterly dark. Jonah wouldn't have been able to see his hand in front of his face. And the smell." Rick shuddered. "Truly horrific." He turned in a half circle. "One recent account tells of a whale that had died, and when cut open, there was a man . . ." His voice dropped to

125

a whisper. "Still alive." The boys in the back row wiggled with glee. "The man's skin was wrinkled as a prune and bleached white by the gastric acids in the whale's belly." He pointed to his head. "And his mind was never the same."

"Oh, that's naught but an old sailor's yarn," Oliver shouted.

Peg stood up, leaned over the row in front of her, and swatted him on the back of his head. "Would you let the preacher preach?"

Rick didn't seem at all bothered by Oliver. He didn't miss a beat, adding more vivid details about Jonah in the fish's belly. Maddie was shocked to realize that information was straight out of the Bible.

"Pretty grim moment in a man's life, wouldn't you say?" Rick set the Bible on the podium that he never used. He walked down from the platform to be on the same level as everyone else. "I'm not sure I would have had the presence of mind to pray like Jonah did, if I were in his place. Imagine how frightened he must have been." He lifted his hands. "We don't have to be in a fish's belly to be scared out of our wits, do we? There's plenty of things to be afraid of." He leaned slightly forward and pointed to Oliver. "Did you know that 'Fear not' is mentioned three hundred and sixty-five times in the Bible? One for every day. The Lord knows we have problems with fear. Every one of us. No one is immune. All of us have fears of some kind."

He looked over at Maddie's dad. "Fear of getting older." His eyes shifted to Cam. "Fear of not being significant." He smiled at Cooper. "Fear of being left alone." His eyes grazed down the row to Blaine. "Fear of holding people to account."

Whoa. Whoa whoa whoa. How did he know her family so well?

Maddie braced herself, waiting, but Rick moved on without adding another customized fear.

"Jonah wrote this book. He wanted his story remembered. He

wanted you to remember. God hears you. In every fearful circum-
stance in your life, God can hear you." He put his hands together.
"Let's pray."

While Rick prayed, Maddie became increasingly attuned to
his commanding presence. Noticed the cadence of his breathing.
Noticed how he kept his shoulders held back, as if there were a
wooden ruler down his back. Noticed the way his hands were
loosely clasped in front of him; the tip of one thumb rested against
the center of his other palm, his nails short and clean.

For some reason, once again, he looked up and caught her staring. Oof! She ducked her chin to her chest, her skin flushed with
heat. For goodness' sake. What was her problem?

A little boy's shriek broke the stillness of the moment. "I am
NEVER going near water again! I don't want to get EATEN like
Jonah!"

Cooper.

Twelve

STARTLED BY COOPER'S OUTBURST, then by Cam swooping him by the hand and hustling him outside as he continued to yell, Blaine made a beeline straight to Maddie as soon as Rick closed the service.

"I need to talk to you," she said, steering her by the elbow. "Privately." She slipped through the crowd and went outside, across the street, and down to the door to Maddie's office. She waited for Maddie to unlock it. Once inside, she could barely hold back her anger. "You told him!"

"Cooper?"

"Not Cooper! Pastor Rick."

Maddie looked thoroughly confused. "Told him what?"

"About the instructor at school. You told him!"

"No, I didn't, Blaine. Why would you even say that?"

"Did you see the way he looked at me when he was talking about fears? He looked right at me—*right at me!*—and said, 'Fear of holding people to account.' You heard him as well as I did."

"I heard. And it was spot-on. Eerily so. But I did *not* tell him

128

anything." Maddie looked offended. "How could you ever think that I would betray you like that?"

"Because . . . because . . ." Blaine plopped in a chair. "Sisters do that kind of thing. To get back at each other." But that wasn't really fair, not true. Cam did that kind of thing, sometimes, so did Blaine, but not Maddie. Never Maddie. "Did you tell Cam?"

"No, of course not. You told me not to and I promised I wouldn't." Maddie folded her arms against her chest. "Why would you think I'd say anything?"

"Cam seemed to know something's wrong."

Maddie flipped on the light. "That wouldn't take a rocket scientist. You're prickly and distant. You never sit still long enough to finish a conversation. You're pushing hard for Cam to set a wedding date." She leveled an I'm-right-about-this face at Blaine. "And then there's your missing palate."

Blaine leaned forward in the chair and put her head in her hands. "I am sure I will get my sense of taste back soon. It's just a blip on the radar. Peg thinks it's an allergic reaction. Once I leave this island, I'll be fine. It's this island. It does stuff to you." She rolled a finger around the side of her head, like a clock. "It messes with you."

"It's not the island, Blaine. Haven't you ever heard? 'Wherever you go, there you'll be.'"

Blaine rolled her eyes. "No. It's the island. It's being here. I need to get away."

"No-oooo. It's secret keeping. It's making you sick. You're scared. Scared and shaken. And when you're scared, you've always done a great job of creating all kinds of noise that acts as a decoy."

"Me? Scared?" Blaine tried to scoff as she said it, but it sounded more like a weak cough. Pathetic.

"I know you're not sleeping well."

"So far, this therapy session stinks." She leaned back in the chair and crossed her ankles.

"That's because you never pay for my services." Maddie gave her a smug grin before she clapped her hands on her knees. "Look, Blaine, you've given that instructor a lot of power. He's been able to silence you, and make you scared, and make you run. Once you start, you'll never stop." She spoke frankly, but Blaine could hear the compassion infused in her candor. "It's not the response I would've expected from you. You of all people. And it's not the one I want to see from you."

"What would that be?"

"Anger. Healthy, righteous anger."

Blaine squirmed. Maddie didn't know the whole story. She didn't know because Blaine couldn't tell her. She was too ashamed. But she knew that Maddie could tell she was hiding something. A warning bell sounded inside Blaine, or maybe it was the horn of the ferry. Either way, it was time to change the subject. "Rick is sure good-looking, don't you think?"

That shut Maddie down.

~⸙~

Cam glanced at the clock. Three a.m. She'd been up twice with Cooper, trying to calm him down because he kept having nightmares that he was getting swallowed by a big fish. Last night, he'd even refused to take a bath.

When Cooper got worked up like this, it was hard to distract him from it. She pulled a pillow over her face, imagining how tomorrow's conversations would mirror today's. Question after question about what would happen if Cooper were to be swallowed up by a whale, a shark, any other big fish. What would it smell like? What should he do if weeds wrapped around his head?

Should he start carrying a pocketknife in his sock, just in case? If he were wearing a watch, could he use that to light the interior of the fish's belly so it wouldn't be so dark?

The reason Cooper didn't want to take a bath, he insisted, was because his skin gets prune-like and that's exactly how Pastor Rick described Jonah's skin after three days in the fish's belly.

Cam sighed. Maybe Seth could help him work it out. He had just the right knack to calm Cooper down, talk him off the ledge. Cam rolled over, punched her pillow. Cooper had been doing so much better this last year. That ball of string he used to carry with him everywhere was long forgotten—and that string obsession was weird. He used to unravel it around a room so that it looked like a spider had cast a giant web. Maddie had a name for it, but Cam could never remember what it was. Something about abandonment, that she remembered.

Cooper hadn't been abandoned!

But in a way, he had.

His mom, Libby, had died in a house fire. And although Cam, as her best friend, had adopted Cooper when he was just four years old, she knew he had memories of his mother, of the fire.

Cam did the best she could, but parenthood didn't come naturally to her. Not like it did with Maddie. Or Seth, for that matter. Cam had always fought a tendency to get preoccupied with things over people. Work, mostly.

Was that why Cooper seemed to be regressing? She had tried to do better. She put all evidence of work away before Cooper got home from school each day, tried not to talk nonstop about it with Dad—tempting as it was, because they were both intrigued by the prospects of sustainable energy and what it could mean for Camp Kicking Moose. She volunteered at school as often as Seth allowed—which wasn't often because he thought Cooper didn't need someone hovering over him. She released a huff of annoyance. She did *not* hover.

Well, sometimes she did.

Argh. Cam pounded on her pillow. It always came down to this. Cooper needed more—and Cam couldn't even figure out what that "more" was. She was just painfully aware that it was never enough.

The principal at the last school Cooper had gotten booted out of had hinted strongly that Cam's shortcomings as a mother were to blame for Cooper's problems. It was a terrible feeling to know that your child needed something you couldn't provide. In her heart, she knew it had nothing to do with the fact that Cooper was adopted. It had to do with her.

In the near dark of early morning, with the wind whistling through the fir trees, it dawned on Cam that *that* was the real reason she kept postponing a wedding date. Seth wanted more children, and he didn't want to wait. He wanted Cooper to have siblings that were as close in age as possible.

More children! More mess-ups. More failures.

Cam just wasn't sure she could live a life of knowing she would never be enough.

⁓

Blaine and Maddie were up early on Monday morning, preparing the buffet for the campers. Blaine poured orange juice into a glass pitcher and set it in a bowl of ice. "Maddie, if you didn't tell Pastor Rick anything about what I'd told you—"

Cutting watermelon into slices, Maddie paused, midcut, to interrupt. "I didn't."

"—why do you think he looked right at me at church and said that thing about a fear of holding people to account?" Blaine genuinely wanted to know. In fact, she hadn't stopped thinking about it.

Maddie shrugged. "I don't know. You should ask him yourself." She set spoons onto a tray filled with ironed cloth napkins.

"It's weird. It's like Pastor Rick just 'gets' people, you know? Like he can see right into your head."

"Yeah, I know." Maddie put the platter on the tray. "Ricky always had the inside scoop. On everybody. You wouldn't believe some of the secrets he knew about me when we were in school. Especially during junior high. It was like he read my mind."

"Oh?" It came out like a whisper. A guilty one.

Maddie set the tray on the kitchen table and turned to face Blaine, fixing her astute gaze on her. A Maddie-stare. "Why did you say that sisters betray each other?"

Blaine felt her cheeks grow warm. Focus, focus, focus. What else was missing for breakfast? She glanced over the large farm table, full of breakfast items they would carry out to the porch. Granola. Freshly cut fruit. Individual yogurts sitting in an ice bath. Coffee cake. Coffee. Cream for the coffee. She snapped her fingers. "Scones. That's what's missing. I knew something was missing." She grabbed the container that held scones she had baked last evening and set them on an oversized dish. Sensing that Maddie was still waiting for an answer, she kept her eyes down and took her time arranging the scones.

"Blaine." It didn't come out like a question.

"I don't know why I said that."

"I think you do. I think there's something you're not telling me."

A trickle of sweat dripped down Blaine's back. Was it hot in here? Or was it the guilt that radiated off her?

"Blaine, I wish you'd open up a little more. You know you can trust me."

"Trust you to forgive?"

Maddie's eyes stayed on her. Slowly, she nodded.

Blaine took a deep breath, then covered her face. "Your missing diary." It came out a little muffled.

"My what?"

She dropped her hands. "Your diary. Junior high."

Confusion filled Maddie's eyes. "You mean . . . *that* diary? The one that went missing? The one I turned the house upside down looking for?"

Blaine bit her lip, nodding. "I sold it to Ricky O'Shea for ten dollars."

Her sister's eyes went wide with horror. "You did *what*?"

"I'm sorry, Maddie. All these years, it's bothered me." She couldn't even look at her. "It's just that . . . you were so mean to me that year you turned thirteen. You acted just like Cam. Like I wasn't important to you anymore. I just . . . I wanted to get back at you." A long moment slipped past. "You'll forgive me, right?"

Stunned, Maddie didn't respond.

MADDIE, AGE 13

Maddie had searched every hiding place in her room for her diary, three times over. She had twelve different spots, each one clever and hard to reach. For the last few months, she'd been sure that Blaine had been sneaking into her room, nosing around, whenever she'd left the house. Maddie could always tell when Blaine had been in her room because things were slightly displaced. She was well acquainted with sister spying, as she'd done plenty of it in Cam's room when she was Blaine's age.

"It looks like a tornado came through."

Maddie turned to see her dad at the doorjamb. "Blaine's been in my room."

"She made this mess?"

"No, I made it. Because I knew she'd been in here and now I can't find my diary." She loved that diary. Her entire inner life was poured into that diary—all her secrets, dreams, hopes, worries. Lots of worries.

Dad walked in and looked around. "So catch me up to speed here. Why have you turned your room upside down?"

"Blaine's been reading my diary again." She frowned at him. "Dad, I've told you and told you. I need a lock on my door."

"No locks." He sat on her desk chair. "How do you know Blaine's been reading your diary?"

"Three reasons. One, I can't find it, and I know where I hid it. Two, she's always in my stuff."

"I seem to remember Cam had a lot of similar complaints about you when she was thirteen."

"Well, that's how I know Blaine was in here. Something happens to a girl when she's thirteen. She gets fascinating. Little sisters sense that."

Dad nodded, as if he understood, which he didn't. "And reason three?"

"Blaine is mad at me. Stealing my diary is her way to get back at me. Very passive-aggressive. That's Blaine. I know, Dad. I've been reading all about this behavior." She pointed to a book about psychology on her nightstand. She'd gotten it out of the public library to analyze her family.

Dad picked up the book and looked at its spine, put it down, then leaned back in his chair. "So why is she mad at you?"

Maddie bent down to check under her bed, then ran a hand between the mattress and springs. "Who knows?"

"You do."

She pulled back from under the bed and sat on her heels. "My opinion, as a future therapist, is that Blaine is suffering from a lack of attention. As a result, she acts out."

"I see. And what is causing this lack of attention?"

"Well, Dad, since you asked . . . I think it's because you travel too much." The baseball season had finally ended and Dad was home for the winter, until spring training started up again.

"So Blaine is mad at you because I travel too much."

"Yes. Well, no. She's becoming thoroughly obnoxious and that's because you travel so much. She's desperate for parental attention. Dad, I'm serious. She is really a head case."

"She's only eight. That's pretty young to be diagnosed as a passive-aggressive head case."

Maddie lifted her palms in the air. "Sad but true."

"I'm still unclear. Why is she mad at you?"

"She's mad at me because I wouldn't let her come with me to the mall the other day."

"Why not?"

These were the moments when Maddie thought it was a pity her father only had daughters. He really had no clue about girls. "Honestly, I don't think you want to know."

"I do. I really do. Why couldn't she go with you to the mall? Were you meeting a boy?"

Maddie shook her head vigorously. "No! Why would I meet a boy at the mall? Dad, don't you know that the emotional maturity between a thirteen-year-old young woman and a thirteen-year-old disgusting boy . . . why, we're decades apart. There's no comparison." She shuddered. The boys in her class were appallingly immature. Worse than most boys in America, she was convinced.

"Then why couldn't Blaine come to the mall with you?"

"If you must know, it's because I was buying my first bra." She watched her dad carefully to gauge his reaction. He was trying so hard to look cool, but a telltale red streak had started up both of his cheeks, and he shifted uncomfortably in his chair. He cleared his throat, glanced at his watch. Any second now, he would think of a reason to bolt. And sure enough, ever so predictable, he jumped from the chair like a cricket and made for the door. She shouldn't feel pleased at embarrassing him, but she did.

Then he surprised her. At the doorjamb, he spun around. "Maddie, I want you to think about one thing. Try to remember how you felt when Cam was thirteen and treated you like a nuisance. And then do the opposite with Blaine."

Maddie leaned her back against the bed. Hmm. This was a rare moment, one she wouldn't soon forget. Her father had imparted some relational wisdom. *Do the opposite.* In a flash of self-reflection, Maddie realized she was turning into Cam. Sisterwise, anyway. According to her psychology book, older siblings had a powerful impact on younger ones—good and bad. Cam had always made Maddie feel inferior, insignificant, barely tolerated. *Oof!* She didn't want to do that to Blaine.

From that day forward, Maddie did her best to treat Blaine with more kindness and understanding, to include her whenever she could. To try, anyway. But Maddie never did find her diary.

Thirteen

MADDIE PRESSED THE DOORBELL OF THE CHURCH OFFICE on First Street at eight o'clock on Monday morning, as early as she dared to confront Rick and definitely prior to Tillie's prompt arrival at nine o'clock.

This wasn't church business. This was business-business. Her business. Him getting into it.

She knocked and knocked and knocked until she heard a sound inside the house.

The door finally opened and Rick popped his head in the crack. He hadn't shaved this morning, and dark stubble covered his lean cheeks. He looked different. More handsome. Was that even possible? "Maddie! Good morning." His voice sounded sleep-roughened, like he hadn't used it yet.

Oh good grief. She had woken him up and roused him out of bed like a crazed woman.

He opened the door and Maddie drew in a shallow breath, pulse quickening.

Whoa. His chest. Drawstring pajama bottoms. Had he noticed her staring? Even her ears heated at the thought. Her flush moved from her ears, her cheeks, down her neck. "Let me change and I'll be right out."

For a split second, she got distracted with the serious purpose of her visit. "Don't bother," she said, pulling her stray thoughts back into line. "I'm not staying. I just have one thing to say."

He squinted as he watched her. "Are you angry with me?" he asked, finally picking up on her vibe, and it hit Maddie all over again with full force: Yes! She was furious with him. Eight years, give or take, of bottled fury.

She struggled to meet his eyes, to keep herself composed. "I am, in fact."

"I kind of remember that particular look on your face from school days." His expression turned mock somber. "So what did I do now?" He lifted a hand. "Hold it. Come on in. I'll make coffee. Then you can tell me what caused such aggravation on a beautiful morning in Maine."

He opened the door wide so she could pass through, which she did, a little reluctantly. She followed him down the hall to the kitchen.

He flicked on the lights and looked around. "Welcome to my office."

Maddie had been in the house a couple of times when Seth was considering it for a church rental. The kitchen had lacked much then and still did. The cabinetry was tired, painted too many times, and some door hinges were missing. The bright orange formica countertops were a throwback to the sixties. Cringeworthy. Tiles were missing in the linoleum flooring. The appliances were a cheap brand to start with; now they were cheap and old. A little card table with two folding chairs served as a table. "You're using this for your office?"

"Office. Kitchen table. Anything else." Rick grinned. "The formal dining room . . . that's become Tillie's domain." He put his hands on his hips and peered around the kitchen, as if hoping something might magically appear. "I'm not really sure where a coffeepot might be that isn't meant for thirty-five people on a Sunday morning. To tell you the truth . . ." He smoothed a hand over his head and turned to her as he finished his thought. "To tell you the truth, most mornings, I just go on down to the Lunch Counter."

Their eyes locked. She looked away, breaking the contact. She needed to distract herself from her attraction to him. School days, all over again. So frustrating! "You go change and I'll make coffee."

"Deal."

She hunted around to find coffee. She opened the fridge and saw six or seven assorted pans, covered in tinfoil. She lifted the foil off one corner of a pan. Tuna casserole. She read the piece of tape on top of another casserole. Nancy's meat loaf. She slammed the fridge. It figured! The whole island was bringing him casseroles. They were all turning into his groupies.

She rummaged through a cupboard and finally settled on tea instead of coffee, heated in water in the microwave. In record time, Rick returned to the kitchen wearing jeans, shrugging a white T-shirt over his shoulders. Much bigger shoulders than she remembered he'd had in high school, when he played point guard on the varsity basketball team. Stronger abs too. She didn't even like basketball, but she had made her friends go with her to every game. Just to watch him, without anyone knowing why she was there. They all thought she loved the sport. She didn't. When the microwave beeped, she handed him a mug of hot tea.

He took a sip, then tilted his head and pointed a finger at the mug. "I'm ninety-nine percent sure this isn't coffee."

"It's as close as I could get." She glanced at the fridge. "Well, at least you're not going to starve."

He exhaled. "The casseroles. I'm grateful, but I don't know what to do with them all."

"Try freezing them."

"They can freeze?"

"Most everything can freeze."

He smiled. "Thank you for that suggestion." He opened a cupboard. "Hungry? I don't have much other than casseroles, but I do have granola bars. Want one?"

"No." She was starving, actually. Planning to confront him soundly this morning had kept her too wound up from eating anything for breakfast. Too wound up.

He handed her a granola bar—her favorite brand. "Eat. Don't want you feeling hungry on top of angry when you have something important to tell me. What's that called again?"

"Hangry."

"That's it. I don't want you feeling hangry. Food is fuel, you know. I want to hear what you have to say. Everything."

Stop being nice. Stop acting charming. She accepted the bar and unwrapped it. It tasted sweet and salty and fruity and nutty and . . . wonderful.

He hopped up on the counter. "Okay. Go ahead. Lay it on me. What's got you so fired up this morning?" His dark eyebrows rose, and a playful grin lit his face.

Darn. She'd lost some of her fire. Calmer now, she took a sip of tea. "It's come to my attention that you paid my sister Blaine to read my diary."

"Wow." He rubbed his jaw. "You're talking about . . . you mean, way, way back. Like, middle school years."

"Yes." From the look on his face, he wasn't denying it. Nor had he forgotten. "So you admit it."

He lifted his hands in mock surrender. "Guilty as charged."

The slightly amused look in his eyes only stoked her fire. "That year . . . I thought I was going crazy. Every single thing I was afraid of . . . they all came true."

His eyebrows lifted. "Seriously?"

"Yes! Some of the things you did to me—spiders in my backpack, bra pads stuffed in my locker—triggered lifelong anxieties."

"You're still afraid of spiders and bras?"

"Yes! No! Spiders, I mean. But that's beside the point."

He dropped his chin to his chest for a long moment, then lifted his head to look straight at her. "Maddie, I owe you a heartfelt apology for buying your diary from your sister."

"You think a heartfelt apology is what I'm after?"

"It's not?"

"How about coming clean? Admitting that you did a terrible thing to read my diary. I only found out because Blaine confessed what she'd done in a weak moment." Her fists were clenched. Her fire was coming back. "You're a pastor, for goodness' sake!"

He nodded solemnly. "You're right. You're absolutely right. Maddie, I am sorry. I was actually trying to apologize to you the other day at Moose Manor, but you cut me off."

"You were going to apologize for paying my little sister to read my diary?"

"Well, to be honest, I probably was not going to confess about that particular transgression. Junior high was a long, long time ago and I blocked most of it out of my memory. But I know I did a lot of annoying things to you when we were kids. And I am truly sorry. For those things." And then his expression grew serious. "And . . . the other . . ." He dropped his eyes, studying the floor. He couldn't say it.

But his forthrightness threw Maddie off. She stumbled to know what to say next, and out came words she hadn't meant to say. "Why me? What did I ever do to you to make you want to be so mean to me? Why weren't you terrible to the other girls? They all had crushes on you."

His eyes filled with amusement. "You weren't like other girls."

"How so?"

"You had a maddening way of being right for the wrong reasons." Then he tilted his head in a way that made him look so appealing that Maddie once again lost her train of thought.

Stop it! she wanted to shout. *Stop looking so cute. Stop trying to charm me off topic.* Her brain was getting scrambled; she searched for something to hang on to. "And now you're making Cooper go crazy."

"Cooper? Oh, you mean, after yesterday's Jonah sermon?" He clasped his hands together. "What was that about? He sure did get upset."

"He's in a complete tailspin. Terrified that a fish will swallow him if he gets anywhere near water. Even a bathtub."

Rick looked thoroughly confused. He scratched the back of his neck. "But those other boys—the ones in the back row—they seemed to like hearing about Jonah in the fish."

"Cooper's not like other boys."

"Right." His brown eyes softened as he looked at her. "Kinda like his aunt."

Her anger started slipping away again. It was hard to argue that comparison. Her entire life, people had warned Maddie about her ability to seek out the worst-case scenario in any situation. This moment was no exception. "Okay, so maybe Cooper and I are a little high on the anxiety scale."

"A little?"

Memories of the many, many other conversations she'd tried to have with Rick—just like this one—moved through her mind. Ones in which she felt embarrassed, made fun of. "Never mind." She turned to go, but he jumped from the counter, reached out, and grabbed her hand. When his hand touched hers, she felt a jolt. Her heart raced, her knees felt soft and unsteady.

"I'll talk to Cooper. Maddie, I didn't come to this island to upset you. I came . . ."

"Why? Why *are* you here?"

"I came because . . ." He paused, looking right into her eyes with such tenderness that she had to look away. Her eyes focused on their two hands, joined together. She should tug her hand out of his grip. She should! But she couldn't make herself do it. It felt like there was some kind of invisible magnetic field around him, pulling her toward him despite her best efforts to resist. That's how it felt from her perspective, anyway. He probably didn't feel what she felt. He cleared his throat and started again, but something had changed in his tone. "I came because it was the right job at the right time."

No. No, he definitely didn't feel what she felt. He never had. She slipped her hand out of his grasp. "I need to get to work." She left him in the kitchen.

As soon as she entered her basement office, she set down her purse and flopped into a chair, closing her eyes. It was hard to have so many feelings for Rick O'Shea. Good ones, bad ones. Just . . . such strong ones. She'd had years of stuffing down her push-pull emotions toward him. Attraction, even fascination, pulling her to him. Exasperation and futility pushing her away. During high school, she'd gotten very good at it. Pretty good. She'd tried her best, anyway.

MADDIE, AGE 16

Maddie was on her way up the stairs to ask her parents if she could borrow the car when she overheard their conversation. Dad, in his deep and loud baritone voice, mentioned her name. She slowed, then crept to the top of the stairs to eavesdrop through their open bedroom door.

"I've never known Maddie to seem so prickly," Dad said. "Usually, it takes a lot to get her mad. This whole week, she's been snapping at everybody."

"She's going through a difficult time," Mom said.

"So I gathered. But why? When I asked, she said nothing was wrong and that I should stop trying to be an amateur psychologist." She could hear her dad thump his chest. "Me!"

"My guess is it has something to do with Ricky O'Shea. Maddie saw him holding hands with Jessica Stewart down at Main Hall the other day."

"But Maddie can't stand Ricky O'Shea. She's done nothing but complain about him for as long as I can remember. Longer. Bring up his name and she looks like she's about to explode."

"Paul, *think*."

Silence, then a big Dad-sigh. "I wouldn't think it'd be a big deal to Maddie if Ricky had a girlfriend or not."

"It *is* a big deal, Paul. Do I have to spell it out?"

"Yes. Always."

"Because deep down, Maddie's always been smitten with Ricky."

Maddie's fists clenched. She had *never* told her mother such a thing! Never.

"Frankly, I'm relieved Ricky has a girlfriend," Dad said. "She'll keep him away from Maddie. I know, I know, don't give me that look. My paternal instincts are not the point of this conversation. Well, if Ricky doesn't appreciate Maddie's charms, she should find someone who does. Show ol' Ricky what he's missing."

Hmm. Maddie hadn't thought of that. Now and then, Dad could surprise her. The one guy who had never been a Ricky O'Shea fan, who could outperform Ricky in every sport and outdo him with every girl, was Chipper, Lacey's older brother.

He wasn't her type, not at all. Though . . . Chipper did like to flirt with Maddie. She thought he just flirted with every girl. Hmm. Maybe she'd have to think twice about him.

Fourteen

As NICE AS IT WAS TO SEE ARTIE'S DAD SO FREQUENTLY, Blaine was more than a little offended when he didn't finish the shepherd's pie she'd made especially for his supper at the Lunch Counter on Saturday night. Last time she had made it for him, he loved it. Raved about it for days. Bob Lotosky was particularly fond of potatoes, being a potato farmer and all, and had asked her to make it for him. She'd been so careful to follow her mother's recipe, to not vary it in the slightest way. "What's wrong with it?"

In his usual blunt way, Mr. Lotosky had pushed it away and said, "Doesn't have that special something. Not like the last one."

The last one. Last summer. Made before Blaine's sense of taste had gone missing.

This was so frustrating! She assumed that if she followed recipes exactly, not varying anything in the slightest way like she normally had, her dishes would still turn out well. But more customer complaints were piling up, fewer people were coming into the Lunch Counter. Peg said not to pay any attention to fickle patrons, to stop overthinking and to just cook.

147

Blaine tried. And it wasn't working.

As soon as the morning breakfast crowd at the diner thinned out, she tossed the rest of the shepherd's pie into the bin.

Man, she missed her mother. She missed getting her help in the kitchen, missed her encouragement. They'd been so close, especially because her dad had traveled so much for his job. After her sisters left for college, it was just Blaine and Mom, most of the time. Just the two of them. They would spend hours in the kitchen, cooking and baking, tweaking old recipes and inventing new ones. Her mom had been gone four years now and Blaine still had moments when she forgot her mom had died. When she remembered, it felt like a kick in the gut all over again.

And now it seemed she'd lost the one gift her mother had taught her to trust: her palate. The very essence of her cooking.

⁓

Only nine in the morning, and it was already hot and humid. Maddie set her coffee on her desk and crossed the room to open the casement window when her sister Blaine arrived. No warning knock. She just burst in and plopped in a chair.

Maddie scowled at her. "Blaine! You can't just walk right in. I might have had a client with me." She needed to get a sign to put on her door so her sisters would stop coming in without making an appointment. OCCUPIED. STAY AWAY. I'M BUSY.

Blaine turned in a circle around the small basement office. "No one's here."

"Not right now, but I anticipate a full day of clients. Eventually."

"Well, until that happens, I need you to practice on me."

"What's wrong now?" She noticed Blaine's eyes were shiny. Was there something more about that awful instructor?

She pointed to her mouth. "I've lost my sense of taste."

"Seriously?" Maddie grabbed her coffee cup and sat across from her.

"Plus my sense of smell. Gone." She reached out to take Maddie's coffee mug from her, took a sip, and made a face. "Nothing. I'm doomed."

"What do you think is causing it?"

"Peg thinks it's the culinary school. They've altered my taste buds. Too fancy, she says."

Maddie's face pinched doubtfully.

"I know. I don't think that's the cause either."

"So what do you think is the reason?"

"You're the shrink. You tell me."

Maddie paused at that, slightly irritated. *Let it go, let it go.* "Have you seen a doctor?"

"No. Should I?" Blaine tilted her head in confusion. "Why? Are you thinking it's cancer? Cancer of the taste buds? Is there such a thing?"

"No. Of course it's not cancer of the taste buds."

"But we do have weird stuff in our family. Look at Dad's voice. Who gets a case of laryngitis that never leaves?" She rubbed her throat, as if it was sore. "Maybe I've inherited some kind of auto-immune disease from Dad."

"Dad doesn't have an autoimmune disease. He had a bad case of laryngitis that damaged his vocal cords."

"Still . . . it's weird."

"Blaine, maybe you should just talk to a doctor. It's always wise to start with a checkup. To rule out the obvious."

"Cancer of the taste buds is not obvious."

"Burned taste buds could be. Any chance you made something outrageously spicy lately?"

She frowned. "Spanish paella."

"Could be something simple, like that."

"So do taste buds regenerate?"

"Pretty sure they heal." Blaine was quiet, though Maddie noticed her foot couldn't stop twitching. "Could there be anything else that caused this?"

"What do you think?"

"Blaine," Maddie said in a no-nonsense voice.

She focused on the contents of her coffee mug. "I know you're thinking that it's all in my head." She pointed to her head. "Psycho . . . something or other."

"Psychosomatic."

"So, is that what you're thinking?"

"Let's just stay in *your* head for now. Is that what you think?"

Blaine straightened the edge of her T-shirt. "If so, if I don't have terminal cancer, then maybe it's a sign. That I'm not meant to be in the world of food." She glanced up. "Evidence of a need for redirection."

"Or . . ."

"Or what?"

"What else could it be a sign of?"

Blaine sighed. "Maddie, stop doing that."

"What?"

"Answering a question with a question. Just tell me what you think."

There was a reason Maddie hesitated to answer Blaine directly. It had been drilled into her during her licensing internship to be cautious of advice-giving because clients, even though they asked, didn't really want to hear advice. They wanted to be understood, or to understand themselves. A good therapist could help people sort out their lives, but they couldn't—shouldn't—dole out advice. It would be taking away essential steps of growth from a client. "The truth shall set you free." She believed those words from Christ, and knew that it was best of all when people came to truth on their own accord.

But when Maddie was with her sisters, she forgot all that, along with everything else she'd learned about advice-giving from her training. Besides, Blaine wasn't really her client. She was her little sister, coming to her with a problem. "I wonder if it's a sign of . . . fear."

"Fear?" Blaine scoffed. "I'm not exactly the fearful-girl type. For Pete's sake . . . I'm planning to travel through Europe all alone."

"True, you're not easily frightened. Not of everyday, run-of-the-mill fears. You try all kinds of new things. Look at the recipes you invent. But, Blaine . . . I think your missing palate has to do with being afraid of this instructor."

She jumped up. "That's all behind me. Done. Over with. I'm moving on."

"Hear me out. I'm not lecturing you or trying to tell you what to do—"

"Yes, you are! You want me to go back to culinary school and blow the whistle on that instructor and ruin his marriage. That is *not* happening!" And with that, she stormed out the door, leaving it wide open.

Maddie stomped to the open door and shouted at Blaine's receding figure, "Then don't expect your missing palate to return anytime soon!" She wanted to yell more—things like, "Stop bursting into my office!" and "Next time, I'm charging you!" but Tillie was at the bottom of the church office steps, staring at her with a frown.

⌒

Sadly, Paul was coming to the realization that last summer, the first year that Camp Kicking Moose had been reopened under new management—which was him—would probably always be remembered as the best summer. He'd had no expectations for guests, grateful they had come to fill the cabins, and he was eager to keep everyone happy so they'd return the following year. This summer, he felt a little differently about many of those repeat guests. Partial to some, much less so to others.

If he knew the guests and liked them, he would put them in cabins close to Moose Manor. If not . . . well, it could be a long walk to the Manor for breakfast on the porch on a rainy day.

This week brought in a couple who drove him crazy last year and even more so this year. The Sweetmans from Long Island. They asked for the cabin Never Enough Thyme, just like last year, but they were absolutely, positively certain it wasn't the same cabin. Like Paul was trying to pull a fast one on them and had swapped the quarter boards over each cabin's door.

Every morning, the Sweetmans felt the need to list out their complaints to him. The sunlight didn't pour through the windows the way it did last summer. (Had they considered that this year was a different week in the summer than their visit last year? No!) The granola had changed (no, it hadn't—Blaine made all kinds of variations from the basic recipe), and it was so rainy compared to last year (which it was, but Paul couldn't control Mother Nature). Nothing was ever quite right for Ernie and Elsie Sweetman.

So why did they even come back to Camp Kicking Moose? Last year, they'd had different complaints. Same whiny tone in their voices, same vague general disappointment. Why come back? *Leave!* he wanted to say. *I'll refund your money if you'll just go. Go and never come back.*

But Cam had put the kibosh on that idea. "Some people just like to complain. If they're coming back, they like being here. They just don't tell you the good stuff." She wagged a finger in his face. "It's one week, Dad. One little week. You can deal with them for one week."

Walking back up to the house from the cabins, he reflected on his eldest daughter's business sense. He couldn't keep this camp going without Cam. He couldn't build a future without Blaine's talent in the kitchen. He needed Maddie's hub-of-the-wheel heart to keep them working well together. He felt cheered up, thinking about his three beautiful girls and how much he appreciated them, how he loved them.

As he came into the wide, grassy clearing of the house, he saw Blaine storm down the front steps to her car, get in, then honk impatiently. Late for work again. It irked him when she honked the horn, disturbing the quiet of the morning. It irked the Sweetmans too. Blaine's impatient morning honks topped their list of complaints.

Next Maddie shot out of the front door, head tucked down, looking like she was thoroughly preoccupied. She got into the passenger side of Blaine's car and they zoomed away without even noticing him. As Paul climbed the front steps to the house, grateful the guests hadn't started to wander sleepily from their cabins to the Moose Manor porch for breakfast yet, he stopped to get a cup of coffee from the buffet table, admiring the inviting spread Blaine had laid out. Cereals, granola—excellent recipe, he thought—blueberry muffins with a cinnamon streusel topping, yogurt on ice, a platter of red, ripe strawberries, freshly squeezed orange juice, hot coffee.

Through the open window he could hear Cooper calling to Cam in a loud, insistent voice. Paul turned the spigot on the coffee urn as his mug filled. Did he really want to go straight from the malcontented Sweetmans into the kitchen of Moose Manor, with Cooper and Cam and the ongoing dilemma of Jonah and fear of water? Nope.

Coffee in hand, he pivoted and headed down the steps toward the boathouse for a little peace and quiet. From the roof of the Seas the Day cabin flew a duck, landing a few feet from Paul. He didn't really think much about it and continued across the large grass lawn, but the duck waddled right behind, honking once or twice like he was trying to get Paul's attention.

Paul stopped and turned back to face down the duck. "No more complaints. You hear me? Or I'll get Captain Ed out here and you'll end up on the menu at the Lunch Counter." They stared at each other, until the duck gave up and waddled off.

At least someone around here listened to him. Cheered up, Paul slapped at a mosquito on his neck, and his smile faded. Good grief. He made fun of Bob Lotosky for talking to potatoes and here he was, talking to a duck.

⁓

"Mom-mom-mom-mom-mom."

Cam jerked her head up. "What?"

"My waffle's up." Cooper was glaring at her. "I tried to tell you, but you aren't listening. You never listen."

She glanced at the toaster. "So it is." Cam took the waffle from the toaster slot, buttered it, poured some syrup over it, cut it up, then put the plate in front of Cooper. "Here you go."

Cooper immediately stabbed a piece and popped it into his mouth, still glaring. He was upset with her. Seth was upset with her. Blaine was upset with her.

Cam had always done an excellent job with work. Relationships . . . not so much. She knew Seth seemed distant lately, and she knew why—she'd been too busy, too preoccupied with this energy project—but it was one thing to know and another thing entirely to get things back on track. That part eluded her.

Besides, this was who she was. She'd always had a tendency to go overboard when she was excited about something. And this energy project *was* exciting. Just imagine what this island would be like if bringing energy into homes wasn't sporadic and unpredictable. Imagine the winters! Warm and cozy, instead of grueling and endless.

It was important, this project. Seth, Blaine, even Cooper, they needed to cut her a little slack. *Right, Lord? Could you nudge them a little?* Cam's faith had been dormant for most of her life, though last year it had woken out of hibernation. Still, she knew her relationship with God had remained pretty shallow; it was nothing like Maddie's rock-solid faith. Or Seth's. They talked about God as if he were right there.

So could you help me out here, Lord? Cam was trying to pray more, about everything. *Can you get them to give me a little margin?*

If it's grace you want, start by giving it.

She popped her head up, looking around the kitchen. "What did you say?"

"Nothing," Cooper said, chomping away, still glaring at her.

"Did you hear something?"

He swallowed. "Hear what?"

Oh wow. Was that a word from Above? Maddie was always getting those. Seth, too. Same with Peg. Not an audible voice, but a voice, just the same. Loud and clear, right to the point, popping into her mind from a different direction than she was thinking. Oh wow, wow, wow.

Cam closed her laptop. "Coops, let's leave early for school and go down to Boon Dock. Maybe Seth is taking Dory for a walk. Grandpa can handle refilling the breakfast buffet until I get back." Cooper nodded, his glare softening a little. "I saw Grandpa head down to the boathouse. Would you go tell him we're leaving? I'll meet you at the car."

A reluctant smile escaped from Cooper as he grabbed his half-eaten waffle and headed to the door.

Twenty minutes later, Cam parked on Main Street and stopped a moment to admire how much better the road looked. The grass growing in the middle of the street was gone. The storefronts were painted, most were filled, open for the season. "Look at that, Cooper. Even the Baggett and Taggett has a new coat of paint. Not the color I would've picked for them. In fact, I wish they would've asked me. Still, it's better than that awful moose-brown color it was. Don't you think so?" When he didn't respond, she spun around and saw he had already headed down to the dock.

Cooper went straight to a bench and sat on it as if he'd been told to, though he hadn't. She plopped down next to him. "Want to go down by the water? I'll be right here."

"No," he said. The bench was big enough that his legs stuck straight out. He seemed content to sit and watch the birds. She wished . . . she wished . . . she wished he would run along the sand and chase the noisy seagulls and dip his toes into the cold surf, like most little boys would do. All little boys. Just not her little boy.

They sat for a while, watching the fishing boats start coming in from the day's catch. "Want to walk down the dock with me? See the lobsters?"

He shook his head. Still committed to his anti-water obsession.

"I don't see Seth," he said.

"Guess he's already come and gone." Absently, she smoothed down his untamable rooster tail. "Last few days of school. Are you excited?"

He ignored her question. "Is Seth mad at you?"

"No. Why do you say that?"

He shrugged. "He doesn't come around Moose Manor as much."

Was that true? Cam didn't think there'd been a change in the amount of time she and Seth spent together. She didn't think so. But . . . maybe?

"When school gets out, I might not see him at all."

"Coops, not true! You'll see a lot of Seth this summer. Like the overnight to the lighthouse that you two have been planning."

He brightened a little at that thought.

A half hour later, Cam walked Cooper up Main Street to school. He dropped his backpack by the gate and crossed the yard to the tetherball pole to join his friend Quinn.

Seth greeted her with, "How's Cooper doing today?" Not a hug or kiss, not even a hello.

At least Dory seemed excited to see her. The big yellow Lab bounded over to jump up on Cam. "Cooper is . . . so-so," she said, pushing Dory down. "I talked to Maddie about his water thing." Her sister was Cooper's self-appointed therapist.

"What did she say?"

"She said it was important to let Cooper seek out experiences commensurate with his level of development."

"What does that mean?"

"Not totally sure, but I think it means to let him work this out by himself."

Seth gave her *the look*. Seemed like she was getting it a lot from him lately. A look that said, *Are you kidding me?* "Cam, I want to get Cooper to a child psychologist."

"Hold on a minute. Just because of that Jonah sermon? It'll pass, Seth. Watch and see. Cooper gets like this sometimes. But he'll forget about it."

"He needs to bathe, Cam. In this warm weather, the kids are starting to tease that he smells like overripe fruit."

"This morning, he was willing to take a washrag bath." She snapped her fingers. "Progress!" When he continued to give her the look, she became serious. "You're the one who's always saying to give Cooper a little space. To not overreact to every little thing. There's nothing wrong with him. He's not sick. He's just a little boy." With a tendency for odd quirks.

Seth shook his head. "I didn't say he was sick. But this sudden fear of water, it does seem different."

"How?"

"I don't know. It just is."

He walked away from her without saying goodbye, something he'd never done before. Not ever. Seth was the one who never wanted to part without clearing up a misunderstanding. "Don't let the sun go down on your anger." It was one of his verses to live by.

Cam turned to walk to her car, but instead she went up First Street to the church office and around the side to the basement door. She knocked once and went inside.

⟳

Maddie recognized Cam's distinctive knock, but before she could answer, her sister walked in and sat down. She was just about to scold her but stopped when she saw Cam's face. "Come in, sit down, I'll make coffee."

Maddie made a cup of coffee just the way she knew Cam liked it. She handed her a ceramic mug and sat across from her. "What's going on?"

"I don't know." Cam took a sip of coffee. "I really don't. Everything was fine . . . Cooper, Seth, all fine. And then suddenly, it wasn't." She dropped her chin to her chest. "And I just don't know why things have slipped off the rails."

"So what seems to be different now?"

Cam shrugged. "I have no idea. Things were going so great until . . ." Her eyes widened. "Until Blaine arrived. Something changed when she came back. She's been pushing me to set a wedding date, and Cooper's overheard her—you know how hard change is for him—and I think it's made him get nervous. That's probably why he had such a strong reaction to the Jonah sermon. And then Seth seems worried about him—and Seth never worries."

"So you think Blaine's to blame?" Maddie was well accustomed to her sister's cluelessness.

"Don't you?" Cam took another sip of coffee. "I love Blaine dearly, but she changes the household's dynamics. Don't you agree? I mean . . . she's so twitchy this summer. Restless."

"Cam, what other things could be causing anxiety for Cooper?"

Cam peered at the ceiling for a long moment. "Honestly, I think it started when . . ."

"Blaine arrived."

"Yes."

Okay. Time to switch tracks. Maddie took out a pad of paper and drew two large rectangles, one above the other, with space in between. "Our brains are made up of two boxes. The top box is emotions. The bottom box is our rational thinking. Logic." She drew a two-sided arrow in the space in between. "Most of us go between the boxes, using our emotions to understand logic, or logic to understand emotions."

Cam peered at the paper, interested.

"Then there are some people who spend most of their time in one box, and they need to have windows that allow them to access the other box." She drew a thick line on part of a box. "And sometimes those windows are too small."

Cam, who was brilliant in so many ways, looked at Maddie in utter confusion.

Spell it out. "Cam, you live in the logic box. Your windows are tiny." She squeezed two fingers together. "Very, very tiny."

Cam tilted her head. "So, you're saying that I have trouble accessing emotion?"

"Yes! Accessing it for yourself. Understanding it in others."

Cam leaned back. "So if someone lives primarily in the emotion box, they would have trouble understanding logic."

"Yes."

"Someone like Cooper."

"Exactly."

Bingo. She got it. Cam's shoulders dropped, discouraged. After a very long pause, she said, "What can I do?"

"Open those windows. Make them bigger. Wider. You can do this, Cam. Plus, you've got Seth by your side. You're pretty lucky. He's a guy with big windows."

"So I should listen to him. His worries, I mean."

"Yup."

"He said that he wants Cooper to see a child psychologist." She shrugged. "No offense."

"None taken."

"Maddie, do you think Cooper needs counseling?"

She grinned. "I think everybody needs counseling. I wish people wouldn't wait for crises. Good counseling raises awareness and understanding, and that can trickle into benefiting all relationships."

Cam's foot was tapping in the air, just like Blaine's had, in that very same chair. Strange. Her two sisters didn't really resemble each other, but in this moment, Maddie could see how alike they really were.

Eyes down, Cam smoothed out a wrinkle in her T-shirt. "I guess what I'm asking is . . . have I messed Cooper up?"

"Messed him up? Oh Cam. No. Of course not. You're doing the best you can."

"Maybe," Cam said in a quiet voice, "my best is not enough."

Maddie's lips lifted in a gentle smile. "I'm pretty sure that's the eternal story of parenthood. When is it ever enough? You're only human. That's why we need to rely on God to fill in the gaps."

Cam scoffed. "I don't think Mom ever felt like this—like she wasn't enough."

"Oh Cam. Not true. Don't you remember the year she went to counseling?"

"What? Mom? She . . . went to a shri—um, counselor?"

"Yes. That was the year Mom joined Mrs. O'Shea's neighborhood Bible study and we started going to church every Sunday."

"Huh." Cam had a thoughtful look on her face. "How about that? I never knew." She rose to her feet and went to the door but stopped to turn back. "Thanks, Maddie. I always feel better after we talk."

Maddie lifted a hand in a wave, but Cam had already left.

So strange. All three sisters grew up in the same household, shared the same two parents, generally had similar life experiences well into high school, yet they all had completely different memories of their childhood.

MADDIE, AGE 12

Mom was late picking Maddie up from school again. *Again.* Wednesdays were their day together. Blaine had ballet, and Cam stayed after school for cross-country practice, so Mom picked up Maddie and they went to get a piece of berry pie together before Blaine needed to be picked up. It was their "thing." It had been working nicely until the last three Wednesdays. By the time her mom finally drove into the junior high school parking lot, Maddie was steamed. "Mom, there are druggies loitering out here."

"Where?"

"They're . . . hiding. But they're all around. Obviously, they don't want you to see them smoking or selling drugs or sniffing cocaine or . . . stuff like that."

"Obviously," Mom said. "Isn't that Ricky O'Shea standing by the post? Should we offer him a ride?"

"NO." Maddie slammed the car door. "Why are you always late?"

"Ricky's going to get soaked. Look, he's waving to us. Sure we can't take him home before we get berry pie?"

"Ignore him. Keep driving." Maddie ducked her chin so she wouldn't have to look at Ricky.

"Madison, you're very hard on Ricky."

"He deserves it."

"He has so much potential."

Maddie scowled at her mom. Whose side was she on? "Today he got everyone in PE class to call me the Table."

"What does that mean?"

"Oh Mom." Maddie huffed. Sometimes her mom missed such obvious stuff. "Skinny arms and legs. Flat chest."

"Oh."

"Just because you're friends with his mother doesn't mean I have to be friends with him." As the car turned onto the road, Maddie sat up to look over the dashboard. "So why are you late again?"

"I have an appointment on Wednesday afternoons."

"What kind of appointment?"

"To tell you the truth, Maddie, I've been seeing a counselor on Wednesday afternoons. Sometimes, she runs a little late."

162

"What kind of counselor?"

"A therapist. Someone trained in understanding people. And listening."

Interesting, Maddie thought. She was good at those things too.

"She's helping me think through some changes I'd like to make."

Maddie felt a swirl of anxiety. "What do you mean?"

"Dad's work is taking him away for longer and longer stretches."

"Oh my gosh! Mom, are you divorcing Dad? Is this 'the talk'? Lacey's parents did the same thing to her. She was minding her own business when suddenly, out of the blue, *kaboom*!" She brought her fingertips together and exploded them. "The talk."

"No! Not at all. No divorce talk. Dad and I love each other and we're committed to each other."

That was a huge relief. Huge. As they waited at a red light, Maddie spoke the question that seemed to fill the car. "Then why do you need to see a counselor?"

"I've just been feeling a little, well, out of sorts lately. Like everybody needs more of me than I have to give. The counselor is helping me think through some ideas to make some changes."

"Might be *the* change. Lacey's mother hardly ever gets out of bed. Lacey says she's going through the change."

"It's a little early for that, thank you very much."

Maddie scrunched up her face. "What exactly *is* the change?"

"Maybe we could save that talk for another day."

"So what ideas did the counselor give so you don't feel unhappy?"

Mom glanced at Maddie. "I didn't say I was unhappy."

"But that's what we're talking about, isn't it?"

"Um, maybe so. I guess you're right."

"Did she have any good ideas?"

"Well, if you're really interested—"

163

"I am."

"She says that women in my age group tend to get out of balance. Their children and husband need them. Their parents are aging and need more help. Women give and give and give until there's nothing left. Like a bucket that gets empty, or a well that runs dry. She thinks I should start looking for some activities outside the home that might, you know, help to fill the bucket."

"You mean, like that Bible study that rotten Ricky's mother keeps wanting you to join?"

"Oh, I'd forgotten about that. She just asked again too. She can be kind of persistent."

Maddie threw her hands in the air. "That's where Ricky gets it! He's persistently annoying."

Mom rolled her eyes at that. "The counselor thinks I should consider working outside the home."

Oh great. If Mom ran consistently late now, imagine what it would be like when she worked. "Like where?"

"Not sure. I never really had a career other than taking care of you girls."

The rain was coming down in sheets. For a long moment, Maddie watched the windshield wipers go back and forth. "Mom, I don't think working outside the home is the answer you're looking for."

"Because you'd have to walk home from school in the rain?"

"Besides that. I don't think the counselor has figured out a long-term solution."

Mom smiled. "Now *you* sound like a counselor."

"I know!" Maddie held up her palms. "People don't listen to me, but I do have very good advice."

"So what's your advice?"

"When a well runs dry, you don't just move on to another well.

You have to dig deeper to find the good water." Maddie thumped her flat chest. "In here."

"Where'd you learn that?"

"I learned about dry wells in geography class and it made me think of people. How they're always looking for the next well. Looking, looking, looking. Never finding it. They should have just stayed put and dug deeper."

Her mother pulled the car into the bakery's parking lot and turned it off. She put the key in her purse, then took out a tissue and dabbed at her eyes.

Oh no! She didn't mean to make her mom cry. "Did I say something wrong?"

Her mom balled the tissue and put it back in her purse. "No, honey. Not at all." She reached out to stroke Maddie's wet hair, giving her a tender smile. "Let's go get that berry pie."

Fifteen

NORMALLY, MADDIE LOVED MONDAYS. Normally, it was her favorite day of the week. She would wake up, eager for the week ahead, yet also relaxed with a sense of abundant time. But on this particular foggy gray Monday morning, she woke from a restless night to the unwelcome return of an all-too-familiar swirl of worry. She wanted to stay in bed until Tuesday.

She'd been doing so much better with her anxiety over the last year, working diligently to take her worrying thoughts "captive" before they consumed her. She avoided Google so she wouldn't be tempted to search for troubling evidence to confirm her inclination toward catastrophic thinking. She made a point to exercise daily. Even in the winter, she jogged along the overgrown carriage trails that circled Camp Kicking Moose. She meditated on God's Word each day, memorizing verses that settled her heart. She even developed a sequence of breathing techniques that she used when she felt hints of panic nip at her heels. Those techniques helped. They all helped. She'd worked so hard at controlling anxiety, thought she'd bested it. But there were still times when it burst through all her strategies and took over, like a bossy houseguest.

Why now? Why today? What triggered it?

Argh. She pulled a pillow over her head. *The Phinney boys.*

The very thought of them sent her anxiety rising and her heart pounding.

Sons of former mayor Baxtor Phinney, the brothers had served a jail sentence for stealing lobsters from their friends' and neighbors' lobster traps—a serious crime in the state of Maine—and were now released on probation. Part of their probation status, deemed by the judge, was to get some therapy. The Phinneys' attorney called and asked her to be willing to accept Porter and Peter as clients. Even if they didn't show up, she would be paid. She agreed, because she was so sure they would never, ever follow up.

And then on Friday, they cornered her in front of the Baggett and Taggett store and made an appointment for today, despite her best efforts to discourage them. "Maybe you should go over to Mount Desert," she had told them. "I'll get you names of good therapists. Male therapists." She didn't care about the money. She'd return it, as long as they left her alone.

"Too fah," Porter said in his thick Maine accent.

"Yeah," Peter said. "We don't wanta go that fah."

"Besides," Porter said, "Mother says you take our insurance."

Ugh. Double ugh.

Full disclosure: Maddie couldn't stand the Phinney boys. Peter and Porter shared similarities. Same height, same heavyset bodies with rounded beer bellies, same shade of brown hair, same scraggly beards, though Porter's was longer. She dreaded the thought of spending any time alone with those horrible Phinneys.

She pulled the pillow off her face. Could she cancel their appointment and not feel guilty for the rest of the day? She blew out a puff of air. Probably not.

An hour later, she was mentally rehearsing her opening paragraph with the Phinney boys as she parked her car. Rick stood in front of the church office door, and all words and thoughts dropped out of Maddie's mind. It was suddenly an empty canvas.

He hurried down the steps to greet her. "Everything OK? You look like something's wrong."

Did she? Probably. She could never hide her feelings. "Challenging clients."

His eyebrows lifted. "So I gathered. They're waiting for you. I let them go into the church kitchen and get some coffee." He beamed. "I found an old can of coffee. From 1997."

"No! The Phinney boys? They're already here?" Drat. Drat, drat, drat. She wouldn't even have time to get organized, get a cup of coffee, sit at her desk . . . or to dread their visit even more than she did.

"So they really are your clients?" Rick frowned, concern clouding his eyes. "They seem like . . ."

"Fishermen. Without a boat."

"I was going to say . . . they seem pretty interested in you. A little too interested." He regarded her with an even expression, just a hint of tension around the mouth. "They asked if we were dating."

"Ugh. Those buffoons. I hope you set them straight."

"I told them we have an understanding." He lifted his palms in mock surrender. "I thought it might help. They said they just got out of jail and you're the first girl they wanted to see."

Maddie dropped her chin to her chest. She should have listened to her warning system and canceled their appointment.

"I'll stick around this morning, just in case you need any help."

"Thanks," she said, a little wobbly sounding. "I'm hoping they'll behave. They're not exactly on the top of my Christmas card list."

"They told me they had a skirmish with the law over a minor misunderstanding."

"Hmm. That's how they phrased it? The community has a different perspective on their lobster thieving."

"Whoa. They stole lobsters? From traps? I'm new to Maine, but even I know that would get me thrown in the pokey."

"That's the difference between a self-aware man and the Phinney boys."

He grinned, slapping a hand against his chest. "You think I'm self-aware?"

"I . . . you . . . that's not what I meant . . ." His grin spread with her discomfort.

In the distance, the Never Late Ferry tooted its horn. The island clock.

"I'd better get ready for them." To brace herself. "Give me a few minutes and then send them down."

Inside her office, she put her purse in the chair closest to the door. A territorial claim. That would be her chair. It was a strategy she'd learned during her internship, just in case a session with a volatile client went south and the therapist needed to make a quick escape. A deep sense of panic rose within her. It swirled and clawed, causing her chest to tighten. Dratted anxiety.

Maddie gripped the armrests of her chair and screwed her eyes shut. Breathe. She should breathe. In for a count of six, hold for six, breathe out for a count of seven.

It wasn't working. She stuck her head between her knees to keep herself from hyperventilating.

She heard the church door open and the sound of men's heavy footfalls. *Oh God*, she pleaded. *Help me.*

Paper bag. Where had she hidden a paper bag?

A knock sounded on the office door.

She reared upright. "J-just a moment, please." She shook out her wrists and sucked in another breath. With trembling fingers, she smoothed back the curls from her forehead and opened the door to Rick. Behind him were Porter and Peter, and they were all chuckling over something sports related.

"These guys are going to come to church this Sunday," Rick said. "Aren't you, guys?"

The brothers grinned at each other. "If it means you'll sign off on our probation papers that we've done our community service hours for the week, then sure."

The other one echoed, "Sure we will."

"Hey, Maddie," Porter said, "you got something going on with this tatted-up preacher dude?" He stuck his thumb in Rick's direction.

Rick fixed his gaze on Maddie, and she on him. "Oh, there's something all right," she said. Rick flashed the Phinney boys a big "I told you so" grin.

Peter cursed, and Porter scoffed, and Rick went to the door. "I'll be right upstairs, sweetheart," he said with a wink, blew her a kiss, and then was gone.

Sweetheart. Good grief! Maddie left the door slightly ajar and pointed the Phinney boys to the chairs farthest away from her. "So, Porter and Peter, tell me why you're here." She flipped open their folder and clicked her pen, ready to take notes like this was a normal therapy session and she was a seasoned professional. *So far from it.*

"It was Mother's idea," Peter said. He pronounced it Moth-ah. "Mother told us you'd put out your own shingle and then told our lawyer we'd agree to getting our heads shrunk."

Porter gave her a smug smirk. "Then the judge cut our sentence. So here we are."

"I realize all of that. The court sent your file to me." She'd rehearsed her opening lines last night and was pleased that she actually sounded like a somewhat competent therapist. Just moments ago, she'd had her head between her knees. "What I want to know is why you agreed to therapy. What do you hope to get from our sessions?" As soon as that last sentence was out of her mouth, she regretted it.

The two brothers looked at each other and burst out laughing. What a way to start a Monday.

⁓

Morning sunshine fell through the windows of the Lunch Counter and illuminated the polished formica tabletops, the scrubbed-clean black-and-white tiles of the linoleum floor. Coffee was brewing, bacon was sizzling on the stove top. A few tables were filled with quiet customers. Blaine heard the Never Late Ferry toot as it eased away from the dock.

These were her most favorite moments, ones she missed sorely when at culinary school. This sight should have calmed her. Instead, her surroundings only reminded her of how peaceful she ought to feel, how peaceful everyone else around her seemed to feel. But they could smell the strong scent of brewing coffee, and the smoky aroma of sizzling bacon. She could not.

Earlier this morning, she had talked to Artie during their weekly scheduled phone call. It was something he had set up for them because his time was so jam-packed. She had told him about her missing palate and how distressed she was and that she didn't know what to do about it. There was a long pause, so long that Blaine thought he might have fallen asleep on her—after all, it was three a.m. on the West Coast. Finally, he spoke.

"Blaine, palates don't go missing. They might change or adapt or mature, but they don't go missing."

What in the world did *that* mean? Artie was no help.

Behind the counter, she finished chopping potatoes she'd boiled when she first arrived this morning. Yukon Golds, the best for potato salad, according to Artie's dad. They held their firmness when diced, unlike a baking potato. It was amazing how much she had learned about potatoes from Bob Lotosky. Following the recipe carefully, she scooped bacon grease out of the frying pan into a separate bowl, added apple cider vinegar and celery salt, and whisked. She sampled the dressing with a fresh spoon. Nothing. It was like she had a bad cold, but she didn't. She poured the dressing over the diced potatoes and stirred carefully, just enough to moisten them. She dropped some crumbled bacon bits into the mixing bowl that held the potato salad, and garnished it with chopped parsley. Then she called for Peg to come and sample.

Peg's head poked around the corner of the storeroom. "What's up?"

"Can you try this?" Blaine held a forkful of the potato salad out to her. "See if it needs anything."

"My favorite part of this job." Peg emerged from the storeroom in her customary outfit of black leggings, an oversized T-shirt, and bright red sneakers. Today's tee had the words scrawled across her ample chest: *I don't care how you do it at home. I'm from Maine.* She tasted, swallowed, took another bite, looked up at the ceiling as if she were searching for something, then said. "Perfect."

"Really? Doesn't need salt?"

"Bordering on too salty."

"Oh no! Maybe I shouldn't have salted the water I boiled the potatoes in."

"Bordering, I said. It's fine. Don't touch it."

Blaine covered the bowl with film wrap and put it in the refrigerator. She washed her hands and went to work slicing cantaloupe.

Peg filled a mug with coffee, regarding her with sympathy. "So, honey, what's going on with you this summer?"

She set down her knife and propped her hip against the edge of the countertop. "Peg, after Cam and Seth get married, I'm going to take a break. Leave the island for a while."

Peg scoffed. "So far as I can tell, Cam's not in any hurry to tie the knot."

"She wants to get a couple of things done first. But she promised she'd set a date soon."

Peg folded her arms against her chest. "You're not talking about a couple of days off island, are you."

Blaine shook her head. She couldn't even look at Peg. She knew how much Peg counted on her.

Peg didn't speak for a long time. Then she let out a sigh and said, "Honey, I don't know what you're looking for out there, but I sure do hope you find it."

Tears filled Blaine's eyes. "Yeah. Me too."

~⌒⌒~

The next therapy session with Porter and Peter Phinney went much like the first one. Maddie sat near the slightly ajar door with her yellow pad of paper and a concerned look on her face, trying to gather history on them. She was doing her best to establish some kind of professional rapport with them, going through a specific set of questions designed for intake. They ignored her questions and spent most of the time delivering lame jokes, high-fiving each other.

Her mind wandered. She glanced at the clock on the table next to the chair. Thirty-two minutes had passed . . . eighteen minutes to go. It felt like an eternity. During her internship, she had discovered there was a pattern to each fifty-minute therapy session. It was a little like a meal: appetizers (chitchat) at the beginning, the main entrée (the real subject) took the bulk of the time, and then came dessert (putting the client back together again). With Porter and Peter, it all stayed with appetizers. Not good ones, either. More like . . . an abundance of greasy pork rinds.

Finally, Maddie set her pen down and looked at them. "Gentlemen," she said, practically choking on that word choice, "I don't think this is going to work."

"What do you mean?" Porter asked.

"You're wasting my time. I'm going to give your probation officer a call and let him know."

Peter leaned forward, eyes wide. "You'd send us back to jail?"

"Me? I haven't done anything. You sent yourself to jail by breaking the law and stealing from your friends and neighbors."

"You're supposed to find out why we did it," Porter said.

Maddie stilled. It was the first time either of them admitted they had stolen the lobsters. Everybody knew they were guilty of the crime, but they still denied it.

"I can't go back to jail," Porter said, and his voice quavered. "I can't."

Maddie looked at him. She heard a thin thread of desperation in his voice. She might have just found something to work with. "Why do *you* think you stole from people whom you've known all your life? You know how hard the lobstermen work. You know the families they are trying to support. You know their children. How could you do this to them?"

"We didn't do it to hurt anyone," Porter said. "They's plenty of lobsters in the ocean."

"Nevertheless, you did hurt people's livelihoods."

"They all hate us here. We'd leave if we could." Peter lifted his leg and jiggled his foot to reveal the ankle monitor.

"Have you considered that it's good for you to come back? Character building? After all, you have to face the very people you'd rather avoid."

"Yeah? Well, it don't feel so good," Porter said.

Maddie observed a noticeable change in their bodies. Porter's leg was shaking, Peter shifted his weight in the chair. Both men avoided any eye contact. They were extremely uncomfortable, despite their bravado. "Why not?"

"I told you," Peter said. "They hate us here."

"They feel you betrayed them. They did the work of trapping lobsters and you stole from them. The court of law agrees. I think it's important to get to the heart of the reason about why you cheated your friends and neighbors."

Porter's foot hadn't stopped twitching. "What would it mattah?"

"When you know better, you do better."

Maddie looked to Peter. He was tougher than Porter. "Do you agree? You'd rather leave the island than stay here? Do you think people hate you?"

He shifted back and forth in the chair, as if he were sitting on a tack. "Don't mattah to me."

Resistance. But Maddie knew resistance could be an indicator. *What you resist, persists. Follow it. Don't fight it*. Figure out why resistance was there in the first place. "Peter, what does matter to you?"

Quiet crackled through the room. "Not this," he hissed. Peter stood at his full height. "Porter, let's get out of here."

Porter paused for a second, looked at the ceiling. Then he looked up at his brother. "I can't go back to jail, Peter. If this keeps me out, I'm staying."

Furious, Peter scorched him with a few unrepeatable words and stomped out the door.

The quiet in the room was simultaneously awkward and profound. She regarded Porter with skepticism. "I'll give you a few sessions, but no guarantees. I'm not doing this just to keep you out of jail."

"Please," he said.

And with that single word, the scales tipped in Porter's direction.

Sixteen

ALL MORNING, COOPER HAD UNDERGONE an entire battery of tests with a child psychologist in Bar Harbor, one Seth had found. The psychologist also spent time observing Cooper in a playgroup with other children. Midafternoon, while Cooper played a video game in the waiting room, Cam and Seth sat in the psychologist's office. Dr. Beamer, a thin, bookish type, held a yellow notepad in her hand and a look of deep concern on her face. "I'm sure it's no surprise that Cooper has a very high IQ."

"Yes," Cam said quickly. "Exactly. Bright children are often . . . a little . . . different. But that doesn't mean he's not perfectly normal. A few quirks here and there."

"More than quirks, Cam," Seth said. "Weird stuff."

Cam frowned at him before turning back to Dr. Beamer. "That's to be expected, right?"

"Maybe . . . but maybe not," Dr. Beamer said. "Give me an example of what you consider a quirk of Cooper's."

"Well, he can be a little fearful. He'll focus on something . . . odd . . . for a while." Cam lifted her chin. "But then he moves off it."

"And on to something else." Seth leaned forward in his chair.

"Cam's right in saying that Cooper's compulsions come and go. I didn't used to be concerned, but lately . . ."

"Go on," Dr. Beamer said. "What's happened lately?"

"Two weeks ago, he heard a sermon about Jonah and the whale," Seth said, "and now he won't go near water. It's causing me . . . us"—he choked up a little—"some concern."

Dr. Beamer nodded thoughtfully. "Has anything changed recently in Cooper's life?"

"No," Cam said quickly. "If anything, it's more stable than it's ever been. And he's been doing so much better than last year."

"Nothing's changed?" the doctor repeated. "Nothing at all?"

Cam lifted her palms in the air with a shrug of her shoulders. "I can't think of anything."

Seth looked at her as if she were speaking another language. "Cam, are you kidding?"

"What?"

He leaned back in the chair. "For the last six weeks, you've been traveling to Augusta at least once a week."

"Just a brief overnight trip." She resented the accusing tone in his voice and tried not to respond with defensiveness. Tried, anyway. "If anything has changed, Seth, it's you. You've started to overreact to Cooper the way Maddie does." She folded her arms against her chest and locked eyes with Dr. Beamer. "Cooper is perfectly normal. Lots of kids go through funny anti-something-or-other phases. Cooper, for now, is just anti-water."

"But this is a kid who lives on an island," Seth said softly. "Water can't be avoided."

Dr. Beamer nodded once in agreement. "I think you've got a problem brewing that you can't ignore. Cooper's abnormal behaviors—what you call quirks—are a sign of distress."

"But why?" Seth asked. "What's at the core of it?"

"Fear. It's out of balance for him. Almost anything out of the norm is perceived as a threat to Cooper's brain. It's like his brain is constantly signaling the need for self-protection. If it isn't properly dealt with in a child, it can become far more serious when a child reaches adolescence or young adulthood. It can turn into . . ." She hesitated.

"Obsessive compulsive disorder," Cam supplied. Maddie had already warned her. Many times.

"Yes, but that diagnosis is based on models of adult scenarios. We don't like to put labels on children. They're changing and maturing. Most grow out of their concerning behaviors."

"There, see?" Cam was pleased with Dr. Beamer.

"Not all, though," she continued, ignoring Cam. "In fact, later in life, their behaviors may become more severe. For many adults, all of life becomes a fear-based trap. Anxieties take over their lives. Certain circumstances can trigger behavior they can't control."

"In other words," Seth said, "full-blown OCD."

"OCD is a way for a person to try and create safety through overevaluation—that's the obsessive part—and then through repetitive behaviors or actions or—"

"Compulsions," Seth supplied. "Like staying away from water."

Cam dropped her chin to her chest. "Like when he would wrap a room up in string."

"He wrapped up a room in string?" Dr. Beamer had a look on her face as if to say, *If there's any doubt about potential OCD, that just confirms it.*

Seth rubbed his forehead with his thumb and forefinger, like a headache was starting. "The other day, Cooper refused to play tetherball with his friend. That's new, because he's always loved tetherball. I asked him why he couldn't play and he said he didn't want to lose."

"Risk aversion," Dr. Beamer said. "The only way to win is to stay off the court." She scribbled down a few notes on her pad. "Well, there's an example of how he is starting to put limits on himself."

"You didn't tell me about tetherball," Cam said, and Seth only shrugged. Why hadn't he told her? Just a few weeks ago, they told each other everything.

"When Cooper feels distress," Dr. Beamer said, "he can't control or regulate his . . . quirks."

"But he could grow out of them, can't he?" Cam asked.

"Yeah," Seth said. "Cooper's not stuck like this, right?"

"That's why we want to catch it in children like Cooper, redirect thinking that leads to abnormal behavior, before it's chronic. But if you don't do something now, it will likely only get worse."

"How?" Seth asked. "How can we help him? What can we do?"

Dr. Beamer bit her lip and squinted. "It's going to take a lot of work. One-on-one time. And he's going to need therapy. I might suggest some medication too."

"No way," Cam said, palms raised. "I'm not putting him on anti-anxiety meds."

"Cam." Seth's voice held a warning tone. "We need to be open-minded."

Dr. Beamer wrote a few more notes on her yellow pad. "And it might be helpful if the two of you had some counseling."

Cam looked at Seth, stunned. To her surprise, he was calmly nodding at Dr. Beamer. "Us?" she said. It came out like a squeak. "What's wrong with us?"

Dr. Beamer gave a vague response. "I just thought it might help to get in sync so that you can best help Cooper."

In sync? "Are we out of sync?"

"Oh yeah," Seth said, with a sideways chuckle that scared Cam a little. "We'll do whatever it takes to help Cooper, Dr. Beamer."

On the way back to Three Sisters Island, Cam and Seth were silent; Cooper had fallen asleep in the back seat of the car.

They'd tried to time their trip to coincide with low tide, so they could drive the bar that held the islands thinly together. It was the only way Cooper agreed to leave the island, if they promised he wouldn't have to cross on water. The narrow central portion of the bar was starting to emerge, but they were a little early and had to wait for the tide to finish going out.

Seth pulled the car over to the side of the road to wait. "Looks like our timing," he said with a sigh, "is just a little off."

Cam had a feeling he wasn't talking about the tide.

<hr />

Somehow, Paul had completely misjudged the tide. Such a rookie error surprised him, because he'd become attuned to the tides. He stood at Boon Dock, Dory beside him, waiting for the Never Late Ferry to return to Three Sisters Island with a package from Pottery Barn. One of the cabins needed a new overhead light because the old one—only one year old, mind you—had been broken by the McLean family. All boys. Captain Ed said he was planning to wait for the UPS delivery truck and would bring it over this afternoon. At least, he thought Captain Ed had said the afternoon. Maybe he meant this evening? Sometimes he wondered about Captain Ed's memory.

If Paul squinted his eyes, he could see the ferry docked over on Mount Desert Island. He glanced at his watch. The tide was going out, the bar was emerging. There was a certain smell to the air during the changing of the tides—dank and musty.

He had two options. He could wait a little longer, just walk across it to get the package from Captain Ed. But he wasn't wearing the right shoes for it. These loafers would get soaked. He could take his own flat-bottomed boat—not much more than a rowboat with an engine—that he kept in a slip at the dock. Getting bitten by mosquitos, he considered a third option: to spend a little time at the Lunch Counter.

These were the kinds of moments when he loved this island life. Time seemed to slow down. After nearly thirty years of a career that kept him on the road, he was grateful for the leisurely pace of life. Turning to face Main Street, he clapped his hands. "Come on, Dory. Come on." But she wouldn't budge. She was waiting for Seth to return from Bar Harbor.

He gave up and walked up the hill to the Lunch Counter. Once inside, he blinked a few times as his eyes adjusted to the dim light from the bright sunshine.

"Paul Grayson," Peg said in her cheery way. "If you're looking for Blaine, she's out back feeding Lola some raw chicken while Seth's gone."

"No thanks. Lola gives me the creeps." He sat on a stool and pointed to the large container of iced tea.

"Coming right up." Peg filled a tall glass with ice and set it under the spigot. "Lemon slice?" When he shook his head, she turned off the spigot and handed him the glass. "Can I talk you into a slice of blueberry pie?"

Paul grinned and gave her a thumbs-up. He'd chosen the right option for his afternoon. "There's an annoying duck out at Moose Manor. I want Captain Ed to come out and shoot it."

Peg handed him a slice of pie, with dark blueberries oozing out from under a flaky crust. "What kind of duck?"

"Sooty brown. Three spots on its head." He took a bite of the pie. Tart but sweet. Perfection on a fork.

She tilted her head. "Hmmm. So just one duck?"

Swallowing, he lifted one finger. "It thinks it owns Camp Kicking Moose."

182

"No wonder, if it's missing its mate. How big?"

He stretched out his hands to show its size.

Her eyes went wide. "Oh dear. Must be a juvenile. Got left behind somehow. Oh Paul, you can't shoot it." She crossed her arms. "I wonder what kind of duck it might be. Around here, we mostly have loons and mallards and cormorants." She clapped her hands. "I have a bird book. I'll figure it out."

"Not to worry." He wasn't all that interested in the duck. He just wanted it gone. His mind had already moved on to a second slice of blueberry pie, until he saw the empty pie plate on the counter.

"Is that what brought you to town today?"

"Camper broke a light," he said, and despite its normal gravelly sound, he could hear the annoyance in his voice. "Waiting for the ferry to bring a new one." He took a sip of iced tea. Hit the spot.

Peg's blue eyes twinkled. "Sweetmans or Witherspoons?"

He shook his head. "The McLeans. They let their boys play soccer inside their cabin." He took another sip of iced tea and set his glass down decidedly. "Not their fault, they said. There's been too much rain lately and the boys needed to play." His voice was ground down to a whisper.

Peg wiped her hands on her apron. "Paul, I wasn't going to mention it, but you seem a little cranky this summer. Are you sure the hospitality industry is right for you?"

He froze. "Say what?"

"Camp Kicking Moose is a little like running a diner. You're serving customers, same as me. Our job is to deal with people, the good and the bad. Hopefully, more good than bad. But once you start nursing a bad attitude, you lose 'em all."

"Bad attitude?" He clapped his hand against his chest. "Me?" The words were scarcely audible.

"Folks can tell if you're not a people person."

"I'm a people person." He thought he was, anyway. He used to like people. That was before he could barely walk across the yard of Moose Manor without some camper wanting him to fix something or get something or change something. From May through September, he hardly ever had a moment to himself. Shocking himself, he realized he had loved the winter. Even with the cold, the snow and ice, even with the power outages, there was something magical about winter on an island. A quiet, a calm, a stillness that felt almost holy. An abundance of time—to read, to putter, to dream. He was already looking forward to the first snowfall.

"Over the years, I've seen a lot of people move here. Big dreams on a little island. They start out all excited, full of plans." She waved her hands enthusiastically in the air to illustrate her point. "Island jobs are service jobs. One year later, most of 'em fold up their businesses and leave. Head back to the mainland." She shrugged. "Not everyone is cut out for island living. Or for serving people."

But I am, Paul thought. *Or . . . I thought I was.*

Peg leaned on her elbows to look him right in the eye. "And then there are those rare ones who know how blessed they are to live here. Blessed to wake up each day to the smell of salty air from the ocean or balsam pine warmed by the sun, or see the wildlife, or hear the ferry. Those are the ones who are meant to be here. The ones who say to themselves, *Wow. I can't believe I get to live here.*"

The bell over the door tinkled and Peg went to greet Nancy with a warm smile. Paul watched Peg for a long while, noticing how she connected with each of the customers. She had a knack for dealing with people and they all loved her. Even the annoying ones.

Not everyone is cut out for island living, Peg had said, almost as a challenge.

But I am! I'm sure I am. At least, I know I want to be, Paul decided.

~

It was late in the day. A sparkling day of flawless blue sky and warm sun. Perfect June weather, without even a single mosquito to ruin the moment. Maddie was planning to head home to Moose Manor with Blaine, but her sister needed another half hour to finish something up. Rather than wait in the diner, Maddie decided to walk down to Boon Dock. The tide was out, the bar had emerged, and the area was crowded with people out walking along it, just for fun.

"Maddie."

She spun around at the sound of Rick's voice.

"Mind if I walk down to the dock with you?"

"I'm just waiting for Blaine to finish up." She turned and started toward the bench on the thin strand of beach. Cooper's bench.

Matching her stride, he said, "I made a list of the things I need to apologize to you about."

Maddie stopped in her tracks and stared. "You did what?"

"Well, you said there's nothing worse than an insincere apology. I listened."

He listened to her? Since when? Her gaze flew to his. He was looking at her with such intensity, such warmth, that her heart melted to see it. *Hold it, Maddie. Stay resolved. Stay immune.*

"I want you to know that I am genuinely sorry for teasing you throughout our childhood."

"Tormenting." She put out her hand. "Let me see the list." He handed it to her. She sat down on the bench and he followed suit.

"You're the reason my bike tires were always flat?"

"Yes. Fifth grade. I let the air out during every lunch period."

"And you're the reason I was stuck as class monitor for eighth grade?"

"Yes. You were sick on the day of elections. I nominated you."

"It was a terrible job. Everyone hated me."

"I know, I know. I didn't always treat you well." He hung his head. "Ohhh . . . There's something else I just remembered." He lifted his eyes. "I was the one who submitted your poem to the high school yearbook."

"That was *you*?" Maddie's hands clenched in tight balls. That mortifying event happened during her Emily Dickinson phase, when she wrote depressing poems about the tortured love/hate feelings she had for a certain boy at school. She hadn't named the boy, thank heavens. Oh, *how* she thanked heaven for that! She'd misplaced her notebook of poems, only to discover later that one of her poems had been published in the yearbook for everyone to read.

"It was me." He could tell that fury filled her. "Maddie, I am truly sorry. I was annoying and attention-seeking. It's no wonder you couldn't stand me."

Her mind was swirling with emotion and tangled thoughts. She needed to get away and process, before she said something she would regret, or worse—forgave him too easily. She felt like she couldn't trust herself around Rick. He brought out all the strong feelings she worked to keep tightly bottled.

"As long as we're talking things out—"

She bolted off the bench, waving her hand between them. "We are *not* talking." She pointed to him. "You're confessing."

"—there's something else."

What now? What more could he say?

He rose to his feet and faced her. "Now it's your turn."

She splayed her hand against her chest. "My turn?"

"Come on, Maddie. Are you really going to pretend you didn't cut me in two when you had the chance?"

"What in the world are you talking about?"

"About the night of Senior Prom."

That night? That humiliating night? "What about it?" She hated the faint wobble in her voice.

The muscles along his jaw hardened, and his dark eyes glittered with pain. "Don't tell me you've forgotten."

"No, I haven't forgotten that night." Tried to. Couldn't.

"After . . . well, you know . . . when you told me you loathed me forever."

Maddie froze. Sound amplified suddenly. She heard a boat engine turn off, the shriek of a seagull, the cry of a baby. "You remember . . . *that*?"

He scoffed. "It's not something a guy can forget. In fact, it was a pivot point for me. A moment that changed my life. A guy's heart can get broken too, you know."

She stared at him, her senses reeling, her mind staggering with the ramification of what he *thought* she had said.

———————⟨❈⟩———————

MADDIE, AGE 18

Maddie couldn't believe that she was in Ricky O'Shea's car, driving to the Chatham Lighthouse.

He glanced at her. "Are your folks expecting you at midnight?"

"No, actually not." She was planning to spend the night at Lacey's and knew her friend would cover for her, if necessary. Wow . . . she'd never needed a cover before. She shivered nervously. Why now? Why with Ricky O'Shea, her archnemesis? She couldn't say

. . . she just knew that tonight she wanted to be here, with him, more than with anyone else.

He drove down Highway 3, crossing the Bourne Bridge to connect to Highway 6, the route that went down the Cape. "So what are your plans, Maddie?"

"You mean, next year?"

"Next year. The next ten years. I'm guessing you've got it all mapped out."

She did, actually. "Well, in the short term, I'll be going to the state university, because my parents let Cam go to a super-expensive private college and they're still paying off her loans."

"So you have to give up what you'd like because of Cam?"

"No, it's not like that. My parents would let me go anywhere I want. I just could see the effects of Cam's decisions. I can get all my requirements done at the JC, then transfer."

"Doesn't seem right."

"It does to me. I'm part of a family. And I have a little sister who's coming behind me. The last thing I want to do is to saddle my parents with loans so that Dad can't retire until he's an old man."

"Okay, I get it. So ten years from now. Where are you going to be?"

"Working as a mental health therapist in a highly renowned clinic in New York City. Making a difference. Changing the world."

"Whoa. You do have it all figured out."

She did. "What about you? What are your plans? Your dreams for the future?"

He was silent for a very long time. Finally, he said, "I've joined the Marines."

Maddie felt odd, light-headed at the news. His choice shouldn't matter to her, but it did. "Why?"

He shrugged, as if it was no big deal. It was a huge deal. Plus, it was counterintuitive. Ricky O'Shea was not the kind of guy who took orders from anyone.

"Is it too late to back out?"

"Why would I back out?"

"Ricky, what made you join up?"

Again, a long silence before he spoke, as if he was gathering his words. "It's probably hard for someone like you to understand. You've always known who you were, what you were about. A straight path. For the rest of us, it's not so easy. Figuring out the road ahead."

"What did your mom say?"

"I haven't told her. I plan to tell her tomorrow, after church."

Maddie's jaw dropped. "Doesn't she have to sign something?"

"Not when you turn eighteen. I've been eighteen since March. A bona fide man." He grinned. "So thinks the Marines, anyway."

His cavalier attitude made her mad. Had he even thought this through? Talked to anyone who had been in the Marines? Weighed the consequences? Made a pro-con list? "Ricky, why can't you just be normal?"

He laughed at that. "Normal is boring."

She scoffed. "Thanks a lot."

"You? Boring? You're a lot of things, Maddie Grayson, but not boring. Fussy, girly, overly earnest, ridiculously responsible . . . but you're not boring."

That was the closest thing to a compliment she'd ever gotten from him. "Tell me why you want to join the Marines. Be serious for once. Tell me the truth."

"The truth?" He took in a deep breath of air. "Because it frightens me. To be sent overseas to an unknown area. To not be in control of my own destiny. I'm not easily scared, but this scares me." He exhaled. "So I am going to face down that fear."

She clapped her hands against her cheeks. "That's crazy! Why do you need to face it down?"

"Because . . . I don't think we're meant to be safe. To live a life with guardrails." He chuckled. "I know that you can't understand that . . . that gut need for living on the edge of danger. In sixth grade, I remember you gave a speech that chalk dust wasn't good for children to inhale. You handed out studies to prove your point."

"I remember. The entire school switched to dry-erase boards after my speech."

He chuckled.

"So then, you're prepared to die?"

His chuckle turned into a cough. "That's pretty intense."

"Well, isn't that what you're talking about? Toying with death? Turning life into a game of chance?"

"No, Maddie," he said, sobering. "That's not what I'm after."

"Then what?"

He had no answer for her.

An uneasy quiet followed, until a passion rose up in her and burst out. "You know what I think? You're not facing down a fear. You're running *from* it."

"Oh yeah? From what exactly?"

"Not what. From whom. From God." She looked through the windshield at the night sky. "'Where can I go from your Spirit? Where can I flee from your presence? If I go up to the heavens, you are there; if I make my bed in the depths, you are there. If I rise on the wings of the dawn, if I settle on the far side of the sea, even there your hand will guide me, your right hand will hold me fast. If I say, "Surely the darkness will hide me and the light become night around me," even the darkness will not be dark to you; the night will shine like the day, for darkness is as light to you.'"

Again, he didn't respond. She knew she sounded preachy, but

good grief, he was joining the Marines! For no good reason other than to be contrary. Ricky continued to stare straight ahead at the road. The only change she noticed was that he kept squeezing the steering wheel, so tightly that his knuckles looked white. But he didn't say another word until they reached Chatham.

They walked around the lighthouse, then down to the beach facing Nantucket Sound. In front of a big log that must have floated in from the sea as driftwood, Ricky laid a blanket he'd brought from the car. The May night was unusually warm and the ocean was calm and the moon reflected on the waves, casting a shimmery glow around them. Maddie slipped off her shoes and dug her toes in the cool sand. They sat so close together that their shoulders and arms touched, and they talked and talked, about everything and nothing. Maddie had no idea what time it was. It felt like only minutes, yet hours had passed. The beach was completely deserted. They were the only two people in the entire world.

Ricky turned to Maddie, and their eyes locked. He regarded her with those intense dark eyes. "You are so beautiful," he breathed, before slowly bending his head to kiss her. The shock of his mouth against hers was stunning, all glowing, sparkling warmth. Soft, firm lips. His lips. Against hers. Ricky. Ricky O'Shea—her nemesis, her schoolgirl crush—he was kissing her. And oh my. What a kiss. The most perfect kiss a woman could ever hope for: tender, ardent, passionate, full of longing and unspoken promises. His hands burrowed into her hair and her own hands wove behind his head to draw him closer. She couldn't believe she was kissing him. She'd had no idea, no idea that kissing Ricky O'Shea could set her on fire like *this*.

When the kiss ended, she leaned back on the blanket, pulling Ricky with her, toward her. An invitation. His eyes, full of longing, swept down her body, then to her face. "Maddie," he said in a husky voice, "are you sure?"

Slowly, she nodded, ignoring little pinpricks of conscience. She never wanted this moment to end.

Too soon, a pale apricot light filled the sky, then a spot emerged, glowing but not distinct, low on the horizon. "Get ready," Ricky said, his arm wrapped around her as they watched. "Here comes a new day." For that moment, the entire world seemed to hush, stop, and notice the spectacle of light that announced the sun's arrival. Held tenderly in Ricky's arms, lying together on the sand, cocooned in privacy, Maddie felt more alive, acutely aware of every detail surrounding her, than ever before. Even the morning air, smelling of salt and a changing tide, seemed fresh and new. A symbolic moment of leaving girlhood behind.

Ricky sat up on one elbow to face her, tracing her jawline with his other hand. Something about the way he looked at her, his eyes as earnest as she had ever seen them, caused an emotion deep inside Maddie to bubble up and spill over. Before she could stop, the words "I've always loved you" blurted out.

Startled, he flinched, his chest hitched with a breath, and he dropped his hand from her cheek. And then there was silence. An excruciating silence.

Oh no. No, she didn't. Did she really say she loved him out loud? She did! She could tell by the stricken look in Ricky's eyes. Utterly stricken. As if he was going to be sick.

Why did she say such a thing, oh why? Could she take it back? Say she was kidding? After all, she hated Ricky O'Shea. And she loved him. And she never wanted to see him again. And yet she did. Her face grew warm, then hot. What had she done? What had she *done*? She felt as if she had given him her most precious gift and he threw it away. It meant absolutely nothing to him. To her, it was everything.

All at once she thought she might be violently ill. She swallowed the clot of nausea that threatened, dug her nails into her palms, shifted her legs and turned away . . . from Ricky, from the sunrise. From God. She grabbed her wrinkled periwinkle dress and tugged it over her head, awkwardly, clumsily. Tears stung her eyes; her teeth chattered so hard she could hardly breathe. She was utterly, thoroughly embarrassed. Ashamed.

And so, it seemed, was he. "I should never have let things go that far," he said at last, his voice a gruff whisper now, roughened by remorse or regret—she couldn't tell which one. "I'd better get you back to Lacey's house." The sun had risen now, bold and bright and accusing, and the night of Senior Prom was over.

Ricky O'Shea left for boot camp on Monday morning.

Maddie spent the next week terrified that she might be pregnant, mortified with herself, full of shame and remorse and confusion and despair. On the morning when her period arrived, she wept with relief, but the heightened anxiety she'd experienced that week never left.

Libby was the only person Maddie ever told about the night of Senior Prom, because she could understand how, given the right circumstances, a girl could forget everything she held dear. The only piece of wisdom Libby had to offer, besides listening, was, "Maddie, one chapter does not write a book."

Maybe so, but Libby said it with baby Cooper in her arms. Sometimes a chapter did change an entire book.

Seventeen

MADDIE HAD TO SIT DOWN ON THE BENCH, drop her head into her hands, elbows on her knees. Loathed? All these years . . . she'd been angry with herself, with him. Ashamed that she had given herself to Rick, humiliated that she had said she *loved* him. Even worse . . . that *look* on his face when she said it—disturbed, disgusted. Like he was going to be sick to his stomach. And all this time, all these years, he had thought she had said *loathed*. She felt as if the world had abruptly stopped making sense. "Oh wow."

"It's kind of nice to know that you feel a little remorse about saying such a mean thing. Even after all these years." He sat down beside her. "A guy heading off to boot camp . . . and that was what you left me with. It stung. Bad."

Really? Her conscience pricked her. *Honesty, Maddie.*

Hold it, she argued back, as if she had two mini-Maddies on her shoulders—one with a halo, one with horns.

Halo Maddie: *Honesty has always been your policy.*

Horns Maddie: *Let's think for a moment. This information changes everything. Rick and I, we can actually have a clean slate. Start fresh.*

Halo Maddie: *Start fresh on a lie?*

She swallowed. Loathed. Loved.

Horns Maddie: *Tomato, tomahto. Pretty close in sound. Let it go.*

Halo Maddie: *Couldn't be further apart in meaning. Tell him the truth. Come clean.*

Stall. Buy some time to think. "You said the night of Senior Prom changed your life. How so?"

"Two things. First, when I told you I was joining the Marines. Facing down a fear. You challenged that by saying it was God I was afraid of. That I was running away from him . . . and that I could never outrun God. He'd always find me."

"I remember."

"And the second thing . . . later . . . when you told me you loathed me."

She shifted on the bench after getting a sharp jab from Halo Maddie.

"All through boot camp, I thought about those two things. That God was right there, alongside me, no matter what I thought or did to push him away. I couldn't escape him. I couldn't hide. And then I thought of you. Loathing me. After what we did. I realized that I had stolen something precious from you."

"You did?" It came out like a squeak. He hadn't stolen it. She had given it.

"I realized I'd never be a man you could respect until I got things straight with God. And I wanted your respect, Maddie. Even when we were kids, even as I . . . what word did you use? Torment? Pretty harsh. I would call it gentle teasing."

"You wanted my respect?" She leaned back. *Me?* "Why?"

"You were always true to yourself. No one could influence you."

Oh, that wasn't entirely true.

"Like, kids made fun of you for still being a Girl Scout as a senior in high school, but you never wavered."

"Girl Scouts shouldn't be underestimated."

"See? That's what I mean. You knew what you wanted and you stuck to it." He gave her a gentle nudge with his elbow. "Pretty rare bird."

"Me?" She wasn't accustomed to compliments from Ricky O'Shea.

"There."

She looked up to see a bird rocket past them. "Oh, that's Lola. Seth's pet goshawk." She shuddered. "Personally, I think a puppy would've been a better choice. That goshawk glares at you like she's wondering how to eat you."

He laughed. "Actually, you're a rare bird too."

She looked over at him. "So then, I guess you did get things straight with God. I mean, you are a pastor now."

He nodded. "It started for me in boot camp. Got locked in later."

"No atheists in a foxhole?"

He shrugged. "Maybe. Or behind a desk."

Her head tipped slightly. Suddenly, she shifted into counselor mode. Listening for what he wasn't saying. "Something happened while you were in the Marines."

He looked away.

Yup. Something had happened.

"And now . . . you're a pastor? You?" She spread her palms. "That, I just don't get."

He gave her a sideways look with a grin. "Wonders never cease."

The Never Late Ferry was heading toward Boon Dock. As Maddie watched it dock, and the water ripple around it, she fought the tug of war within about whether she should tell Rick she hadn't said she had loathed him, but that she had loved him.

She believed in honesty . . . but she also believed in restraint. Discernment.

Avoidance, Halo Maddie whispered. *Circumvention. You're doing it again.*

Some things are better left unsaid, hissed Horns Maddie.

"I'll always be grateful to you for giving me that kick in the butt when I needed it, Maddie. I'm not sure where I'd be today if we hadn't had that jolting . . . uh . . . time together after Senior Prom." He jerked his hands in the air like he'd been electrocuted. "It shocked me. It shamed me. It changed me. Eventually, it set me on the path to becoming a pastor. And that led to my coming here."

"How so?"

"I met a chaplain in the Marines who'd been born in Thailand. He taught me something I've never forgotten. In the Thai language, the word for 'connector' also means 'welding.' That's what we're meant to do with our lives, he said. Connect others to God. Weld them to him for eternity."

Maddie could not believe those deeply spiritual remarks were coming out of Ricky O'Shea's mouth. "But . . . you're not here on the island *because* of . . . me. Right?"

"Well, yes and no. I wanted the job. And I knew I owed you an apology for that night. It was wrong of me to . . . well . . . I hope you can forgive me for being a jerk."

An odd disappointment filled her. What was that?! Where did that come from? She loathed him. *Liar*, whispered Halo Maddie. She wiggled her shoulders to knock those two Maddies right off.

That settled it. She would *not* tell him she had loved him. Not ever.

"But as long as we're both here, I'm hoping we can start over. A new beginning at a later stage of life. Hopefully, you'll discover that I'm a more mature version of myself. I'd really like to be friends."

"Is there anything else you need to confess?"

"Probably. But for now"—he pointed to the paper in her hand—"that's all I've got." He tipped his head. "Can we start again?"

With a shrug meant to convey all the indifference she knew she was supposed to be feeling but didn't feel at all, she stuck out her hand. "I'm Madison Grayson. Friends call me Maddie."

He grinned and took her hand. "Hi, Maddie. I'm Rick O'Shea. Your new pastor." He didn't let go of her hand until she tugged it away. "And now that we're finally talking, I'd like to run some ideas past you for the church."

"The church?"

"You. Me. Teaching a class together. Clicked into place right now like a key in the ignition. I thought we could call it 'Look Fear in the Eyes and Smile.'"

"I don't get it," she said, clearing her throat, buying time.

"I got thinking about it because of Cooper and Jonah and the whale. I think everyone has a Jonah moment. Everyone."

"A Jonah moment?"

"Yeah. You know. The worst-case-scenario moment. Some deep-down fear that holds you captive. For Cooper, fear of separation. For many others, it's fear of death." He held her gaze. "For some, fear of rejection can stop wholeheartedly loving."

She drew in a sharp breath. "Loving?"

"Living." He shook his head. "I meant wholeheartedly *living*."

"You really think people would come?"

"I sure hope so."

Maddie lifted her palms in a gesture of reluctant willingness. "I'll give it some thought and get back to you."

From outside the Lunch Counter, Blaine whistled to her. Maddie rose from the bench, gave a casual goodbye to Rick, though she didn't feel at all casual about it. She felt a little gutted. On the way up the hill to meet her sister, she weighed out the pros and cons of teaching a class with him.

It would be good exposure for her counseling practice. Fear was a good topic to address, to study, if for no other reason than to be more helpful with Cooper's anxieties. And there would be plenty of other benefits: Blaine and her fear of this slimy instructor. Cam and her fear of slowing down, being still. Dad and his sudden inability to make decisions. *And then there's me.* She knew she had plenty of fears she barely kept the lid on.

Loving wholeheartedly. Her top fear.

She suddenly knew why she needed to say yes to Rick. *We teach what we most need to learn.*

A few days later, Blaine was closing up the Lunch Counter when she heard the toot of the Never Late Ferry as it pulled into Boon Dock. She took in the chalk sandwich board and paused for a moment when she noticed Cam walking up the hill from the dock. Her head was tucked, her shoulders dropped. Blaine felt a well of sympathy rise for her sister, a rare feeling to have for Cam. "You look like you've lost your best friend."

Cam's head jerked up and she waved. When she drew closer, she said, "Just a disappointing day."

"Need a ride home? Seth is out at Moose Manor with Cooper."

"In that case, I do." She shifted her big leather messenger bag to her other shoulder. "I thought a grant was a sure thing, but it's not happening."

"For sure?"

"For sure. The grant was given to a potato farmer in Aroostook County."

"Yikes. Hope it wasn't Bob Lotosky."

"I don't think so." Cam held the diner door open for her. "Unless he's working on an invention to ferment mashed potatoes into fuel."

"He would consider that a desecration to a potato." Blaine set the sandwich board against the interior wall. "Cam, why don't you just give up on those stupid grants?"

Cam frowned. "Impossible."

"Why?"

"The locals don't have the resources to provide all that this island needs."

"Why don't you just pay for this energy project?" Blaine tilted her head. "You've got the money."

Cam sent her an annoyed look. "Blaine, I don't just *have* the money. It's all invested for the future. For Cooper's future." She glanced at her watch. "The grants are the best way to go. I just have to look for more."

Blaine let out an exasperated sigh as she flipped off the lights. "You and Seth are *never* going to get married."

"Yes, we will. When it's the right time for us. Not when it's the right time for you." Cam stayed at the open door. "Ready? I want to get home."

Blaine hung her apron on the hook, grabbed her purse, shouted goodbye to Peg, and joined her sister. The shallow well of sympathy she had for Cam had run dry.

⌒

Maddie could hardly believe her first month as a practicing therapist had passed. And she could actually pay July's rent without borrowing money from her dad. She'd had five clients come through her office, which was four more than she'd expected. Credit went to Rick. He kept referring people to her, giving her high praise as a therapist even though he really had no idea, and those referrals actually made appointments with her. Not only did they show up, but at the end of the fifty-minute hour, they made appointments for the following week.

This afternoon, Porter Phinney sat opposite her on a chair. Maddie had to dig deep to feel compassion for this particular client, calling to mind the words of her internship supervisor: There's something to like in everyone.

Really? Even the Phinneys? Maddie tried to imagine Porter as a chubby child—but all she could conjure up was a fat bully.

On this warm afternoon in late June, she heard Rick's footsteps pound up the front steps and wondered where he'd been. Working in such close proximity to him, she'd become ever aware of his movements. Where he might be at various times of the day, looking for him to head to the Lunch Counter for meals, listening for when he came up or down the stairs.

"Ah you listening to me?"

She jerked her head up. "Of course. Taking notes." She'd asked Porter a few questions about his childhood, and it was like opening up a shaken bottle of soda pop.

Porter seemed to enjoy talking about himself. "We never measured up to our father's expectations. We were never good enough. If we washed the windows, Father would find the one spot we'd miss. I remember bringing home a report card of nearly all Cs once, only two Ds, and he tore it up. Straight As or nothing. That's how it always went."

"So did you quit trying to please him?"

He shrugged, like it was no big deal. "School was hard for us. We didn't have a chance of getting into a big-name school."

"Did you want to go to college?"

"Nah. We only wanted to start lobstering. It was plenty good enough for us."

"But not for your father."

Again, the careless shrug. Porter generally betrayed little, if any, real emotion. His face was a mask, his words, diversions. Core characteristics of someone with *alexithymia*—emotional unawareness. She scribbled that observation down in his file.

"I don't know your father very well, but his reputation seems pretty important to him. Porter, do you think you and Peter were trying to get back at your father by stealing lobsters?"

Blank face. Completely empty. "How's that?"

"Imagine the public humiliation your father felt when you and Peter were thrown in jail. Isn't it possible that you wanted to embarrass him?"

"You mean, be a loser on purpose?" His face scrunched up in confusion. "Wouldn't that be kinda like shootin' yerself in the foot?"

Maddie had to suppress the urge to blurt out, *EXACTLY! You and your brother are on a self-destructive course of action, all with the intent of shaming your father. Ironic, when what you really long for is for your father to be proud of you.*

But she didn't say any of that to Porter.

She remained quiet as he started to fidget, played with the pattern of fabric on the arm of the chair. "So, what now?"

"Once you know a truth, Porter, you can't unknow it."

That completely befuddled him and the fifty-minute session had just come to a close. Maddie was okay with leaving him to ponder it. As she closed the door behind him, she caught a glimpse of Rick, standing on the front porch, and she felt a little jab in the ribs from Halo Maddie. *Once you know a truth, you can't unknow it.*

Ouch.

⌒

The Lunch Counter was open but empty as Paul stopped by one rainy afternoon. It was the last day of school, a later-than-usual date because of so many snow days, and he had promised Cooper that he'd come to the annual year-end party to be held at the diner. "Where is everyone?" he said.

Peg took off her oven mitts and leaned her palms on the counter. "And a good afternoon to you, too, Paul Grayson."

He smiled, settling on a stool. "Sorry. Hello." Bright blue head-band today. It brought out the blue in her eyes. Blue like blueber-ries.

"They should be coming down the hill any minute, soon as the rain tapers off."

Paul spun on the stool to look out the plate glass window. The sky was lightening, the rain was slowing. It disappointed him a little. He liked being in the diner when it was quiet, when Peg was free to talk. And he had been hoping Cooper would get a sound drenching by the rain. That boy needed a bath.

She slapped an open book about birds on the counter. "Paul, look through these pages and find a picture of your duck. It's still at Camp Kicking Moose, isn't it?"

He nodded. "Still nipping at my heels." Every time he left the house, that duck appeared. It flew toward him and waddled behind him, squawking, like a noisy shadow.

"Blaine said it thinks you're its mother." A giggle burst out of her, then another, and then it mushroomed to a full belly laugh.

Paul was shocked. This duck situation was not funny. It wasn't at all funny.

"The sandwich board," he said, trying to change the subject. "That's a lot of potatoes on the menu." He wondered if she no-ticed his voice was improving. *Not quite like ground gravel today,* he thought. *Definitely better.*

Peg sighed, wiping tears of laughter from her cheeks. "I know, I know. Bob Lotosky sent over a couple of bushels of potatoes from last year's harvest."

"Old potatoes? Odd."

"Not so odd when Bob Lotosky is the one who stores potatoes for the winter. They're just as good as if he just pulled them from the ground."

Paul wondered if she might be growing a little smitten with the potato man.

She sighed. "There's just a lot of them. Blaine searched high and low to find as many dishes as she could find to make. Recipes I've never heard of."

Ah. That explained why they'd been having so many potato dishes for dinner at Moose Manor. Swiss raclette. Leek and potato galette with pistachio crust. Crispy gnocchi with razorback clams. "Don't like potatoes?" He tried not to enjoy that thought quite so much as he did.

"Sure, I like a loaded baked potato now and then, but bushels of 'em? So many varieties I can't keep 'em straight. Good grief, I can't even walk in the storeroom." She pointed to the glass display cooler. Stacks of plastic containers, filled with something beige looking, lined the shelves. "Interested in trying four different varieties of potato salad? On the house."

He shook his head. He was a little potato-ed out from this week's dinners. "I'll save myself for cake." He had already spotted three different rounds of cakes, cooling on wire trays. It smelled like a bakery in here, a scent that reminded him of coming home to Corinna's baking. It occurred to him that such memories didn't create that sharp sting he'd grown to live with. Now, they evoked a sweetness. When did that change? He wasn't sure.

"That particular cake," Peg said, "isn't for the school party. It's

Blaine's tenth try to get Cam and Seth's wedding cake just right."
She bent over to examine them, poking gently on one. "They sure
look perfect to me. But so did try number one." She straightened
and shrugged. "You know Blaine."

Did he? Sometimes he wondered.

~⌒~

Blaine had dodged fat raindrops when she ran across Main
Street to buy more eggs from the grocery store. She had barely
gotten in the door when the skies opened and rain pelted down.
She decided to wait it out, walking up and down the aisles, mentally editing Nancy's terrible end-cap display decisions. Cans of
soda right above bottles of bleach. Jars of dill pickles shared shelf
space with bags of marshmallows. Boxes of toothpaste next to
bottled orange juice.

Man, what she could do with this store if Nancy would give her
free rein, the way Peg had given her at the Lunch Counter. She'd
offered! But Nancy liked things the way they were. Argh. Why did
people resist change so much? She just could not understand it.
Blaine loved change. *Loved* it.

~⌒~

Elizabeth Turner was due this morning for a therapy session and
Maddie half expected her to cancel. Or be a no-show. She knew
she'd shocked Elizabeth by turning the responsibility for a good
relationship with her daughter-in-law over to her. Frankly, Maddie had surprised herself when she pushed Elizabeth in a different
direction than she wanted. But to Maddie's way of thinking, the
one who was in her office was the one who had the capacity to
make changes. So that's where the work began.

And there was something else too. Maddie considered herself

an astute judge of character. She had a good hunch that Elizabeth Turner would be willing to make the changes she needed to make in order to keep her family.

Through the window, she heard the ferry's arrival. If Elizabeth was on the ferry, she'd be here in a few minutes. Maddie took out her Bible and read a few verses, asking the Lord to bless this hour and guide the conversation. Just as she said *Amen*, she lifted her head and saw Elizabeth turn up the front walk. She smiled, relieved.

Elizabeth came into Maddie's office dressed very similarly to their previous session, as if she were attending a formal tea. Her face, though, didn't seem quite as tight and drawn.

"Come in, come in," Maddie said. She sat down and waited for Elizabeth to join her. "How are things going?"

"I had a talk with my daughter-in-law. I invited her out for lunch, and at first she said no, but changed her mind when I suggested we go to Jordan's Pond. She's crazy about their popovers."

"Smart. So . . . how did lunch go?"

"Awkward. Uncomfortable."

Oh dear.

"I told her exactly what you told me to say. That I was doing the End Zone Run without meaning to." Elizabeth looked away. "I learned a few things."

"Such as . . ."

"Vivienne admitted that she feels guilty when I am filling her role with their daughter." She pursed her lips. "She chooses to work, you know."

"What exactly does your daughter-in-law do?"

"Vivienne? She's a doctor." Adding in a somber tone, "So is my son. They're both quite busy. Busy and tired. There's not much time left over for Sophie." Elizabeth leaned forward in her chair.

"That's why, you see, I have wanted to live near them. I can be there for Sophie when they can't."

And . . . here they were . . . right back at the End Zone Run. "Elizabeth, did you share your feelings with your daughter-in-law . . . Vivienne? Did you tell her that you never had help as a young mother?"

Elizabeth leaned back. "I did. I told her I was trying to give her what I'd never been given." She let out a breath. "She listened. She said she was willing to start over. But only if I was willing to accept some boundaries." She frowned and held up a finger—a signal to Maddie to wait for her before responding. "Imagine such a thing. Me! Needing boundaries."

Maddie tried not to smile, even looking down at her hands in her lap so her eyes didn't give away her amusement. Elizabeth might not have much self-awareness, but she was here. Something inside her knew she needed to get help, to make changes. And this daughter-in-law did go out for lunch with Elizabeth. That meant there was something left to work with.

Maddie lifted her head. "Elizabeth, I am so proud of you. I know this isn't easy, but if you're willing to work at it, I'm fairly confident that your entire family is going to be appreciating each other in a way you'd never imagined possible." She smiled at the look of hope that lit Elizabeth's eyes. "Did Vivienne describe the boundaries?"

Elizabeth nodded. "First, she said I have to get a cell phone."

"A cell phone?"

"Yes. Something I abhor. In my opinion, technology is destroying relationships."

Interesting point. A little dramatic, but interesting.

"Next, she said I had to learn to text."

"To text," Maddie repeated.

"And finally, I am not allowed to come to their home or go to Sophie's school unless I have been approved to come, by Vivienne, with a text message." She slapped her hands on her knees. "I don't even know what that *means*."

Maddie swallowed her amusement. "Well, then. We're going to get you up to speed." She rose to her feet. "We're going to Bar Harbor and get you a cell phone." Not every therapist would make this same choice. Most wouldn't. Her supervisor would caution Maddie and warn her not to cross a line, not to get overly invested. But it felt right to her.

Elizabeth blinked, twice. Weary hope sprang to her face. "You'd do that for me?"

"Absolutely. By day's end, you are going to not only learn how to text, but how to insert emoticons. You are going to shock Vivienne with your intentionality."

"Emoti-what?"

Maddie flashed a smile. "I'll explain on the ferry." She went to the door and held it open. "Let's go."

Eighteen

AT THE CONCLUSION OF CHURCH ON SUNDAY, Maddie was floored when Rick announced the first "Look Fear in the Eyes and Smile" class would be held this Wednesday evening. Was he serious? In just four days? She assumed it would start in the fall, to allow for plenty of time to think it through, to plan, to ponder. When she objected to Rick afterward, he dismissed her worries like he was shooing a fly. "I have no doubt you could teach this class in your sleep."

Hardly!

With some reluctance, Maddie agreed to meet up on Monday morning to map things out. She woke with something that resembled . . . nervousness? Excitement? Anticipation? Almost as if she was actually looking forward to this time together. She'd been sternly talking herself out of stray feelings for Rick, residual emotions left over from teen years. Neutrality, detachment, impassiveness, objectivity . . . those were the feelings she aimed for.

They planned to meet for coffee at the Lunch Counter, but Maddie instantly discovered that was a mistake. Some of the female customers hushed at the sight of the new pastor, watching them as they settled into a corner table. And they kept on staring at them. Inwardly, Maddie cringed. Everyone on this island, it seemed, had joined the Ricky Fan Club, casting starstruck glances in his direction. After Nancy and her friend stopped at their table and pulled up chairs to stay for a while, Rick finally picked up on Maddie's exasperation, helped along when she looked at her watch and let out a big sigh, as if she had a client waiting for her. She didn't, but she couldn't stand this much longer.

Adroitly, Rick ordered and paid for coffee for Nancy and her friend, with an apology for having to leave so soon. "Another time, ladies," he said, and Maddie thought she heard them sigh with happiness.

He steered Maddie through the Lunch Counter by the elbow toward the door. "Sorry about that."

She rolled her eyes. "Be sure to duck your head as you go through the door. Wouldn't want your crown to get knocked off."

He grinned and dimples appeared. Both cheeks. "A crown is merely a hat that lets the rain in." He held the door open for her. "Let's go up to my church office."

"You mean, the card table in the kitchen?"

He laughed. "I fixed the wobble."

The church office was also the wrong place to be. Each time the phone rang, Tillie would interrupt in a serious Tillie-tone. Rick asked if she'd take a message, and he would return people's calls later in the day, so she did just that and then interrupted to give him the phone message. Each time. Plus, Tillie felt it wasn't enough to hand Rick the message, she needed to explain each one. The latest one took the prize. Captain Ed's eldest sister was in the MDI hospital and he wanted Rick to go visit her and read her last rites.

Rick looked at the pink message, puzzled. "Does Captain Ed realize I'm not a Catholic priest?"

"He said do whatever needs to be done so that his sister gets a ticket to Heaven."

Rick exhaled. "A rather tall order."

Just as the phone rang again, Maddie suggested they go down to her basement office. Nobody ever came there without an appointment. Even Tillie was intimidated by a counseling office. As they walked down the path, she said, "You're going to have to improve your management style with Tillie."

"I don't really have a management style yet. I've never had an admin to manage." He sighed. "Tillie's just trying to be helpful. Her daughter and grandson moved to the mainland and I think she's lonely. She reminds me a little of my mom. Trying to help by overhelping."

At her door, Maddie stopped and turned. She understood Tillie's situation, but still, she took her volunteer job a little too seriously. "You can't tell someone what they're doing wrong? Since when? First day of kindergarten and you made sweet Miss Apfelbaum cry. A brand-new teacher. Younger than we are now."

"Oh, yeah. That."

"You led a strike against the cafeteria food in freshman year of high school."

"Man, that cafeteria food was terrible." He scrunched up his face. "Wow, you sure have a long memory. Do you remember every single thing I did?"

"No, of course not." Absolutely not. She certainly didn't want Rick to think she'd kept tabs on him. She stopped that after Senior Prom.

"You know, Maddie, people can change. That's what your business is all about, isn't it?"

Without responding, she opened the door and flicked on the light. Good, the power was still on. The kitchen light had been flickering up at the church—that was usually a warning sign that the power was about to go.

Rick followed her inside and walked around. "Well, this is . . . really nice. Very welcoming."

"You seem surprised."

"I guess . . . I'm not sure what I thought it would be like in here, but not this."

"Let me guess. Did you expect a shrink's couch?"

He laughed. "Not that, so much. If anything, I would've expected it to be frilly. Lace curtains. Doilies on the couch."

"Like your grandmother's living room? Smelling of mothballs?"

"Yeah! That's it. That's it exactly." Rick turned in a circle, his hands in his back jeans pocket. "It's really cool, though."

She sighed, leaning her chin on her palm. "I'm always so underestimated."

"Oh, I didn't mean it like that. I just thought it would be . . . feminine. Like you are."

Oh? Cheeks growing warm, she busied herself with finding a pad of paper. "Help yourself to a cup of coffee."

As they began the process of collaboration, Maddie was surprised—impressed, even—that Rick had a pretty clear idea of what he wanted this class to look like. Four sessions, he thought, should cover the basics. After that, he hoped people would form small groups. Such groups, he believed firmly, were the way to build lasting community in a church.

The time went quickly and soon they had the outline designed for all four classes. "I hope people come," she said as he packed up his papers. "I hope you're not going to be disappointed. Change comes slow here."

"I could never feel disappointed being here," he said. The way he looked at her made her stomach feel tied in a knot. "I'm connecting with some ministers on Mount Desert later today. I'll extend an invitation to their church members."

"Wow, do you ever slow down?"

He grinned. "Too much to do. Too little time."

"There's time, Rick. Plenty of time." She grinned. "It's only Monday."

Something sad flashed through his eyes, so sad that it caught in her heart. Then just like that, it disappeared and his familiar confidence returned. "You know what they say. Live like there is no Monday."

As the door closed, Maddie pondered that odd remark. It didn't make sense to her. She loved Mondays.

On the wide green lawn of Moose Manor, Blaine tore yesterday's croissants into pieces and tossed them to the little brown duck. Her dad's pet duck. She smiled, thinking of how flustered he got when she called it his pet.

"Stop calling it that," he told her. "I want Captain Ed to come out and shoot it. Serve it up at the Lunch Counter as duck à l'orange."

Fat chance. Her dad was all bluster. She'd seen him chase the resident coon cat away from stalking that duck more than a few times.

She watched the duck nip at the croissant and bite it down, then look to her for more bread. She tore a piece off and tossed it on the grass. "I'm going to miss you, little brown duck. I hope you'll still be following Dad around Camp Kicking Moose when I get back."

Artie told her the other day that he was worried if she left, she might not come back. She reassured him that she'd be back. Of course she'd be back. Three Sisters Island was her home. Her family was here. Peg was here. Her future was here.

"Then why are you leaving?" he had asked. "I know, I know.

You've said you have to find your culinary voice and all that. Blah, blah, blah. Tell me the real reason. I know how much you love Three Sisters Island. I know how valued you feel by Peg. I know how important you are to your dad and sisters, and how much help you give the camp during the summer. So tell me the truth. Why would you leave the one place you love?"

She had no answer for him.

~⌒~

Maddie was so convinced no one would show up to the Wednesday night "Look Fear in the Eyes and Smile" class that she made her family promise to attend. That way, at least a few people would be sitting in the room. Rick, the eternal optimist, said to prepare for fifty. It ended up somewhere in between with an audience of twenty-five, give or take a few. Not bad at all. Some pastors and their spouses from Mount Desert Island, a handful of campers from Camp Kicking Moose, some locals like Peg and Nancy and Captain Ed and, of course, the Graysons.

Maddie wished she had presented her part first because Rick was such a hard act to follow. He had a gift for teaching. Well prepared, with riveting content, intelligent, with a knack for comedic timing in his humor. He started off with a quote from Babe Ruth, which automatically disarmed and relaxed the audience, especially the men: "Never let the fear of striking out get in your way."

He stayed with the baseball metaphor for the introduction, sharing statistics about the average number of strikeouts per batter. Staggering stats. "We have to be willing to face being up at bat. Think of what we'd miss if we let fear stop us. Babe Ruth wouldn't have hit 714 home runs."

"WHOA!" Cooper said. "Mom, is that really true? Did Babe Ruth hit seven hundred and fourteen home runs?"

Rick laughed. "It's true, Cooper."

As she observed the audience's engagement, her heart started to sink. She was the opposite of Rick in every possible way. She didn't like public speaking and she wasn't any good at it. Why had she agreed to this? Agitation tightened her shoulder muscles. She would be a complete failure, and her practice would suffer. Her five clients would dwindle to two, then one. Then none. She would have to give up her beautiful little basement office.

Maybe she could work for Peg at the Lunch Counter. Or Captain Ed's Never Late Ferry.

And suddenly Rick was introducing her, telling everyone that this class was all her doing—it so wasn't—and that he had known Maddie since she was a little girl and she had always inspired him, through her honesty and integrity, to be a better person. A better man.

She rose and went to stand beside him. He gave her a wink and sat down. As she opened her folder, she sent up a little prayer. *Lord, bless my efforts. Bless those who are here tonight.*

She lifted her head and caught Rick watching her, an encouraging look in his dark brown eyes. *Don't think about him, don't think about him.* She made herself look away, took in a deep breath. "Worry is not all bad. It's the brain's alarm system, a way of warning you to be alert. The body responds by acceleration of the heart rate and breathing, constriction of blood vessels, and releasing nutrients for muscular action. You might recognize all of those as fight or flight. It's designed to stimulate rapid bursts of intense physical activity. In fact, worry can even cause your pupils to dilate. The purpose is to enhance vision in the dark. So you see, worry is not necessarily a bad thing. It's a God-given design to help us." She dared a glance at Rick and saw his eyebrows lift in a silent plea: *Where are you going with this?*

"But many of us," she continued, "myself included, have an overactive alarm system. It works too hard. If we allow our alarm system to remain stuck in overdrive, it will wear us out. It's like a copper penny soaked in acid. The most effective way to calm your overactive alarm system depends on how you pray. And that's what we're going to address this summer. Effective prayer will teach you how to deal with worry."

She glanced again at Rick. Eyebrows down. Big smile.

Cam hadn't planned to go to the Fear class at church tonight until Maddie begged her. Seth had been eager to attend, insisting they needed to hear what was said. "We're not immune, Cam," he said. "Cooper isn't the only one who needs it. We need it too."

How so? She wasn't sure but thought she'd better go.

Rick's portion of the evening was much like his sermons—interesting, relevant, even a bit entertaining. Pretty much what she had expected from him.

But Maddie. Wow! Her sister seemed to have transformed into someone Cam barely recognized. She spoke with a quiet authority, providing strategies to pray in a way that calmed a body's stress response.

And then there was something else about the evening that Cam hadn't expected. She sat across the room from Pastor Rick, and noticed how his eyes never veered away from Maddie. It was more than polite attentiveness. The way he was looking at her! As if she hung the moon.

How about *that*.

She grinned. Well, well, well. So Pastor Rick was smitten.

Her grin slipped away. Rick had grown from a cute boy with an edge into a lean, handsome man. Cam was always willing to root for the underdog, but she doubted Ricky O'Shea could ever claim Maddie's heart. Not a chance. Too much history between them.

Seth gave her a nudge. "So what'd you think about that?"

She looked at him. "I know! Do you think Rick came to Three Sisters Island to woo Maddie?"

"What?" Seth's face scrunched in a question. "I meant what did you think about their suggestions? Prayer and meditation, for one thing?"

"Oh. Yeah. Yeah, those were good. We should remind Blaine about those ideas."

Seth gawked at her. "Blaine?"

"She sure needs something to calm her down."

Seth's expression turned troubled. "Blaine," he repeated in a flat tone. "You think Blaine needs something to calm her down."

"Blaine," Cam said with a nod. "She sure does."

～⌒～

Blaine took notes during Maddie's talk, just as diligently as she did in culinary school. Her sister had some really good suggestions about how to control anxiety before it controlled you. And she liked the part about how anxiety could be camouflaged in different forms: tension, avoidance, restlessness, lack of intimacy, lack of commitment. And this might have been the biggest aha moment of all: Often what seem like trivial worries are manifestations of deeper ones.

She was so glad Maddie had made them all come tonight. Man. Cam sure did need to hear this.

～⌒～

It seemed that each and every time Maddie was coming or going from her basement office, or stopping in at the Lunch Counter, no matter the hour, Rick would appear, almost as if she had summoned him, though she hadn't. He would bring up an idea or two for the Fear class, and the next thing she knew, they were immersed in deep and animated conversation.

One afternoon, they walked along the emerging low-tide bar between Three Sisters Island and Mount Desert Island, and he brought up his time in the military. In particular, he appreciated the disciplined life. "I needed that," he said. "Maybe more than other kids because I grew up without a dad. A lot of the exercises were designed to teach soldiers that we were part of a unit, a whole. Most of us joined the Marines thinking we were lone rangers."

Strolling the bar with Rick, listening to him talk about his life, Maddie realized she was getting to know him, really know him, for the first time.

But as comfortable and familiar as they were growing with each other, as attracted as Maddie felt to Rick, he was careful not to say or do anything that could be interpreted as inappropriate. He never stood too near to Maddie. He never touched her.

On this July morning, Maddie walked toward her office from Main Street, came through the gate that led to the church office, and looked up at the house to see if Rick might be standing at the front window, sipping his coffee. Oftentimes he was, and would wave to her. But not on this morning. Instead, Tillie stood at the top of the porch stairs. "I'd like a word with you."

"Come to my office," Maddie said with a smile, but Tillie did not return it. She wondered where Rick was this morning but didn't dare ask. Instead, she opened the door and let Tillie go in ahead of her. "Please, sit down."

Tillie's gaze swept over the small office. "It's rather feminine."

Maddie smiled. "I think of it as neutral."

"It would take some work for a man to be comfortable here," Tillie said, before settling into a chair.

"So far, my male clients haven't complained." All three of them. Maddie sat across from Tillie, a yellow pad of paper in her hands. "Tell me what's brought you here today."

Tillie folded her hands primly in her lap. "You."

"Pardon?"

"You," she repeated, her lips drawn thin. "You're causing disruption in the work of the church."

"Me?" Maddie cleared her throat. "How so?"

"Pastor Rick. You're taking far too much of his time and attention."

"I am?"

"He is such a caring, dedicated pastor. Having a counseling office below the church office is far too distracting to him. He watches for when you arrive in the morning, listens for when you leave. Whenever the Phinney boys are here for a session, he sits right out on the porch steps until he knows they've left your office." She smoothed out her skirt over her knees. "I'm sure you can understand the dilemma. Our island has waited a very long time for a pastor. At long last, we have one. Pastor Rick needs time to prepare for his sermons and for teaching classes and for meeting with parishioners. You're taking all his time and attention."

"Me."

"Yes, you." Exasperation laced Tillie's tone. "Meetings for that class you're teaching. Lunches at the diner. It's not right. It's just not right for one person to take all his time." She laced her fingers together. "That's why I've come to speak to you this morning. I think it is in the church's best interest if you consider finding another location for your counseling office."

Leave her beautiful little basement office? Maddie bit her lip. "But, Tillie, you see, I signed a year's lease."

"Perhaps we could find a way to break the lease."

Maddie leaned back in her chair and set her pen down on her yellow pad. "I appreciate your concern for the church and for Rick, Tillie—"

"*Pastor* Rick."

"—but I'm going to stay put until my lease is up."

Tillie frowned. "I see."

But she didn't.

"It's my job to protect our pastor from unnecessary concerns."

Maddie worked to keep her voice very soft and sincere. "I know you take your work very seriously, Tillie."

She rose and clomped to the door. She turned to Maddie with a frown. "I trust you won't charge me for this appointment."

"No, of course not," Maddie said. When the door clicked shut and she knew Tillie had gone upstairs, she tossed the yellow pad on her desk. Her mind replayed Tillie's complaints: She was causing too much distraction for Rick. He kept watch during the Phinney boys' sessions. He looked for her to arrive each morning.

She jumped up to twirl in a circle. Oh wow. Wow, wow, wow. Was it really possible that Rick felt about her the way she felt about him? Maybe so.

But then again, maybe not. She came to an abrupt stop. Even after all this time—even after cracking the door to consider how strong his reaction had been to that *enormous* misunderstanding so many years ago—still . . . she still couldn't bring herself to completely believe that Ricky O'Shea wouldn't find a way to break her heart.

Nineteen

ALL WEEK LONG, BLAINE HAD BEEN ARRIVING late to the Lunch Counter each morning. A little later each day. So far, Peg hadn't complained, but today she seemed miffed. Normally chatty, Peg had hardly said a word of greeting to Blaine. She'd even started the coffee, which was a signal that she was not happy. The coffee was Blaine's domain.

"I'm sorry, Peg," she said. "I'll do better." She yawned. "I've just been sleepy lately."

Peg turned her way. "Artie called this morning."

Oh no. "Is it Thursday?" Artie even set his alarm clock for three a.m., Pacific Standard Time, so that he and Blaine could talk before the breakfast crowd started coming into the Lunch Counter.

"Artie strikes me as a guy who always does what he says he'll do."

"Yes. Very trustworthy." Blaine knew what Peg must be thinking: *Unlike you*. Artie knew what he wanted out of life, knew how to go get it, content with who he was and where he was going. The very opposite of Blaine in every imaginable way.

Peg sighed, which said so much. Before anything more could be asked, Blaine grabbed her apron from the hook on the wall, tied it around her waist, and got to work.

$$\sim\!\!\!\circ$$

At the end of the day, Maddie was on her way to the Lunch Counter to catch a ride home with Blaine. On the sidewalk, she passed by Peter Phinney. He glanced up and his glum countenance shifted to righteous indignation.

"What's wrong?"

"Yah sistah . . . she kicked me out the dinah. Told me not to come back unless I go to a shrink."

"Blaine?" Good for her. "Just call for an appointment anytime, Peter. I haven't sent my report to your probation officer yet. I gave you a month's grace." She tapped her wrist as if there was a watch on it. "Time's just about up."

He scoffed.

"Monday, I'm going to send it."

"You wouldn't send me back to jail."

"No? Just try me."

His face paled.

"It's your choice." She passed around him to go into the Lunch Counter and nodded when she saw Porter, enjoying a thick BLT sandwich with another fisherman. She was pleased to see he was branching out with others and making friends, not just living in the shadow of his big bully brother.

Maddie sat on an empty stool to watch her sister at work. The more she noticed, the more concerned she felt. Blaine, who normally carried herself with an effortless elegance, looked downright frumpy. Her clothes were rumpled, her hair looked like it needed a wash, her shoulders slumped. And she didn't seem quite right, either. Her movements in the kitchen, usually quick and decisive, were slow and uncertain, as if she weren't sure of what to do next.

Maddie felt a surge of love and worry for her little sister. Mom's death had hit Blaine the hardest, and sometimes she wondered if that loss continued as a ripple effect on her. Cam had already graduated from college by then and moved on. Maddie was in college. Both had a place to go, a world where they belonged. But Blaine? She was still stuck in high school.

She wondered how it must have felt for Blaine to come home every day to an empty house, or to a father who muffled his grief. Blaine must have felt completely alone. Abandoned.

Maddie waited until Blaine turned the sign on the door from open to closed and they were alone. "Blaine, I know how bold and feisty you can be with the Phinney boys. You put them in their place like nobody's business. So help me understand why it's impossible for you to take a stand with this instructor?"

"The Phinney boys are idiots. They like to woo-woo girls."

"You're not answering my question."

Blaine flinched, stopping abruptly. "I told you why."

"Because you like this instructor's wife."

"Yes."

"Are you really being a good friend to his wife by not being truthful about her husband?"

Blaine strode past Maddie, untying her apron. She tossed it on the counter and spun around. "Whose side are you on, anyway?"

"Yours," Maddie replied. "Always yours."

"I just can't do that to her."

"Oh Blaine. Do you really think she doesn't know?" Maddie watched Blaine as she busied herself behind the counter, sensing a shift happening inside her.

Blaine squirted the countertop with a cleaner, then wiped it down with a clean paper towel. Without looking up, still scrubbing, she said, "You're convinced he'll do this to someone else?"

"Absolutely."

"And that he's done it before?"

"No doubt in my mind."

"I just think that calling him out will only hurt his wife and make me look like an immature schoolgirl with a stupid . . ." Blaine stopped abruptly. Too abruptly.

Oh. Oh, oh, oh. Now, Maddie got the full picture. "Crush," she supplied softly. *An immature schoolgirl with a stupid crush on her instructor.* "Tell me a little more."

Miraculously, Blaine didn't balk. She wasn't fighting her right now. She simply leaned against the counter, took a breath, and began. "I told you I made a mistake." She crossed her arms against her chest. "I think I gave off signals that I was attracted to him. I'm sure I did." Tears pooled in her eyes.

"Because you were."

She nodded.

Ah. "How far did it go?"

"Too far."

Oh Blaine.

"I mean . . . not *that* far. But too far." She paused to catch her breath. "I liked his attention. I liked him. Until *that* day."

"So you made a mistake. Why is that impossible to get over? You're allowed to make mistakes. You can recover from this, get back on track. Go back to school."

"Going back there is unthinkable." She sniffed, eyes filling with tears. "I can't go back. I just can't." She started crying. More like sobbing. It was a complete downpour. Her shoulders shook, her nose dripped, her breathing was wheezy.

It suddenly seemed so clear. Her sister's restlessness, her avoidance with the instructor and his wife, her disappearing palate. When Blaine's sobbing settled, Maddie leaned forward on the stool. "There is a way to solve this problem. It starts with forgiveness." She pointed to her sister. "Forgiving yourself."

Fresh tears flooded Blaine's cheeks. "I can't."

"That's because you don't do it in your own strength. All forgiveness stems from God. He's the one to ask."

"I can't. God and I . . . we're not on the same page." Blaine yanked another paper towel off the holder and mopped her face. "He's gone silent." She sighed. "Like my palate. They're both disappointed in me. They've both gone missing."

"Sounds like you're confusing God and humans. When you disappoint a friend, it's true . . . there's damage. There's work to do to make things right. But God isn't like people. He's faithful even when we're not." She'd been told that once and never forgot it.

Maddie thought Blaine was listening, but it was hard to tell. Blaine kept her chin tucked low, her eyes on the ground.

"Right now it's difficult for you to believe all things are possible with God because you don't see a way out."

Blaine's head jerked up. "I do see a way out. I'm going to Europe."

"That's not what I meant. What I meant was . . . a way back."

"No way. Not happening."

"That's where trust comes in, Blaine. Trust that God can bring good out of bad." She went around the corner to put her arm around Blaine's shoulder and squeeze her into a side-to-side hug. "Think about what we've talked over. Try not to assume you understand the mind of God, especially without bothering to check the Bible."

"I'll think about it," Blaine conceded with a sigh.

The first few "Look Fear in the Eyes and Smile" meetings had gone surprisingly well. Each class was bigger in size than the week before. Maddie even had a few new clients come from the classes. Tonight, after everyone left, she stayed to help clean up. She assumed Rick would be exhausted, but he was charged up. "Do you have clients tomorrow?"

"None. Three on Friday, though."

"Good. I'll meet you at Moose Manor tomorrow at three o'clock."

She was picking up some papers and stopped to look up. "Why?"

He grinned. "Just be ready. And wear hiking boots."

The next afternoon, as Maddie tugged on a pair of thick socks and tied her hiking boots, she wondered what Rick had in mind. She also wondered why she kept accepting his invitations. Why had she said she'd go on a hike with him? It wasn't a date. No way was it a date. She hoped he didn't think it was a date. After all, hiking didn't count as a date. Or could it? And if so, how did she feel about a date with Ricky O'Shea? Conflicted. Uncertain.

Eager.

She heard the high-pitched whine of an engine and peered out the window to see Rick drive up the gravel driveway in an all-terrain vehicle. Her stomach did that tingling thing that it did each time she caught sight of him from a distance.

Shoot. The tingle thing was not a good sign of her resolve to remain unaffected by Rick. To be calm and less reactive. She watched him slow the ATV to a stop.

More tingles. Shoot, shoot, shoot.

He flipped a switch and hopped off the ATV. That was when she noticed a second helmet hanging upside down off the handlebars. ATVs? Oh no. Not her thing. No way. There was no way she was going anywhere on that thing.

She flew down the stairs and opened the front door just as he was walking up the porch steps. "I can't ride an ATV."

"Why not?"

"Too muddy. Too noisy. Too dangerous." Maddie listed them off on her fingers. "I know of someone who drove straight into a tree. Her neck has never been the same." She stroked her neck, already worried, already feeling the whiplash.

"If we were to hit a tree, which isn't the plan at all . . . and I *mean* at all . . . then I promise I'll take the full impact. You'll be in the back. Safe and sound."

She caught herself twirling a lock of hair, something she did when nervous, and dropped her hand to her side. "Why? Where did you get that thing, anyway?" Lots of locals had ATVs.

"Captain Ed traded someone for it. Your dad is considering buying a few for the camp, but he said he can't quite decide. Last night after the class he asked if I would try one out, seeing as how I've had experience on them."

"My dad?" Her father had lots of ideas for Camp Kicking Moose, most that never came to be, but she hadn't heard of this one. She chewed the inside of her cheek.

"He said some guests have asked about taking them on carriage roads."

She straightened, cleared her throat, looked straight at him. "You do know that 'carriage roads' is a euphemism, don't you? They're really overgrown trails."

Rick looked back at her, one brow lifted in amusement. "Come on," he said as he took her by the elbow, leading her down the porch steps. "Let's give it a go. It'll be fun. I promise I'll go slow." He handed her a helmet. "Climb aboard," he said, swinging his leg over the ATV and settling on the seat.

Maddie didn't think this was a good idea, but a deep-down part of her didn't want to miss it either, so she climbed on behind him. Awkwardly, she put her arms around his waist.

"Point me to the carriage road."

She pointed to a golf-cart-sized path between two balsam fir trees. He twisted the throttle and the ATV sputtered to life, and then they were off in a cloud of gravel, rocks flying out from beneath the wide rubber tires. He veered into the trees and onto the dirt road, rumbled over small fallen limbs, thumped into a ditch, and hurtled along the trail farther than she had ever hiked or jogged. He drove straight uphill into thick trees, then downhill, stopping only when they reached a fallen log that was too big to pass.

He helped Maddie off first. She pulled off the helmet and shook her head. Hat hair was the worst. She stretched her legs, feeling like she'd just ridden a horse.

He opened up the ATV seat and took out two cold bottles of water. Holding them in one hand, he unscrewed both caps and handed her a bottle. "Is this still Camp Kicking Moose's property?" He took a big gulp of water.

She stood a good five inches shorter than him. Maybe six. That pins-and-needles feeling started again, prickling her fingers and toes. *Quit it, Maddie! Think about something else before you embarrass yourself.*

She lifted her gaze to the treetops, stilled, listened. "Hear the ocean? Camp Kicking Moose extends all the way to the north end." She took a sip of water, then dabbed her lips with her shirt-sleeve.

"You're so dainty."

"Dainty?"

"Tidy."

"And proud of it." A pair of screeching seagulls flew overhead. "The lighthouse isn't far from here."

Rick walked up to examine the fallen log.

She knew what he was thinking. In her best Maine accent, she said, "You cahn't get the-ah from he-ah."

He grinned. "Someday I want to see that lighthouse I hear so much about. But this log is way too big for you and me to move." He kicked it, but it didn't budge.

Uh, yeah. It was huge. "We had a doozy of a storm in March that knocked a lot of trees down."

"Kind of exciting."

"Kind of freezing, that's what it was. No electricity for over a week. We kept the fire going in Moose Manor's fireplace twenty-four hours a day." She smiled smugly. "This winter, no doubt you'll find out how exciting a northeaster can be on an island."

"Ah, but your sister Cam is going to fix all that."

"Can't imagine it could happen that fast. On the other hand, when Cam gets her überfocus thing going, stuff does happen."

"Yeah, I even remember her like that as a kid. Pretty intense. My mom used to say she hoped Cam might run for president one day. She said she would vote for her." He grinned. "She seems a little"—he seesawed his hand—"mellower now."

"Does she? It's this island. It changes you from the inside out. Slows you down." She'd been looking up at the treetops, at the breeze gently moving the limbs, and a sense of joy and contentment filled her—so full it nearly spilled out of her. "Suddenly you find yourself wondering, 'Now, what exactly was the big hurry?'"

As she spoke, she turned her head to look at him and saw his eyes drop quickly to his water bottle, as if he didn't want to be caught looking at her.

He took a sip of water, then screwed the cap back on. He sat on the ground, leaning his back against the log. "I can see how the island gets hold of you, doesn't let you go. It's like it has a claim on your heart you just can't ignore."

Maddie stilled.

"Take your dad, for example. He had to come here. He couldn't stay away."

She had to look away from those dark eyes. She had a strange feeling he wasn't really talking about her dad. When she finally glanced back at Rick, she found his eyes were still on her.

"So tomorrow I'm going skydiving. Want to come?"

She'd been leaning against the ATV seat, relaxed, but the moment he asked, she jumped up like she'd sat against a pincushion. "Are you kidding? All I'd do, the entire time, is worry about the landing. *How* I would land." She waved her hands in front of her. "No way would I parachute out of a plane. No way. And I think you're crazy for doing it." She hung the helmet on the handlebar of the ATV. "Do you do other extreme sports? Or just jump out of airplanes?"

"Extreme sports? I never thought of them like that. How do you define an extreme sport?"

"They could all end badly. Unlike tennis or golf or walking a dog."

He made a snorting sound. "Can't argue with that. Let's see . . . if that's your definition, then I do probably engage in a bunch of extreme sports." He listed them off.

As she listened to him, her eyes grew wider and wider with each endeavor. "So you're telling me that in the last year you have bungee jumped, skydived, ziplined, rock climbed, and white-water rafted."

"One more. Scuba diving. In caves."

"Why? What's there to see in a cave?"

"Pretty fascinating to be inside a dark cave, to see the life inside." He pointed to his head. "Wearing an LED light on the helmet, of course."

"There's life? Inside a cave?"

"Bats, mostly. There's a certain smell to a cave that's like none other."

"Bats?" she repeated, wrinkling her nose.

"Well, yeah, bat guano has a scent of its own. But I meant the smell of water and earth. Stalagmites. Limestone. Sort of a chalky, bone-deep-cold smell. Very cool. I'd recommend it if you're looking for an endorphin rush. I happen to like the adrenaline rush of risks."

"There are safer ways to get an endorphin rush. Jogging, for example. Playing tennis."

"Dating. Falling in love." He looked right at her as he said the words.

Again, she stilled. Was Rick flirting with her? No, of course not. She wished he'd stop looking at her so intensely. And yet she liked it too.

Halo Maddie: *Ricky O'Shea has changed. Grown up.*

Horns Maddie: *Ignore, ignore, ignore!* The word bleated in her head like a smoke alarm. *This is Ricky O'Shea! Do not let him pull his schtick on you. A leopard doesn't change his spots.*

Halo Maddie: *People do change. He's a pastor now, for goodness' sake.*

She wiggled her shoulders to shrug the two imaginary Maddies off and refocused the conversation on sports. "Swimming. Snorkeling."

"Ah yes! I swam with sharks in Belize. Nurse sharks, so it didn't seem too dangerous."

"Nurse sharks? There's such a thing?"

"Yup. They wore little caps on their heads with a red cross on it."

She gave his bent knee a gentle kick with the top of her hiking boot. "Why do you choose to do things that risk your life?"

"Why do you think life needs to be safe? Or even that it can be made safe?"

He was always doing that, turning questions around. She recognized the tactic because she did it herself. Plus, she was well aware of her hypervigilance. Aka acute worry. Worst-case scenario. Catastrophic thinking. She knew. "Okay, I admit that I'm no risk taker. But you! You're practically toying with death."

"I live without fear. I can do that because I know my days on earth are in the hand of God."

That didn't sound like the logic of a typical twenty-seven-year-old man. "What does that mean?" She tilted her head. "Why do I get the sense that these . . . extreme athletic activities . . . have something to do with what happened to you overseas?"

Amusement lit his eyes. "Nice try, Dr. Grayson, but I never went overseas. I ended up with a desk job. Pretty dull stuff."

"But I thought going overseas was what drew you to the Marines."

"It did. But desire wasn't enough."

"I'm not following you. What wasn't enough? The desire?"

"No. My heart."

"Your heart wasn't in it?"

"My heart was all there," he said with a chuckle, "but it turned out my heart just wasn't up to the job." Then he grew serious. "Maddie, what would change if you knew you only had a year to live?"

Twenty

"What?" A chill went down Maddie's spine. "What did you say?"

"What would change for you if you knew you had a year to live?" Rick said. "Or a month? Or a day?"

Her stomach dropped. Her mind started spinning. Rick was dying. Cancer? Brain tumor? No! It couldn't be true. She sifted through his words, grasping for something to cling to, something that made sense.

Hold on. Think, think, think. Heart. He said it was his heart. She lifted her eyes to look straight at him. "What's wrong with your heart?"

He didn't answer right away, as if he was gathering his thoughts. "Something inherited. A heart condition called hypertrophic cardiomyopathy. HCM, for shorthand."

"Try longhand."

"Over time, the walls of the heart muscle thicken. It can lead to arrhythmia—"

"Irregular heartbeats?" Okay. Okay, that wasn't so bad. That could be fixed. She was sure about that.

"Sometimes irregular. Sometimes racing."

Still fixable. "But manageable, right?"

He seesawed his hand in the air. "Usually, HCM goes undetected. But it can lead to . . ."

"To what?"

"Another problem."

"Like what?"

He seemed lost in thought for a bit. Then he rubbed his forehead before finally looking up. "Like . . . sudden death."

Shock—awful, sickening shock—dropped on her like a bomb. She turned away from him, gripping her elbows. *Breathe in, breathe out.* Her hands felt clammy. "Wait. Wait just a minute." She remembered reading something about HCM and spun around. "Isn't that the cause of those athletes who drop dead?"

He nodded. "That's it. Exactly."

It couldn't be true. God, she pleaded, *don't let it be true.* Chaotic emotions flew around her head like the way Lola would sky-dance around Boon Dock. Her heart was racing so fast she grew dizzy. She could feel herself inching toward a panic attack, right on its cusp. *Reorient, Maddie. Keep to the facts. Rick is here, right now. Right in front of you.* "Then why," she cleared her throat and started again. "Why do you put yourself at risk to die?"

"Because I like living each day as if it were my last. And because I have no fear of death."

She stared at him, unblinking, trying to get her head around what he was telling her, trying to focus, when all her mind could grasp was that Rick might die. Any moment. Anywhere.

"Maddie, all the color has drained from your face. Say something. Anything."

"You've given up," she said in a flat tone.

"Given up?" He laughed. "Just the opposite. I don't think you can fully live until you're prepared to die."

"Rick! Be serious. This isn't funny."

"I know." He sobered. "I admit," he continued, "that it took me a while to get there. Finding out I had a heart condition, well, it profoundly shook me. But that chaplain I've told you about . . . he helped me understand that I'd been given a gift. The best gift a young man could have. It gave meaning to every aspect of my life." He lifted his shoulders in a shrug. "Facing death taught me to realize that every single day is precious, every act is sacred. It truly did help me to live more fully. More fearlessly." His gaze measured her face. "You know why I wanted to do that Fear class this summer? It's because I believe that fear of death is at the core of all anxiety. All of it."

She had been trying to take in all that he had to say. It was hard to argue with his logic, but it was hard to accept it too. "I still don't understand why you tempt fate."

"Because . . . along with this heart condition, God has given me the gift of fearlessness."

"Not everyone considers fearlessness to be a gift. Your mother, for example, might call some of your choices to be based on an absence of common sense. There's even a syndrome named after it."

He laughed. "My mother would call it stupidity."

A smile tugged at Maddie's lips. Her first.

"I have complete peace from God about my adventures. And I've seen some remarkable sights, gone on some wild journeys. Knowing I might not live a long life makes me even more determined to take risks, to be bold about sharing my faith. 'For God has not given us a spirit of fear but of power and love.'"

"'*And* a sound mind!' If you're going to quote the Bible at me, don't leave parts out."

"Touché." He grinned. "Same ol' Maddie. Iron sharpens iron."

"You said it's an inherited condition?"

"My father."

She knew Rick's father had passed, but she never knew when or why. "How old was he when he died?"

"Twenty-nine. Sudden heart attack. Left my mom with a six-year-old girl and a very strong-willed three-year-old boy to raise."

She felt her stomach clench. "Isn't there something that can be done? Something you can do to prevent a sudden heart attack?"

"If you mean 'change my lifestyle' . . . then no. There's nothing I'm willing to consider." He shrugged. "It is what it is. A sudden heart attack is not such a bad way to exit stage left. I can think of a lot worse ways to die."

"Rick. Be serious. You're only twenty-seven." She dropped her chin.

"I am dead serious . . . pardon the pun. Despite what I thought as a teenager, nobody has all that much time. No one." He used a hand to shade his eyes from the sun, then bent down and picked a tiny wildflower. "Smell it. Look at it."

"Jasmine." She breathed in deeply before looking closely at the tiny star petals. It took her back to her grandmother's home on a summer day. Funny how scent could evoke memories. And yes, awe.

"Knocks you out, doesn't it?"

"It does."

"Good. So now, every day, hunt for a moment of awe. It'll change your life."

"That's what you do?"

"Been doing it for years."

"Is that why you jump out of airplanes?"

"Skydive. Big difference. Standing at the open door of a small plane and looking down on this big planet of ours . . . yes. It absolutely fills me with awe. Mind-blowing awe. People seem like tiny ants from up there, yet the Bible says God knows the number of hairs on our head and not one sparrow will drop without his knowledge. He keeps this little planet turning, keeps calling us to redemption, keeps inviting us to spend eternity with him. Blows my mind." He grinned. "Okay. End of sermon." He looked straight at her, waiting for her to respond. "Any reaction?"

Did she have a reaction to what he had confided in her? Did she have a reaction to him? Maddie did her absolute best to keep an unaffected expression on her face, to keep her eyes from revealing her true feelings. Despite her best efforts, despite trying to play it tough and cool, she knew she was in trouble. As a boy, Ricky O'Shea had stolen her heart. As a man, he was back to claim it.

And this wonderful, brilliant, talented, frustrating, exasperating man could die at any moment.

Twenty-One

OUTSIDE, NIGHT HAD ALMOST COMPLETELY FALLEN; darkness enveloped the trees that framed the property. In Maine, Cam thought, sitting on the porch of Moose Manor, the night sky never quite turned black. So many pinpricks of starlight kept the sky a very dark navy blue, but not quite black.

Just thirty minutes ago, Cam returned from a very long day trip to the mainland. After meeting with the child psychologist in Bar Harbor, she had made a point not to be away from Cooper overnight. This time, she'd left early in the morning to drive to Portland in order to meet with a nonprofit company offering grant money for alternative energy. She had arrived in Portland with such high hopes and left the meeting thoroughly discouraged. Not only did the nonprofit deny her the funding, but they shot holes in her plans. "Your island is too small, too remote," they told her. "Too few locals. You're wasting your time with this year-round nonsense."

They didn't understand, she decided. They didn't understand islands, nor locals. Both were tougher than mainlanders gave them credit for.

Cam sat in a rocking chair, waiting for Seth to join her after he finished helping Cooper pack up for their camping trip tomorrow. She had tried to help them, made lots of suggestions, until Seth finally asked her to please leave them alone. "We'd need a pack mule for all the things you want us to bring," he told her. So she gave up and went outside to watch the moon rise behind the balsam fir trees . . . and ruminate about the day's disappointment.

When Seth finally came out to join her on the porch, she told him all that she'd been thinking about. "I might have made a mistake by only pursuing grants and funding from the state of Maine. They seem almost biased against small outer islands." Maybe she should have considered that bias months ago. After all, there were three thousand islands off of Maine's coast. "I think I'm going to seek out federal grants." To the federal government, an island was an island.

Seth sat in the chair beside her and crossed one ankle over the other. "Cam, after we got engaged, you said you needed time to complete the grant work before we set a date." He ran a hand down his trimmed beard. "So I gave you time."

When she heard the defeated tone in his voice, she hurried to say, "Seth, we can go ahead and set a wedding date. This grant work is just going to take longer than I thought it would."

"I wonder if there's always going to be something more important than Cooper and me. Becoming a family."

Cam felt a hitch in her gut. "What do you mean?"

He took her hand, and kept his eyes on their joined hands. "I think maybe . . . we should put a hold on setting a date."

She held her breath, every muscle tight. "What?"

"There's no hurry to getting married."

She forced herself to look at Seth. "What's changed?"

"You're an all-or-none person. Right now, you're all in for the energy project. It's got your full attention."

239

"I thought you supported the project."

"I do. It's a good thing for this island. It's a big undertaking. Like you said, it's going to take longer than you thought."

"I thought you liked that quality in me."

"I did. I do. I admire it. It's just . . . once you get going, you can't be stopped."

She knew that about herself. "You and Cooper . . . you're the most important people in the world to me. I just get . . . I don't know. It's like . . ." She paused, rubbing her forehead. "I'm either on or off. I don't come with a dimmer switch. I go all in or all out."

He inhaled deeply. "Yeah. So I've noticed. It can get a little . . . overwhelming." One second slid into the next, but he didn't say anything more.

A long moment of silence followed. Cam sat for several moments, staring straight ahead. *This wasn't happening. This couldn't really be happening.* Expression cautious, she asked slowly, "You don't want to marry me." It wasn't really phrased as a question, but it was.

He looked away as he considered, biting his lip. Then he turned to face her, and said soberly, "That's not what I said. I do love you, Cam. I do want to marry you. But sometimes I'm not sure how or where I fit in your life, or what a life together would even look like." He took in a deep breath. "That's why I think we need to step back a little." He squeezed her hand. "Let's just put the wedding on ice for a while, until we get things figured out for ourselves. Until we figure out how we can best help Cooper."

Tension vibrated between them and Cam's eyes started to sting. *Do not cry. Do not cry.* She rose to her feet, grateful for the cover of darkness. "You'd better tell Blaine that there won't be a wedding this summer."

"Okay."

Cam walked to the door. She couldn't be near him right now.

"Cam."

She stilled.

"I'll be back to get Cooper at eight in the morning. For the camping trip. He's all packed. Excited to go."

"I heard it's supposed to rain tomorrow."

"Just a small chance of rain. We'll be fine. Maybe Cooper will get a shower after all."

Without looking at Seth, Cam nodded and opened the door. Closing it, she leaned against it, listening for the sound of his motorbike start up, then wane as he drove down the gravel driveway. He was gone.

Involuntarily, Cam lifted both hands to cover the lower half of her face. During their exchange just now, her lungs had tightened as if she were being physically wounded, and her breath had wanted to stop off in her throat. She stood unmoving on Moose Manor's hardwood floor, struggling to comprehend what had just happened.

This morning, she had waved goodbye to both Seth and Cooper, and left for Portland, thinking everything was just fine.

And it wasn't.

~⁓~

Maddie was in the kitchen, making a batch of granola for tomorrow's guests because Blaine had forgotten to make it. She'd watched Blaine do this often enough that she knew how to make it turn out as good as her sister's. Pretty close, anyway. Nothing ever tasted as good as Blaine's cooking. She mixed vegetable oil and honey into a glass bowl of oats and coconut, then stirred it with a large wooden spoon. As she spread the mixture onto a baking sheet, Cam walked into the kitchen. Maddie glanced at her, thinking she looked a little odd. Pinched and pale. Her lips were set together a fraction too tight.

"Bet you're hungry after a long day. There's nothing much left in the fridge tonight. I've started a list to go grocery shopping tomorrow. I think there's eggs left in the carton. You could whip up some scrambled eggs."

Wordlessly, Cam cracked the eggs and started to whisk, as if whisking eggs was the most important thing in the world. In fact, she was beating the life out of those poor eggs.

Maddie slid the pan of granola into the oven and turned to face Cam. "How about if you sit down and tell me what's wrong while I make those eggs for you?"

Cam dropped the whisk and plopped into a chair. "Seth wants to postpone our wedding. Indefinitely."

Maddie's jaw fell open. "Why? What reason did he give?"

"He thinks there will always be something that's more important than him and Cooper. Over being a family." She propped her chin on her elbows. "He says I go overboard on everything."

Maddie tossed out the overbeaten eggs and started again. She cracked two eggs, whisked milk and seasonings into them. She cooked them low and slow, the way Blaine did, waited until they gently set before scooping them on a plate to hand to Cam. "Not quite like Blaine's, but as close as you're going to get with me as the chef."

Cam looked at her plate of eggs with sad eyes. "Do you think Seth is right? Do you think it'll always be this way? The thing is . . . I'm not sure I can change. It's like . . . hardwired into me. Whatever I do, I have to give it one hundred percent."

Maddie watched her, impressed. There was shocking self-awareness in that comment. Normally, Cam wasn't sensitive enough to detect anything. "Is Seth asking you to change who you are?" she said in a soft voice.

"I don't know. Isn't he?"

Don't say it, Maddie. Don't say it. Hold back. Let Cam figure this out. "What exactly was at the heart of his complaint?"

She sighed. "I guess . . . I suppose that he doesn't feel like a priority to me."

"Would that be so hard to change?"

Cam took so long to answer that Maddie had to bite on her lip to stop from shouting: *No! Come on, Cam. You can fix this, you can make things right again.*

Sheer relief smoothed the worry lines from Cam's face. "I get it! I need to prove to him that I'm all in. Maddie, you're brilliant." She jumped off her chair and bolted to the door. "I know just what I need to do. Go overboard on Seth!"

As Maddie listened to her sister's light footsteps tap up the steps, she reflected on their conversation. She was pretty sure Seth didn't want Cam to go overboard on *him*—scary thought!—but it was a start in the right direction.

These were the moments Maddie wished she could bill her sisters for counseling hours. She'd be rich.

$\backsim$

By the time Seth arrived at eight o'clock on Saturday morning to pick up Cooper for the camping trip, Cam was ready to go. Packed, dressed in Blaine's hiking gear. "I'm coming too."

"No kidding?" Cooper said. "Cool!" He seemed pleased.

Seth, not so much. "On *our* camping trip?"

"Sure. Why not? I like to camp."

Seth looked at her as if she might have had a stroke. "But . . . what about the grants?"

"They can wait until Monday."

Seth still seemed skeptical. "Lie down, Dory." The dog flopped onto the rug and let out a sigh. "Cam, you do realize that we are sleeping outside."

"Under the stars," Cooper piped in. "We're going to count them."

"I like stars," Cam said.

"Let me just be clear that we are sleeping on the ground," Seth said. "Hard ground. No tent. No hot showers. No indoor toilets."

Cam swallowed. "Twenty-four hours. How hard can it be? Besides, I love the outdoors."

Seth grinned. "No . . . you don't."

She shrugged. "People can change. I can change."

"She'll do great," Cooper said. He, at least, was thrilled she was coming. "We're going to check out an osprey nest that's near the top of the lighthouse."

"I like ospreys." She did too. She loved watching them soar overhead.

"It'll be an adventure," Cooper said.

Seth scratched his forehead, stalling. "Cam, we're not going to come back early. No matter what. We've got a guys' adventure all planned. Hiking, catching fish to eat."

"Wait," Cooper said. He lifted his palms in the air like a traffic cop. "Hold it a minute. We're not going in the water, right?"

A worried look came over Seth. "Coops, I'll be with you the whole time. It's going to be great."

"But I don't have to go *in* the water, right?"

Seth flashed a look at Cam that said much. *See? I told you this was a bigger problem than you wanted to believe it was.*

"Seth won't let anything bad happen to you." Cam crouched down to look right in Cooper's eyes. "And I'll be with you too."

"And Dory. Mom, you always forget about Dory. She's our watchdog."

Dory thumped her tail at the sound of her name.

Seth still wasn't convinced. Squinting skeptically, he said, "Cam, are you sure you can handle this overnight—"

"Absolutely. I'll be fine," Cam said, trying to project a confidence she didn't feel. "Better than fine. Watch and see." She had something to prove to both Seth and Cooper. She was all in.

〜⌒

Standing at the kitchen sink, putting dishes from the campers' breakfast into the dishwasher, Paul gazed out the window. The bright morning sun was now hidden behind scudding gray clouds with dark underbellies. A strong wind lifted loose leaves off the ground and sent them spinning into the air. The rain began to fall, first in fat drops, then more steadily. He heard gentle rumbles of thunder, off in the distance. Somewhere from the back of his mind came a long-forgotten warning: Maine ranked fifth in the nation for lightning deaths. The reason? So many people were outside, enjoying nature. In the open, exposed—the most dangerous place to be during a storm. Just out enjoying nature. Like Seth, Cam, and Cooper were doing today. *Lord*, he prayed, lifting his head, *watch over them. Keep them safe from harm.*

At that exact moment, a flash of blinding blue light lit the sky, a strange ripping sound like the atmosphere was being torn in two. Then came a deafening boom.

Paul stilled, heart pounding, his own breath ragged. That was an eerie blast of thunder.

The kitchen door swung open and Maddie appeared, eyes wide. "Did you hear that?"

Paul craned his neck around. "Couldn't miss it." He rinsed the suds off his hands and grabbed a towel, surveying his daughter with a canny eye. "You're wearing the look you had as a little girl when something was troubling you."

She walked to the window and peered out. "Since when have you noticed things like that?"

"I notice. Sometimes." He glanced out the window. The rain was coming down in thick sheets.

"I knew there was a chance of rain in the forecast today, but I didn't think it'd be a thunderstorm."

"Me either. It'll pass soon." He hung the wet rag over the sink faucet to dry, just the way Corinna used to.

"Are the campers in their cabins?"

"Hope so." He didn't really know, but there wasn't much he could do about that now. Still, he should have remembered to say a prayer over them too, just in case they didn't have the sense to come in from the rain. He lifted his eyes to the ceiling and breathed a silent prayer. *Lord, watch over those campers!* He dropped his head and stared at his daughter for a long moment. Maddie was twirling a lock of hair, peering through the window at the sky. "What's troubling you?"

"I don't know. I can't really say. I just have a feeling that we're on the verge of something catastrophic."

Paul had picked up a sponge to wipe down the kitchen counter. As her words registered, suddenly his hands went still. "You *what?*"

She looked at him, gravely serious. "I know."

In between thunder booms, cocking his head, Paul thought he heard the sound of a familiar bark. Dory. He bolted through the kitchen and ran to the front door, opening it wide. In flew Dory, soaking wet, shivering, shaking.

"Oh no," Maddie said. "Oh no, no, no. Dad . . . Dory was with Seth."

"Dory's always been terrified of thunderstorms."

"She'd never leave Seth's side." Fear shone in her eyes. "Not unless . . ."

An awful, sickening feeling started to swirl in Paul's stomach. "Maddie, don't jump to any conclusions." Dory was pacing, quivering, nervous, tail tucked, eyes pleading. He tried to stay focused on calming Dory down, but inside, his thoughts were scrambling, flailing, trying to latch on to something firm and sound, something logical. His voice fell to a gruff murmur. "The dog got separated from Seth and Cam and Cooper, got lost, got scared, ran home. That's all."

"Maybe that's not all. Dad, the last time I had this feeling . . ." Her voice drizzled to a stop.

Paul remembered that day. Maddie was in college and had called him at work with a similar feeling of foreboding. She couldn't say what it was that was bothering her, only that she had woken with a sense of utter dread. He had given her a gentle lecture about not putting too much weight on such feelings. Yet that very afternoon, Corinna had died in a house fire. Libby and her grandmother too.

"Don't say it," he said. "Don't even think it."

But as he said the words, he couldn't look at her. Maddie had always had a sensitivity to things Paul couldn't understand.

＿＿＿～◯＿＿＿

Opening the front door, Maddie leaned on the doorjamb to watch the thunder and lightning split the sky. The wind moaned through the balsam firs that lined Moose Manor's expansive lawn, and the rain poured down on Camp Kicking Moose like a fire hose on full blast. It was powerful and terrifying, filling her with dread . . . and awe. She fought a rising sense of panic over Cam and Cooper and Seth, knowing they were in a precarious situation right now. At best, they were in danger. At worst . . .

She shook her head. She shouldn't go there. Couldn't even think about the conditions they might be in. She hadn't felt so helpless, so utterly, completely helpless, since her mother had died.

MADDIE, AGE 19

A month had passed since Maddie's mother had died, and she still felt numb. Thoroughly anesthetized. She hadn't even cried.

In a way, it was a blessing, because she had come home from college this weekend to help her dad clean out the master bedroom closet. Mom and Dad had shared a small closet, and he had mentioned that it was hard to open it up and see Mom's clothing. Hanging there, waiting, like she'd just slipped out to the grocery store and hadn't come back yet. She wasn't coming back. There wasn't a lot that Maddie could do to help her dad get through this lonely time, but she could help with the closet.

Maddie had spent the last two hours sorting her mother's clothing into piles. A pile for Cam, who insisted she didn't want anything, but Maddie didn't buy that; a pile for Blaine, who wanted everything, but Maddie knew that wasn't what she really wanted; a pile for her; and the biggest pile was giveaways. It was slow going. She was about halfway through when she heard the doorbell ring. She froze. In the last month, the family, as if by silent assent, avoided the front door and came in and out of the kitchen door in the back of the house. The house was on a corner lot, so they even parked on the side. Keep your head down, or turn to the left, and you didn't even have to look across the street.

The bell rang again, and Maddie cringed before she pulled the door open, bracing herself.

"Hi, Maddie. I saw your car parked on the side and figured you were home for the weekend. Guessed you probably were facing a tough task today. I wondered if I could help."

Ricky O'Shea's mother.

Maeve O'Shea was a robust-looking woman, a few inches taller than Maddie, with a tanned face that didn't need makeup. Her brown hair, cut just below her shoulders, boasted a wide streak of gray that swooped upward from her forehead, then ran to the tips. A handsome woman, she'd heard her described. There was something about her that Maddie had always been fond of, despite such conflicted feelings about her son. Maybe it was simply because Ricky's mother had always been especially fond of Maddie.

"Maddie, honey, how're you doing?"

Maddie looked up and saw such compassion in her dark brown eyes, so like her son's. Her head was eerily framed by the burned-out remains of the Cooper house across the street. Mrs. O'Shea opened her arms and suddenly Maddie felt a strange tingling, like her mouth felt after a visit to the dentist when the Novocain started wearing off. All the feelings she'd been afraid of were waking up: overwhelming grief, horror at facing a life without her mother, excruciating sorrow, muffled guilt. She dove into Mrs. O'Shea's arms, sobbing. For a long time, Mrs. O'Shea just let her cry, rubbing her back and whispering *hmm-hmm*s and *you poor thing* at just the right moments.

They sat at the kitchen table and drank gallons of tea, and Maddie talked and talked and talked. And cried and cried and cried. It surprised her, actually, that she had any tears left.

She was grateful her dad was intentionally not at home this afternoon, that Blaine hadn't shown up as she'd promised. That Cam had taken Cooper to live in her Boston apartment since the fire. She'd been trying to be strong for her family, to encourage them to talk things out and not stuff their grief. They ignored her advice, and she couldn't blame them because she ignored her own advice. She didn't want to dump her grief on her college friends. Mostly, there was no one to talk to. Until today. Maddie pulled tissue after tissue out of the box to mop up her face, but the tears kept coming.

"You've been holding up like a rock, but maybe it's time to give yourself a little room to grieve."

"I can't. Especially now."

"Why not now?"

"Cam is going to adopt Cooper. Libby's will stated that she wanted our family to care for him if something happened to her, and Cam decided to adopt him."

"Okay. So . . . why can't you let yourself grieve?"

"Cam has no idea how to be a mother. She's going to mess this up."

Ricky's mother smiled. "That's what motherhood is all about. Trying your best and messing it up, but somehow the Lord covers us. Somehow, it works out." She put a hand over Maddie's. "This is Cam's journey."

"But it'll take a village to help raise Cooper. We're the village. We can't be a healthy village for him the way we are now."

"All the more reason for you to stop fighting grief. Let it come, honey. You have to go through it, not around it. I know how it feels to lose someone you love before you're ready. It's the hardest thing I hope you'll ever have to face in your life, but it's harder still to pretend that a major earthquake hasn't occurred."

Major earthquakes. She knew all about those. Tears pricked Maddie's eyes again. "Do you think God might have taken my mom"— she had a hard time talking around the knot in her throat—"as a punishment?"

"How so? Like, for something you did?"

Head bowed, Maddie nodded. "Like . . . a sin." Was she really saying this, thinking this, here with Ricky O'Shea's mother? Of all people?!

Mrs. O'Shea took a long time to respond. "I think your mother's death was an accident. And I also think God is faithful even when we are not. He always stretches out his arms to bring us back to him."

The tears started flowing freely again, running down her cheeks. "I didn't even have a chance to say goodbye," Maddie said in a choked voice. "To tell Mom how much I loved her."

"Oh, honey, she knew." She let Maddie's sobs subside, then added, "Your mom told me something about you that I've never forgotten. She said that of all three girls, you were the one she learned the most from. The most reflective. The most insightful."

"She said that?"

"More than once. She said you had a way of being the heart of the family, keeping everyone together, no matter what happened." She squeezed Maddie's hand. "And you'll keep on doing that, but not at the expense of your own suffering. It's okay to grieve for your mom. The Bible says 'We don't grieve as those who have no hope' . . . but we do grieve. Just don't forget this one thing: Even though you have lost your mother, God remains." She smiled and patted her knees. "Let's you and me both go tackle that closet together."

They finished the closet and the bureau, then cleaned out the master bathroom of makeup and hair products and curling irons and blow-dryers, so Dad could use it without feeling as if Mom were hovering. She wasn't. She was in Heaven and wouldn't be needing hair spray anymore.

They talked as they worked, and Ricky's mom volunteered information on Ricky's life and Maddie tried not to look too interested. He had joined the Marines just to be oppositional because his mother wanted him to go to a Christian college, like his older sister. "I am confident the Lord is going to redirect that boy, but it'll be in God's good timing. And I'm also confident I will be rewarded an extra gem in my heavenly crown because I am Ricky's mother." She pushed up the hair that lay on the back of her neck with a grin. "There's a reason I turned prematurely gray."

Afterward, Ricky's mother took away the giveaway pile so that Blaine didn't riffle through it and take things out. Silly things, like a moth-eaten old scarf. There were better choices of memorabilia for Blaine—some of Mom's jewelry, a favorite hat. It helped Maddie immeasurably to have someone to work with, someone neutral yet someone who loved their mom, who shared a sense of loss. And it felt good to do something concrete, something visible, that moved the family forward. And it was the first time in a long time that she sensed the presence of God back in her life. It felt so good, like the sun on her face on a cold winter day.

When Maddie drove back to school on Monday morning, she changed her major from accounting to psychology.

Twenty-Two

MADDIE HEARD THE SPUTTERING ENGINE of Peg's clunky old minivan on the gravel driveway. It had barely come to a stop in front of Moose Manor and Rick was already out of the car, umbrella open, helping Peg climb out. Maddie felt her heart leap at the sight of Rick. Then she took in his solemn expression, and how ashen Peg's face looked as they hurried in the rain to the front door. Maddie's eyes grew wide with apprehension. "What's happened?"

Peg exchanged a grim look with Rick before she spoke. "Captain Ed says the lighthouse was struck by lightning."

"That boom?" Dad said, holding on to Dory's collar so she wouldn't jump on Peg. "Was that it?"

"Yes," Rick said. "That was the lightning strike. A fire's been spotted."

Peg bent down to pat Dory's head. Without looking up, she said, "This morning Seth told me he and Cooper were planning to hike out to the lighthouse."

"And Cam," Dad said.

"I persuaded her," Maddie said in a dull tone. "She's trying to prove to Seth that she's all in."

253

Rick reached out to put a hand on Maddie's shoulder. "Seth is an experienced outdoorsman. He'll know how to protect them. He'll find shelter."

"But if the lighthouse is on fire," Dad said, "they have no shelter."

Maddie's heart rate started skyrocketing. "You don't think they were in the lighthouse when it was hit by lightning, do you?" When no one answered, she said, "We can't just leave them there. We can borrow Captain Ed's lobster boat and go right now." She grabbed her raincoat off the wall hook behind the door.

"Maddie," Rick said softly. "The tide is in. The storm is still in full force. It's too dangerous."

"He's right," Dad said, his voice huskier than usual.

"Not by water," Rick said thoughtfully, stroking his chin. "It'll have to be by land."

"But we can try to go get them," Maddie said, her spirits lifting. She could see Rick's mind was already spinning.

"Not we. Just me." Lightning lit the sky, and on its heels came window-rattling thunder. Rick went to the window and peered out at the pouring rain. "Maddie, that overgrown carriage path we hiked on . . . you said to go past the huge fallen log to get to the lighthouse."

"Yes. Straight up and over the hillside."

"Rick," Peg warned, "I know that route. It's all granite. Slippery in this rain. And lightning loves granite. I just don't feel right about you trying a rescue on your own. Not in this storm."

"Peg's absolutely right," Dad said. "You'd be too vulnerable." Another crack of thunder rent the sky and Dory ran under a table, whimpering. "We have to wait for the storm to pass."

"I'll be careful," Rick said, taking a moment to give them each a reassuring glance.

Maddie felt a strange peace, a sense that all would be well. It was curious how calm she felt at this moment, because it wasn't a typical response for her, especially in the midst of a crisis. *My grace is sufficient for thee.* That verse circled through her mind, lifting her thoughts to the Source of sufficient grace. "He can do it," she said, eyes fixed on Rick. "If anyone can, he can."

Rick looked at her and she looked at him, for a second too long. Everyone noticed.

"I need rain gear." He grabbed a yellow poncho off the wall hook. "Rope, water bottle, first-aid kit. And prayers."

Maddie grabbed an umbrella to head to the boathouse for rope, just as Blaine came downstairs, still wearing her jammies, yawning. She looked at everyone, puzzled. "What's going on?"

⁓◯

Under a blue morning sky, Cam and Seth and Cooper had hiked up a steep rocky hill to reach the lighthouse. Not an easy hike, not at all, and Cam was puffing as they crested the hill, but they made it. As they went into the lighthouse to check it out, Cam filled her mind with ideas about turning it into the control hub for the island's power. But . . . she kept those thoughts to herself. She was learning! They walked around in the lighthouse, climbed to the top to see the osprey nest—Cooper was disappointed that its residents had vacated—and climbed back down. Dory started barking like crazy and they let her out of the lighthouse. She bolted toward the land's end, and they followed behind, wondering what was making her act so crazy.

As they walked toward the ledge where a metal ladder led down to the small beach, now completely covered by high tide, Cam was startled to see the blue sky was now filled with thick, dark clouds. Wind had kicked up and the foamy surf below was churning angrily. No rain, though.

Somehow, Cam knew lightning was about to strike. She couldn't say how she knew—whether she felt it on her neck or smelled it in the air or heard the buzz of electricity. Something surrounded them, some kind of sizzling energy. She almost felt as if she could reach out and touch it. Seth sensed it too. He grabbed her and Cooper and yanked them away from the ledge just as a flash of white exploded, throwing them facedown to the ground. And then came an ear-blasting *BOOM*!

Shell-shocked, terrified, ears ringing, Cam lay completely still, eyes squeezed shut. Her heart was pounding. Shooting pains coursed up her leg. When the blast threw them to the ground, Seth had landed hard on her ankle, twisting it painfully. It *hurt*.

Cooper popped up. "Whoa! That was a close call." He sounded like it was fun.

"More than a close call, buddy," Seth said, his breath ragged. "Cam, open your eyes. We're all right."

She sat up carefully, eyes still closed. She opened one eye in a squint, her vision resting first on Cooper, then on Seth. Then behind them. "Ohhhh. No! No, no, no, no." The historic lighthouse, the icon of the island, the very place Cam had in mind to use as the headquarters for the energy project—it was on fire.

~⊙

Paul stood by the window at Moose Manor, arms crossed against his chest, staring out at the rain. Only once before had he witnessed such a fierce summer storm. It was his first summer working at Camp Kicking Moose and he was only eighteen or nineteen years old. He remembered that a camper had gone rowing one afternoon, when the sky had been blue just like it was this morning. A storm came up suddenly, out of nowhere. Lightning had hit the metal rowboat and killed the camper instantly. He'd forgotten all about that event. He couldn't even remember the camper—not his face or his name. How could he have forgotten something like that?

How could he have let Ricky O'Shea go out in this storm?

Feet shuffled behind him, and he turned to find Peg standing there with two cups of steaming coffee in her hands. "Blaine made it. Don't worry. It's drinkable."

He took a cup from her, tried to smile but gave up. "Wasn't Blaine supposed to be at work this morning?"

"Yeah, but the power went off so I closed up." She tilted her head. "Paul, Seth and Cam and Cooper . . . they'll be okay. Rick will get to them."

"You sound so sure." But Peg couldn't be sure. She didn't know anything more than he did.

"I'm sure of one thing. They're all in the Lord's care, and there's no better place to be." She put an arm around his waist. "They'll be okay."

To his surprise, without thinking, he folded his arms around Peg and put his chin on the top of her head. They stood there for a long while, watching the rain out the window. It was comforting.

❧

Cam was amazed at Seth's composed demeanor during a crisis. He looped an arm under her knees and carried her far away from the burning lighthouse. He created a shelter for them using their ponchos and found one of those breakable ice packs in his backpack to put on her swelling ankle.

"I wish I'd brought some aspirin," Seth said. "Does it hurt much?"

"Not too much," Cam said, trying to make light of it. Her ankle was throbbing, so much so that she wondered if it was broken. She didn't think she could walk down the hill, which meant they would have to wait until the storm passed, the tide went out, someone noticed they'd gone missing and came to rescue them via water. In that order. She wasn't sure if Cooper could be persuaded to get into a boat, but that was the least of her concerns right now.

"Think the rain will put out the fire?"

"Hope so," Seth said. "The wind doesn't help though."

"Seth, we can't lose that lighthouse."

"Nothing we can do about it." He let out a ragged breath. "Man oh man, I think we were only about forty feet away from that strike." What he didn't add was that they had left the lighthouse only a minute prior to it.

Cooper, tucked between them, was as calm as a cucumber. Strangely calm, Cam realized. Cooper was never calm. "Dad, what about Dory?"

Seth was leaning away, rubbing his hair vigorously to get the rainwater out. "Sorry, what?"

"What about Dory?"

"She ran off like the wind," Seth said. "Don't worry. Dogs know how to take care of themselves. I bet Peg's giving her a biscuit at the Lunch Counter by now. Don't you think so, Cam?"

Cam hardly heard Seth. She was entirely focused on Cooper. "Cooper, you called him Dad."

Cooper's mouth dropped in an O. His eyes went wide. This was his *I'm hiding something* face. Cam waited. Seth waited. And waited. Finally, Cooper tucked his chin. "Aunt Blaine told me."

"What did she tell you?"

"That Seth is my real dad."

Cam stared at Seth, who stared back at her. "She *told* you?"

His gaze went back and forth between them, almost as if he thought he might be in trouble. "She said it was my birthday gift because she won't be here for my actual birthday in August."

258

Seth shook his head and rainwater sprayed from his hair over Cam. "She *told* you? Blaine told you."

Cooper's face grew serious. "Was she lying to me?"

Cam and Seth looked at each other. She gave him a slight nod to go ahead. *Say it.*

"She wasn't lying," Seth said. "We were waiting to tell you until after we got married. We didn't want to overload you. But it's the honest-to-God truth. I'm your father." His voice choked up. "And there's no other boy I'd ever want for a son."

Cooper dove into his arms.

No wonder the cloud over Cooper had lifted so suddenly, Cam realized. Last night, just before she went to bed, she'd gone into his room to check on him and found Blaine there, sitting on the end of his bed with her arms tucked around her knees. At the time, Cam thought nothing of it. Blaine would often read to Cooper if he woke with a bad dream in the night. The only thing that struck her as odd was that Blaine wasn't reading a book to him, and Cooper seemed completely serene. He was sitting up in bed, his hands tucked behind his head, listening carefully to Blaine. No wonder.

But Cam wasn't angry with Blaine; she was grateful. Blaine had been right all along—Cooper needed them, together.

She looked over at the burning lighthouse. All the dreams she had for the island's energy needs, all the grant work she'd been laboring over this last year, was disappearing before her eyes. Like with everything else, she had overdone it. Overfocused on work. She glanced at Seth and Cooper. Look at what she had nearly lost.

Maybe this moment was a gift in disguise. Her mind traveled back to Blaine's sharp comment: *Give up on those stupid grants.* Impossible, Cam had told her.

Impossible? a voice within her asked. *Or could it be entirely possible? What better use of the money from your company's sale could there be than to help this island get on its feet?* These questions shocked her the same way the lightning bolt that hit the lighthouse had shocked her. They came out of nowhere, with a *BOOM!*

Use her money for the island? After her company had been sold, she'd chosen to retain her shares as stock, mostly for tax purposes, but also because she didn't really know what to do with the money. As hard as Cam worked, she wasn't motivated by profit. Only purpose. She'd even offered money to her dad to renovate Moose Manor, but he had refused her.

A little like the moment before the lightning struck the lighthouse, Cam felt a presence surrounding her. A good one. The pelting rain formed a veil around the poncho shelter Seth had created for them, yet she could see, suddenly and clearly, her path forward. She turned to Seth, the man she loved so dearly. To Cooper, the little boy she loved with all her heart. Her family.

Still hugging Cooper against his chest, Seth lifted his eyes to meet Cam's. "What?" he said. "What's that look about?"

Droplets rolled down Cam's forehead into her eyes. Her hair was dripping with rain, her clothes heavy and damp. She knew she looked frightful, mascara running down her cheeks, her ankle hurt like the dickens, yet she'd never been so happy. She tunneled her hands into his wet hair and smiled. "Seth Walker, will you marry me? As soon as possible?"

Surprised, his eyes grew shiny, and he leaned over to kiss her. "Just as soon as we get off this hill."

It wasn't much later before Cam heard someone call to them. She lifted the edge of the poncho to see Pastor Rick, red-faced and winded and soaked by rain, striding toward them, a big grin on his face. He held a water bottle in the palm of his hand like it was on a tray. "Did someone call for room service?"

~⌇~

The storm had passed over Three Sisters Island, leaving behind an innocent blue sky and white puffy clouds. Rick and the missing trio were safely back at Moose Manor, soaked to the skin. Maddie created an ice pack for Cam's ankle as Peg hunted through kitchen cupboards for a bottle of aspirin. Dad got a fire going in the living room to warm them up and dry them off, while Blaine dashed upstairs to grab dry clothes. Seth carried Cam to a chair near the fire. Maddie put a pillow under her swollen ankle and arranged the ice pack around it.

"I don't know how you were able to get down that hill with this ankle," Maddie said.

"Two big men and a brave little boy," Cam said. "They helped."

"Pastor Rick and Dad took turns carrying her down most of it," Cooper said.

"I'll bet." Something snagged in Maddie's mind. "Cooper, what did you just say?"

"I said that Pastor Rick and Dad took turns carrying Mom down the hill."

"Dad?"

Cooper poked his glasses on the bridge of his nose. "Seth is my dad."

Maddie looked at Seth, then Cam, and back to Cooper. "How did you know?"

Cooper turned to the stairs. Blaine was coming down them with her arms full of dry clothes. She froze, pivoted on her heels to turn around, and headed back upstairs.

Cam saw. "Blaine! It's okay. Come on down."

Blaine stopped, pivoted again, then slowly came down the rest of the stairs, arms full of dry clothes, face full of guilt. "I just thought Cooper needed to know."

"He did need to know," Seth said. "You were right. We should have listened to you."

Blaine's eyes went wide with shock. "Woohoo!" She tossed the clothes into the air. "Man. Those are words I don't hear very often around here." She bent down and picked up the clothes in one fell swoop, and tossed a T-shirt of Dad's to Rick. "Dude, your face is as bright red as this T-shirt."

Strangely red. Rick was still breathing hard and fast, as if he'd run a long distance. "I'm fine," he said, waving off Maddie's look of concern. "Just overheated. I need a little fresh air." He walked over to the front door and opened it.

"I just can't believe you're all here, safe and sound," Peg said. "Hoo-ey, I think this morning took a few years off my life."

"And how many years would that be?" Dad said.

"Never you mind, Paul Grayson." Peg wagged a scolding finger at him.

"I wasn't scared," Cooper said. "I really wasn't. Not even when the lighthouse blew up. Mom and Dad were with me."

Seth came up and crouched in front of Cooper, tugging him into a hug. "You don't have to be scared of anything, Coops. We're together, and nothing is going to separate us." He looked up. "Hey, where is that pastor? Let's see how soon he can get us married."

They turned around to discover Rick, sitting on the threshold, forehead resting on his knees.

Maddie dove down on her hands and knees. "What is it? What's wrong? Your heart?" She could almost hear it racing.

"Maddie," he said, gasping for breath, not able to lift his face, "would you mind taking me to a hospital?"

Twenty-Three

Two hours had passed. Maddie sat in the Mount Desert Island hospital emergency waiting room, thumbing through old magazines, trying to distract herself from anxious thoughts. "He has a condition," she had told the nurse who sat at the front desk. "Something called HCM."

She would never forget the grave look in that nurse's eyes, how quickly she moved to get Rick seen by a doctor. It gave Maddie a chill because she understood how serious his heart condition was in a way she had known intuitively. Just as Rick was wheeled away, she squeezed his hand and gave him a shaky smile. He had improved on the long trip over to Mount Desert Island; his heart had stopped racing, and he could talk. He even tried to get her to turn around, to skip the trip to the hospital, but she refused. His color was still a pasty white, but he was definitely better than he was at Moose Manor. He was better, she reminded herself for the hundredth time. He was alive.

But for how long? When would be the next time? A sound filled her ears, like the sound of a wind in the tops of trees. The howl of the rushing wind grew louder. *No, no, no. Not a panic attack. Please no.*

Maddie ducked her head between her knees. Breathe in, breathe out. Six times? Or seven. She couldn't even remember.

Maddie replayed, over and over, the conversation she'd had with Rick about anxiety. She was anxious about pretty much everything. She always had been. She kept it under better control than she used to, but it was still there, nipping at her heels. It took an enormous amount of effort to keep the lid on worry. Breathing techniques, reorienting thoughts, exercising regularly, eating and sleeping well. But after that day with Rick, she'd realized that all the tools she'd gained during this last year were about dealing with the symptoms, not the source.

If she played out all her worries, ran them to their bitter end, they eventually led her to a fear of death. Long before her mother died, she'd felt a perpetual alarm, imagined worst-case scenarios, prepared for every imminent disaster. She wanted to keep everyone safe, all the time. After the fire, she realized she couldn't keep anyone safe. Life was too full of risks. Her anxieties took over her life.

She lifted her head. So if Rick's theory was right, then the opposite must be true. If you had no fear of death, then that vague dread that constantly hovered—it could be vanquished. Not just managed or discounted, but eliminated. Overcome. Conquered. Defeated.

Maddie could sense she was at a spiritual fork in the road. Same ultimate destination, but two different paths to get there. One road was familiar terrain, the other much less so.

"Madison Grayson?"

Maddie reared upright to see a young doctor stand in front of her, a dark-haired beauty, with a concerned look on her face.

"Are you all right?" The doctor spoke in a gorgeous French accent.

Maddie stood and pushed her hair behind her ears. "Um, thank you, yes. Perfectly fine." Perfectly certifiable.

"I'm Dr. Turner. Richard O'Shea said you were waiting for him."

"Is he all right?"

"Yes. His heart has settled down. For now."

"Until the next time, you mean." When the doctor's eyebrows lifted in question, Maddie added, "I know about his heart—about his condition. Isn't there something that can be done for him?"

Dr. Turner motioned to Maddie to sit down and sat beside her. "There is a device, an implantable cardioverter defibrillator. It's a pager-sized device implanted in the chest like a pacemaker that continuously monitors the heartbeat. If a life-threatening arrhythmia occurs, the ICD delivers electrical shocks to restore a normal heart rhythm."

"Oh, thank God." *Thank God, thank God, thank God.*

"He's refused it."

Blast! Blast, blast, blast. "Could this device save his life?"

"It could. And a lifestyle change could help. But when a person has this kind of heart condition, and that person is driven to . . . how does one say . . . ?"

"Heart-pounding adventures."

"Exactly. There is just no guarantee."

"But this device . . . it's better than not having it, right?"

"Yes."

"I'll talk him into it," Maddie said, striving to project a confidence she didn't feel.

⁓◯

Blaine stood on the thin strand of beach near Boon Dock, peering at her iPhone to find the place with the most bars, the golden spot for cell phone reception. She stopped, tapped Artie's number, and waited.

One ring and he picked up. "Blaine? Are you all right?"

She smiled. She loved that Artie would drop whatever he was doing to answer her call, anytime, anywhere. "I'm fine. I just had to talk to you. Are you busy?" Of course he was. He worked as an EMT on Saturdays to help pay off medical school bills. Maybe she shouldn't have bothered him. This could have waited until Thursday's call.

"Someone can cover me for a few minutes. What's wrong?"

"Just a *crazy* day. A pivotal day. This morning, a big whopper storm came through the island and the lighthouse got hit by lightning and caught on fire and Cam and Seth and Cooper got stranded, but Rick rescued them, and Cam has a hurt ankle but Cooper found out that Seth is his real dad and now they're talking about finally setting a wedding date and then Rick nearly passed out. You should've seen his face. Lobster red. Maddie took him to the hospital."

Silence, as Artie took it all in. "So is Rick going to be all right?"

"Yes. Maddie called to say they're on their way home."

"And you're okay?"

"I'm fine. Better than fine. Artie, now that there'll be a wedding, I can leave for Paris." She smiled, so pleased with this turn of events. "That's the reason I'm calling. What would you think of meeting me in Europe sometime this next year?"

"You're kidding, right?"

"Dead serious."

A long pause. "Blaine, I'm in med school. I have student loans that I'll be paying off until I'm . . . so old that I can't even think about it. Just thinking about those loans freaks me out. There's no way I can just flitter off to Europe like you."

Flitter? *Flitter!* "I thought . . . maybe you could come over your Christmas break. I could help pay for the airfare." Not sure how she could do it, but she'd figure something out.

"You can never see a day ahead, can you?"

"Man, Artie. You sound just like my dad. We've got our whole life ahead to pay off loans and stuff."

"Don't you get it, Blaine? I'm working toward my future. You . . . you're . . ."

"I'm *what*?"

"Going sideways. Maybe even slipping backward."

Artie had hit his mark. Wounded, Blaine felt chastised, misunderstood, swamped by remorse. She thought he'd be pleased by her invitation. Instead, he sounded angry. She didn't know what else to say.

Neither did Artie. "I better get back to work. Let's talk on Thursday, regular time. Okay?"

Before she could answer, he'd hung up.

⟿

What a day. The sky was now clear and blue, emptied even of clouds. The sea had a smooth, glassy surface. The lighthouse was badly damaged, if not destroyed, Cooper finally knew who his dad was, Cam and Seth were planning to get married as soon as possible . . . and Rick nearly died.

On the ferry ride back to Three Sisters Island, Maddie glanced at Rick. His eyes were closed, but she didn't think he was sleeping.

"You almost died."

His eyes popped open. "I didn't die."

"You could have died."

"But I didn't die."

"But you could have." She sighed. "Rick, today was a warning." In so many ways.

He shifted on the seat to face her, before letting a grin tip the corner of his mouth. "I'm not worried. Why should you be?"

Why should she care? The truth struck her, hard, like an uppercut. *Because I'm worried that if I let myself go, I'll fall in love with you all over again. Because maybe I never did stop loving you. And it terrifies me to think I might lose you again. That's why I should be worried.*

Those thoughts she kept to herself. "I'm not worried for myself, of course," she quickly qualified, "but I do care about the church. You are a pastor with a church to lead. A church that depends on you."

"The church belongs to God. If something were to happen to me, another pastor will step forward."

"Maybe you're not quite so easy to replace." *Not at all.* "Look, Rick, there is something you can do. An implant to regulate your heart rate. Something called an ICD."

"Maddie, I told you that I'm at peace with this."

"Maybe so, maybe not."

"What's that supposed to mean?"

"If there's something you can do to help prevent the risk of a heart attack, then maybe you should do it. Or . . ."

"Or what?"

"Maybe you should ask yourself why you won't consider it."

"Because," he said, in a patient, professorial tone, "I'm at peace with knowing that my life is in God's hands."

"Right. Or maybe you're afraid of the procedure."

He scoffed.

"You passed out in high school biology."

"What? When?"

"When we had to prick our fingers," she said, "to draw blood for a microscope slide."

"Oh, right. I'd forgotten." A grin started a slow spread across Rick's face. "You have a shockingly good memory."

Only when something concerned Ricky O'Shea. "As I recall, it was a pretty dramatic moment for Mr. Obitt's biology class."

The sound of exuberant gulls drifted around them. The ferry was slowing, preparing to pull into Boon Dock.

He studied her for a long while. "You really think I'm afraid of the procedure?"

"The things most protested against are often the very things that need looking at. As your therapist, I encourage you to face your fear. With a smile." She said it with a chuckle, a little forced. When he didn't respond with a smile, she suspected that she might be on to something.

The line of his mouth took on a grim cast and he kept his eyes fixed on the tops of his muddy boots. Neither of them said a word for several seconds.

"Maddie, am I doing this for you? Because I'd do any—" He stopped. His gaze met hers with such unspoken emotion that her skin pebbled with tingly goose bumps.

Tears pooled and she had to look away. "If you won't do it for yourself, then do it for me." She dismissed the tears with a swipe of her hands across her eyes.

He sat up. "If I agree to have this ICD, then I want you to do something for me. Go skydiving with me." As her eyes widened and her jaw dropped open, he quickly added, "We'll go tandem. Nothing to worry about." He snapped his fingers. "Piece of cake."

No. No way. No way could she jump out of an airplane. No way on earth.

His eyes danced with amusement. "I'll trade you one fear for one fear." He held out his hand for a shake. "Do we have a deal?"

Drat. Drat drat drat drat drat. She released an edgy breath. "Only if the ICD comes first. I don't want you dying on me halfway down."

"Then," he said with a big grin that revealed both dimples, "I believe we have a deal."

Twenty-Four

EACH EVENING THE WEEK BEFORE THE WEDDING, Blaine stayed at the Lunch Counter after closing time and baked. Peg was her taster, because she still had no palate. It took three tries for Blaine to achieve the perfect genoise sponge—light, moist, not too closed a structure—that she wanted for the cake layers. Then came the raspberry jam. Two tries. Almond filling—four tries. Buttercream icing—only one try. That, Blaine could make blindfolded.

Cam promised everyone it was going to be a minimalist wedding. As simple as possible. Pastor Rick would preside. Cooper was Seth's best man, Maddie and Blaine were the bridesmaids. Cam went through their closets and picked out dresses they already had. Even for herself. Blaine didn't particularly care for the dresses her sister had picked out, but she was so happy that a date had been chosen for the wedding that she pasted on a smile, nodded, and agreed to everything Cam wanted.

But not when it came to the cake. Cam tried to give her suggestions and Blaine wouldn't hear of it. Seth had insisted that the only food at the reception following the wedding would be Blaine's cake. He knew of the Grayson girls' tendency to go overboard in all things, and he wouldn't budge. Keep it simple, he said. Just cake.

So if only cake was to be served, Blaine told Cam to leave this one thing entirely up to her. Just this one thing.

The weather was warm and humid all week long, sticky damp air, so Blaine waited until the morning of the wedding to construct the cake, ice it, and then finish with piping. Early Saturday morning, she drove to the Lunch Counter to collect all the cake's components and take them back to Moose Manor to assemble it. As she carefully stacked the cake layers in a box, each one tightly bound in plastic wrap to keep it fresh, Peg came in to say good morning.

She had her hair in giant pink rollers. "I don't know what I'm more excited about—seeing Seth and Cam get married or eating a big piece of that cake."

"I think it's going to be my best cake yet."

"Honey, I know it is. All the love you put into it—that's what's going to make it the best one yet. That's what makes your food so special."

Blaine stilled. How had she missed that?

Cooking and baking were expressions of love for Blaine. It had always been that way for her, taught so by her mother . . . until this last year at culinary school. She'd gotten so caught up with technique, with impressing others, with being the best . . . she'd forgotten why she cooked. Love was missing from her food.

Peg was peering at the coffee-making cheat sheet index cards that Blaine had thumbtacked above the coffeepot. "I'm going to miss you, Peg. Most of all, more than anyone, I'm going to miss *you*."

Slowly, Peg turned to her, eyes shiny. "You're still going to leave us?"

Blaine nodded. "I need to do this. I can't explain why, I just know I need to go. To find myself."

Peg enveloped Blaine in a hug, squeezing her tightly. Her pink rollers jabbed Blaine's forehead. "Honey, you have no idea what kind of hole you're leaving here for me."

Blaine thought she might.

Peg released her to wipe away tears. "Not to mention how many complaints I'm going to get about my coffee." She leaned closer to the card. "Now, where was I? One tablespoon of coffee for each cup. Seems so simple."

It was. It really was. And yet, and yet . . . Peg still made terrible coffee.

Blaine finished stacking all the pieces of the cake into two boxes, took them out to the car, and came back in to help Peg make the morning coffee. One last time.

～⌒◯

On Monday morning, Maddie was at her desk in her little basement office, reviewing information in a textbook. She paused for a moment, reflecting back on Cam and Seth's beautiful wedding. It was flawless. Even the weather had improved, just in time.

Midday on Saturday, a rainstorm had blown through and swept away that awful heavy humidity, leaving blue skies and crisp fresh air for the late-afternoon ceremony that took place on the large grass lawn in front of Moose Manor.

Cam looked radiant, shockingly calm, even serene, as Dad helped her out the front door and down the porch steps on her crutches. She didn't even mind that all the campers in the cabins came out to watch. Or that a small brown duck appeared out of nowhere and walked behind her like a bridesmaid.

And Seth, with Cooper beside him as best man, couldn't stop beaming. He looked like a man who'd just won the lottery.

Maddie wondered how Seth and Cam were enjoying their honeymoon on Cape Cod, considering it included an eight-year-old boy. And considering Cam was still nursing a badly sprained ankle and hobbled around on crutches.

Then her thoughts drifted to Rick's upcoming surgery in August and her happiness faded away. He had to go back and forth to MDI hospital for a number of tests: ECG, an echocardiogram, and now he was wearing the Holter monitor for forty-eight hours. He never complained, he never went back on agreeing to get the implant. She knew she had pressured him into it, but she felt strongly it was the right thing to do. She still did, but worry ate at her.

Yes, Lord? She squeezed her eyes shut and leaned back in her chair. *A word of reassurance, please?*

She waited, listening. Nothing came.

Her eyes opened with a sigh. She noticed a piece of paper in the back of her textbook and tugged on it. She remembered writing it down during a lecture in graduate school. It was an ancient chant used to meditate on, to reorient one's mind toward the Lord's presence.

All shall be well, all shall be well, all manner of thing shall be well.

St. Julian of Norwich

She repeated it aloud, once, then twice, receiving a sense of calm. Of reassurance. Her eyes lifted to the ceiling. *Thank you.*

The door opened and Blaine burst in. "Maddie, I have an announcement."

"Blaine! You can't just come bursting into my office. I might have been in the middle of a therapy session."

"Nobody's here."

Maddie frowned. True enough. Blaine stood wearing a sleeveless lime-green pique cotton sundress with a chunky navy-blue necklace. She'd knotted her hair at the base of her neck in a messy bun. The look was pure Blaine. Casual, self-assured, stylish without trying. Maddie grinned, feeling a surge of joyful well-being. Her little sister was back to herself. "What's up?"

"Two things I wanted to tell you, face-to-face. First, I just mailed a letter to the culinary school supervisor, explaining the unfortunate"—with her fingers, Blaine made bunny ears in the air—"situation."

Maddie leaned back in her chair. "How does that feel?"

"Pretty darn good." She grinned. "When I licked the envelope to seal the letter, I think . . . not sure . . . but I think I tasted the glue." Her smile spread.

Maddie held back from saying "I told you so." She didn't need the validation. "I'm impressed, Blaine. I know this fall won't be easy for you."

"Well, easier than you might think." She held up two fingers. "Because of the second thing. On Wednesday, I'm leaving for Paris."

Maddie's joyful feeling faded. "You're really not going back to culinary school?"

"Not yet. Next year, maybe." She tipped her head back and forth. "I think. Pretty sure." She frowned. "Don't look at me like that. I will be back. I just need time. I need to figure out who I am."

Maddie used that small piece of paper with St. Julian of Norwich's chant to mark her place in her textbook and closed it, noticing the chapter title: Avoidant Personality Disorder.

⁓◌

Paul was in the boathouse, rubbing the underbelly of a kayak with a rag. He looked up when he saw Blaine standing at the open door. She caught his breath, looking so lovely, limned by the sunlight. He wished Corinna could see how their youngest had matured. But maybe she could. Peg said that what separated us from those we loved who were in Heaven was a curtain, not a wall. He liked that thought.

"Hey, Dad. Whatcha doing?"

"Those Morgans. They dragged this new kayak along the shore and scraped it up. Next year, they are banned from kayaks."

"Pretty sure you can't ban a guest from using the equipment they've paid to use."

"I can. I will. I'm starting a list. The Sweetmans are on the top. Morgans right behind them. McLeans too. And then the Witherspoons."

"Man oh man," she said, walking past him to peer out the back end of the boathouse, "you sound like a grouchy old innkeeper."

Argh. She was right. He did sound like a grouchy old innkeeper. He could hear Peg's voice chiding him: *Do you realize how blessed you are to be here? To wake up to the scent of ocean air? Or the unique smell of low tide along the beach below Moose Manor. The bright stars at night, so far from the mainland that they seem to glow.* There were so many things to appreciate about living on Three Sisters Island.

Paul knew he was blessed to be here. He loved this place. He'd been in a slump after the excitement of a new beginning had worn off, but that didn't mean Camp Kicking Moose wasn't the best place in the world to be. Especially in the summer, even with annoyingly high-maintenance campers. They weren't all annoying campers. Most, he had to admit, were good people. There were just a few who always made life a little harder than it needed to be. *That's life*, he could imagine Peg saying, pigtails bouncing under her brightly colored headband. *That's just life.*

Suddenly Paul felt a shift. He was the one who bought Camp

275

Kicking Moose in the first place. Reluctantly, his daughters joined him. Then they caught his vision. But starting something was one thing, living its reality was another. The whole endeavor had been harder, taken much longer, than he'd expected. It took courage to see things through, and he'd let his courage fade off screen.

Good grief . . . how many times had he started to ask Peg to go on a hike with him, only to allow himself to be derailed? It was time he stepped up to the plate. Fully embraced this new life of his—the good, the bad, and everything in between. He stood straighter, feeling lighter, more purposeful than he had in months.

Blaine spun around. Paul looked up to see her take a deep breath, squeeze her hands together, and he braced himself. He sensed an announcement was coming.

"Dad, I know you don't want me to take a year off from culinary school, but I've made my decision. I'm going. I've bought my airline ticket to Paris. I'm leaving on Wednesday."

Stay calm. Stay calm. He couldn't fault her for making her own decisions. A year ago, she couldn't even make a decision about a college major. Maybe this was progress. Not his choice, but progress nevertheless. "Must have had some pretty good tips at the Lunch Counter."

"Noooo, not really. I put it on my credit card. I'll pay it off little by little."

Paul's stomach clenched. By the time Blaine paid it off, she could have bought four airplane tickets to Paris. He blamed himself for Blaine's lack of fiscal responsibility. He had traveled too much during her childhood. Missed too many opportunities to teach her about life. He tried to not overreact, though inside he was steaming. "And you plan to stay . . . where exactly?"

"There's something called couch surfing. All my friends do it."

"Is it what it sounds like? You sleep on strangers' couches for a fee?"

"Yeah. Just a small fee. It's a great deal, Dad. Totally safe."

You bet. He figured he wouldn't sleep at all until she returned home. "Blaine . . . I'm going to go ahead and start the ball rolling on the remodel of Moose Manor."

She gasped and her eyes went wide. "You would redo the kitchen without me? The *kitchen*?" Her voice rose an octave. "Without me?!"

"I don't want to do this without you. But I need to keep the camp moving forward." His voice was fading; he should stop now but he needed to say more. "I don't want to just stand still. Waiting."

She dropped her chin, slowly walked past him to the open door, then spun around. "Dad, I promise I'll be back."

And then she disappeared from view.

A rational thought broke through and brought Paul a thin ray of cheer. Knowing Blaine, she'd give Paris a few weeks, lose interest, and then come home. Maybe she'd even be back in time for the fall semester of culinary school.

And then, around the door, her beautiful face reappeared. "One more thing. I forgot to tell you that Artie's dad is coming to town next weekend. Artie says he's got the hots for Peg." She wrinkled her nose. "Kinda gross to think of old men having the hots."

And *then* she disappeared.

A moment later, he heard a quack and looked over to see the duck in the open door where Blaine had just been. It waddled toward him and sat down about a yard away, staring at him with its beady, needy eyes. Good grief. Most Maine men had a loyal black Labrador retriever by their side. He had a duck.

Elizabeth Turner came in for what turned out to be her last session. "Have you heard of a place on this island called Camp Kicking Moose?"

Maddie barely suppressed a smile. "In fact, I have."

"My son and daughter-in-law expressed some interest in taking a family trip there." Shyly, she added, "They invited me to join them." She lifted a finger in the air. "Separate cabins, of course. I do like my privacy."

Maddie grinned. "I think that sounds like a wonderful idea."

"I do too. But unfortunately, there's a waiting list for the camp. And my son and daughter-in-law only have one week they can take off. They're both physicians, you know."

"Yes, I believe you've mentioned that." Maddie closed the file. "Elizabeth, you are to be commended for repairing the relationship you've had with them. I know it's not easy to be the one to start the healing process, but you've done it. And I'm confident that you'll keep on doing it."

Elizabeth tried to hide her pleased look, but not very successfully. "I had a good guide." She picked up her cell phone, the one Maddie helped her pick out. "And I have put you on speed dial, just in case." She chuckled. "I know how to do it now."

As Elizabeth gathered her myriad of things and prepared to leave, Maddie said, "Let me see if I can talk to the camp's owner and get your family moved up on the waiting list."

Elizabeth's eyes widened in surprise. "You can do that?"

"I can try." Plus, if she could make it happen without it seeming too creepy, she might try to play matchmaker and introduce Elizabeth to her dad. She might be her dad's type. But then, did her dad have a type, besides her mom? She didn't know.

Elizabeth reached out and gave Maddie an awkward hug, then hurried out the door.

It was August. A month had passed since Cam and Seth's wedding. They'd come back from their honeymoon to Cape Cod with T-shirt souvenirs for everyone, including Peg. Seth had moved into Moose Manor, which made Dad happy. He said the family had always been a little too lopsided in favor of women, and he welcomed a son-in-law to balance things out.

There was some truth to that, but Maddie knew what her dad really wanted was a noisy household to crowd out missing Blaine so much. They'd heard from Blaine now and then, whenever she could find an internet café and place a call through a computer. It was a crackling, fuzzy connection, but at least they heard her voice. Dad always seemed especially quiet after Blaine's calls, but it was clear that she was enjoying this time of finding herself. Maddie had been home alone when Blaine last called, and she started to ask if her palate had returned—because that, she felt, would be the sign that Blaine was truly finding herself. But the connection failed before she could finish the question and maybe it was just as well. Maybe she shouldn't ask.

Maddie was pleased that Cam decided to hold off on the energy project until school started. Cam, Seth, and Cooper had plans to spend the rest of the summer having fun together as a family— camping, hiking, canoeing, kayaking, fishing, swimming at the little cove below Moose Manor. Cooper was in heaven. Maddie had never seen him like this—his whole self so settled. No one had listened to Blaine, but she had been absolutely right. Cooper had been in limbo too long. He needed Cam and Seth together. He needed them to become a family.

Today was the day Rick would have the procedure to implant the ICD in his heart to regulate its beating. The doctor had determined that Rick was a candidate for a newer type of ICD. It would be implanted at the side of his chest under the armpit—less invasive than those attached to the heart. Maddie had offered to stay with him, especially when she found out that he'd need to spend at least one night in MDI hospital. Tomorrow, the ICD would be checked. If all went well—and the entire church was praying for a smooth procedure—they'd be back on Three Sisters Island tomorrow evening. Oh, she hoped so. She felt very responsible. Rick wouldn't be undergoing this surgical procedure if she hadn't insisted.

The nurse came in and gave him a sedative. "This will help relax you. The orderly will be in soon to take you to the operating room."

As soon as the nurse left them alone, Rick said, "Goggles. And sneakers."

Maddie looked at him. Even on a gurney with a tube attached to his arm, even in a hospital nightgown, he looked utterly masculine. Maddeningly calm. "What in the world are you talking about?"

"You'll need to wear sneakers for the skydive. No high heels. No flip-flops. And you'll wear a jumpsuit and goggles."

Oh, *that*. "Why goggles?"

"To protect your eyes from the wind. We're falling at one hundred twenty miles an hour."

The very thought sent her anxiety rising, fast and jagged. *Cannot . . . think . . . about this . . . now.*

"When the plane reaches about thirteen thousand five hundred feet, then we start our freefall. That'll last about sixty seconds."

She peered at the IV. The nurse must have forgotten the sedative.

"I'll deploy the canopy around five to six thousand feet, then we'll have five or six minutes of flying under the canopy." He dropped back on the pillow and closed his eyes. The first sign she'd seen that the sedative was working. "Exhilarating. Best feeling in the world."

"Why do we have to talk about this now?"

"Helps me relax."

"Helps trigger a full-blown panic attack in me."

He opened his eyes and grinned.

All morning, Maddie had felt needled by how she had never come clean with him about the love/loathe misunderstanding. She took a deep breath, deciding it was a good time to go with the truth. "Rick, I have a confession to make. I didn't say I loathed you."

He tilted his head and stared at her in confusion. "What are you talking about?" Uh oh, the sedative was kicking in. His speech was a little slurry.

"The night of Senior Prom. After . . . well . . . you know. I didn't say I'd always loathed you. You misheard me. I didn't say loathed."

He squinted, like he hadn't heard her clearly. "Then, what did you say?"

"I said . . . I *loved* you."

His forehead furrowed in total confusion. "And now?"

She brushed his head gently with her fingertips. "Still do."

He tried to say something but gave up and laid his head back on the pillow. His eyes drifted shut just as the orderly arrived to wheel him away.

Maddie stood in the hallway and watched him go. She felt better having told him the truth before he underwent surgery. But she also felt a pinch of relief that he wouldn't remember a word of what she'd confessed.

"Maddie."

She swiveled around to find Maeve O'Shea standing a few yards away from her. "You came!"

"Only because you let me know about it. Rick never said a word."

Maddie had sneaked a peek at Rick's contacts to get his mother's phone number and give her a call. She risked his indignation but felt it was still better to let his mother know.

"When I listened to your voicemail, I hopped in my Buick and started driving up 95." Mrs. O'Shea beckoned her into an embrace that brought with it peace, somehow settling Maddie's spirit. She wondered if her mother had felt the same way in Mrs. O'Shea's presence too. Probably so.

Mrs. O'Shea released her and stepped back, hands holding on to her upper arms, clucking and crooning. "Look at you, Maddie Grayson. All grown up. Such a lovely young woman."

Mrs. O'Shea looked a little older than the last time Maddie had seen her, a little grayer, a few more wrinkles, but so much the same. Calm and comforting.

"Let's sit down and catch up while we wait until Rick's out of surgery."

"You missed Rick by just a moment. I wish he could've known you were here."

"Actually, I was here. Since he didn't tell me he was having this procedure, I just thought it would be best if I waited until he woke up before he saw me. He thinks I worry too much."

"Me too. I mean, he thinks I worry too much too."

They sat down in the waiting room and faced each other. Mrs. O'Shea had a thoughtful look on her face as she leaned back in her chair. "I'm glad you're here today."

With a shaky sigh, Maddie turned to her. "Mrs. O'Shea, you should know that I'm the one who pushed Rick to have this surgery. I'm not sure how you feel about it. I know there are risks."

"All of life is a risk." Mrs. O'Shea laid a soft and wrinkly hand against Maddie's cheek. "Ricky's lucky to have you."

No. No, Maddie was the lucky one.

"Want to know a secret?" Mrs. O'Shea's brown eyes, so like her son's, brimmed with good humor. "Do you know what my boy predicted about you after the first day of kindergarten?"

"I can guess." Maddie smiled. "Probably that I would be a future meter maid."

She threw back her head and laughed. "He said that one day he was going to marry you."

Maddie coughed, stunned. "But he spent most of kindergarten throwing crayons at me!".

"That boy." Mrs. O'Shea rolled her eyes heavenward. "He told me that you were the only girl in school who stood up to him." She squeezed her arms. "I can see that you still do." Then her expression turned serious. "Ricky doesn't tell me much, Maddie. I don't even know if you're dating each other. But I do know that heart condition of his is serious business. Ricky's just like his father, in every way imaginable. My husband and I didn't have the long marriage I had envisioned for us. Even still, a few years with John O'Shea beat out a lifetime with any other man." She patted Maddie's knee. "I just wanted to tell you that, woman to woman." Her eyes locked with Maddie's. "And never forget this . . . you're stronger than you think."

Was she? She hoped so. She wanted to be.

Still, it brought Maddie deep, deep pleasure to hear Mrs. O'Shea's thoughts, to sit with her during Rick's surgery. Hoping, praying, waiting. Trusting. This summer, it seemed as if God kept whispering into her heart this fundamental truth about his sovereignty. *We live on borrowed time. Our lives belong to God.* It was worth repeating several times a day until it went bone-deep, into her very marrow.

After a few hours, Dr. Turner came to find them, still in her surgical scrubs. A smile wreathed her face.

Twenty-Five

AUGUST GAVE WAY TO SEPTEMBER. Labor Day weekend had come and gone. Days were growing noticeably shorter, there was a chill to the morning air, leaves were already changing color. And Camp Kicking Moose was wrapping up its second season. Bob Lotosky, came over from Aroostook County to help the Grayson family close up the camp for the winter. Rugs in cabins were rolled up and hauled over to the carriage house. Bed linens were washed and stored in an extra bedroom in Moose Manor. The kayaks and canoes were cleaned and hung from the rafters in the boathouse.

Today, Paul walked from cabin to cabin, checking to make sure windows were shut tight, nothing forgotten. He felt pretty pleased with how things had turned out this year. Better than how the summer had started. He felt he was finally getting the swing of this camp business. And next summer, if all went according to plan, Moose Manor would be remodeled. Campers could eat three full meals a day in the formal dining room. Aside from a successful remodel, all he needed was his missing youngest daughter to return as the camp chef. If Blaine didn't come back by next May, he would find someone else. He would prefer Blaine to be in that role, but he also preferred that she finish culinary school and stay on track . . . and look where that was. Completely derailed. If he waited for Blaine to finish something she started, he might be waiting for a very long time.

As he closed the door to the Our Tern cabin, he saw Peg's battered green minivan rumble up the long driveway and walked over to greet her.

"Can't stay," she said, leaning out the car window, though she turned off the car's engine. "Captain Ed is watching the diner for me and that's always a worry. Last time he forgot to charge everyone." She handed him the bird book, open to a page. "Is that your pet duck?"

Paul looked closely at the picture. "Not sure. Might be." As if it was summoned, the duck emerged from underneath a hydrangea bush that lined the manor and waddled toward them.

Peg squinted to assess the duck, who stared back at her. "Well, I'll be. Paul, that duck of yours is a Harlequin duck. A juvenile female." Carefully she enunciated, "A threatened species."

"So I can't have Captain Ed shoot it?"

"If you did, you'd both end up in the slammer. If that duck is happy here at Moose Manor, you leave it be."

Paul looked down at the duck, standing right beside him, preening her feathers. "Well then, if I have to have a duck as a pet, then I'm going to give it a name. Little Peg Legg."

Peg turned the ignition on her minivan and it roared to life. "Do that and you'll be banned for life from the Lunch Counter."

She drove off with a wave, and Paul and his duck watched her go.

⁓

The first frost came over Three Sisters Island in late September, ushering in the most beautiful season there. The whole island took on an autumnal array of color: brilliant red, orange, and gold leaves clung to trees, reflecting like a mirror in the harbor. In the sky, flocks of migrating birds filled the air. In the ocean, pods of whales swam south. All seemed quiet, peaceful. All but Maddie Grayson.

It was with great difficulty that Maddie sat in a small airplane, gripping the edge of the straddle bench for dear life. Rick was directly behind her, the epitome of calmness. She'd insisted he check the harness three times. The canopy and the reserve canopy, she asked to be checked five times.

"It's going to be great, Maddie," he shouted as they sat together, waiting until the plane reached the right altitude. "You're going to love it."

No. No, she wouldn't. She had researched skydiving accidents and printed out a page of warnings: skydiving was high-risk and ultra-hazardous. "Look at that," she said, pointing out the cautionary notes from the page. "It says it's not for everyone. For example, if you have poor health."

"Ah, but your health is excellent."

"Very fragile mental health, though. Getting worse by the minute."

Rick laughed, as if she were joking.

"Rick, don't make me do this." The whine in her voice, even to her own ears, made her sound like an annoying six-year-old girl.

"Oh no. No you don't. We had a deal. A deal is a deal. I have a scar under my arm to prove I held up my end."

She spun around to face him at those half-gentle, half-harsh words. The look in his eyes was a mixture of amusement and encouragement. And something else that she couldn't quite pinpoint. Something sweet.

He patted her shoulder. "Tandem jumping isn't so terribly dangerous."

"It's that *terribly* part . . . that's what worries me."

But he only laughed.

Rick had a friend with a small plane who was starting a skydiving business. He offered to take them up for the cost of fuel and let them use his equipment, as long as they promised to sign waivers. Maddie had wanted to read the waiver thoroughly before signing, especially the part about "in event of death" . . . but Rick wouldn't let her. "Just a precaution. Legal mumbo jumbo. Trust me, Maddie." He gave her the pen and pointed to the numerous places where her signature belonged. Her hand trembled as she signed.

Rick spent a lot of time going through all the instructions with Maddie while still on the ground. So much so that his pilot friend asked if he'd give up the ministry and come to work for him as a skydiver instructor.

"Can't," Rick said. "Too many souls to save."

The pilot friend pointed out that he could give short sermons just before people jumped. "You'd have their attention," he said. "Imagine talking about Heaven or Hell right as someone is ready to jump out of the airplane. Mention a few skydives gone wrong."

Rick laughed and said that shed a different light on things, and that he'd consider it.

Skydives gone wrong? Maddie felt as if she might be sick, right then and there. Better still, maybe she could just pass out. Remain unconscious for the whole thing. Rick might not ever know she had fainted until they landed.

When they reached a certain altitude, the pilot and his copilot— also an enthusiastic skydiver—gave them a five-minute warning. At this point, Rick scooted closer behind Maddie. The copilot hooked together the four points of the harness that bound Maddie to Rick . . . and his canopy. And the reserve canopy. *Oh Lord, please hold those metal hooks tight. Don't let me go, Lord.*

"Remember," Rick said, "we can't talk during the freefall. But as soon as the chute is open, then we can talk."

Talk? She couldn't imagine what she had to say at that point that would sound even marginally intelligent. Scream? Now that sounded more likely. The thought of jumping out of this airplane sent her anxiety rising, sharp and fast. *No no no no no no. Why did I agree to this?*

When it was their turn to exit, Rick moved them toward the opening of the airplane. Maddie had to squeeze her eyes shut so she couldn't look down. "Maddie, let go of the doorframe. Let go." He peeled her hands off the doorframe. "Remember to arch your body to get in the freefall position. Belly forward, arms at an angle, face to earth."

Face to earth. What a haunting visual. A full-fledged panic attack was chasing her, gaining on her. "I can't do this." Her throat tightened with fear, her pulse thrummed fast in her ears. She was just about to die. And she'd done it to herself!

"I'd never let anything happen to you. You've got to trust me. I'm going to count to three. One, two, three . . ." And he wrapped his arms tightly around her and jerked them forward, out of the plane. TERRIFYING!

Wind blasted Maddie's face and a loud roaring sound rushed through her ears. Rick yanked her arms out at an angle. She kept her eyes squeezed tight, sure she was soon to crash to earth in a splat. *Please, Lord, a quick death. No lingering.*

Suddenly, Rick must have pulled the canopy because a shock caused them to lurch upward . . . upright . . . and then there was quiet. Her ears felt like they were going to explode and she was so light-headed she thought she might faint. Or throw up.

"Open your eyes, Maddie."

"D-do I have to?"

"I don't think you want to miss this."

She opened one eye, then another. "Oh . . . oh wow." The earth below her looked like a quilt—patches of green, lines of gray roads, blue ocean in the distance. From up above, it all seemed strangely small.

"Are you comfortable? Hooks not digging in?"

She nodded, her gaze scanning the jagged coastline, the crashing waves, the tall pine trees on the island. "All good." Was this how God saw his world? Such beauty. So precious.

"It might seem slow, but we're really going pretty fast."

"Smooth and steady, right?" she said, amazed they could carry on a conversation. She'd made him promise not to turn it into a roller-coaster ride, the kind he liked.

"Smooth and steady."

"How's your ticker?"

"Beating like a marching drum."

Just as she was starting to not feel quite so terrified, he told her they would need to prepare to land in two minutes. So soon?

"We'll glide in like an airplane. Feet in front, lift up legs." When she lifted her legs, he said, "Not quite yet. There's still time."

This was the most daring, most bold experience of her life . . . and she was surviving! So far, she hadn't died of fright. She didn't have a panic attack. Close, very close, but she kept it from blooming into a full-fledged one.

And she felt no fear. None! She was floating in the air, held up by a thin piece of fabric and strings, wrapped in Rick's arms, and for the first time in a very long time, she felt as if she had nothing to be afraid of. Relief spiraled through her. *Thank you, God!*

"Rick, if we don't die at the landing, let's do it again."

He burst out laughing. "It's a pretty awesome feeling, isn't it? Living without fear."

"It's . . . incredible." Exhilarating. Freeing. She never wanted to go back to that anxious state she had lived with since . . . well, she couldn't remember not feeling some level of anxiety. Not ever. She was born with it, an acute sense of imminent disaster.

"Before we land, I have a question to ask you. It's facing the biggest fear of all."

She turned her head slightly to hear him. She'd never have done this for anyone but him. Never could've experienced this kind of freedom. She'd do whatever crazy thing he asked of her.

"Maddie Grayson, will you marry me? Be my wife?"

Stunned silent, she could hardly breathe. They stayed that way for several long moments. When he finally spoke again, his words emerged ragged against her hair. "Okay, time to get ready. Lift your feet now and I'll guide us in for a gentle landing."

Still in shock from his question, she lifted her knees up.

And slowly, carefully, he guided them down to the ground. He took the shock of the landing in his legs and kept running forward as the canopy dropped behind him. As they came to a stop, her feet landed on solid ground. *Thank you, God. Thank you, thank you, thank you.*

And then there was quiet again. Rick held her tightly against his chest to whisper, "Maddie, I don't know how much time the Lord has planned for me, but I know I want to spend it with you. I've loved you since the first time you scolded me back in kindergarten. You make me a better man. Whether it's a long life or a short life or something in between," he said, so softly she almost didn't hear, "I want to spend it with you." He unclipped their harnesses and spun her around, looped his hands under her arms and pulled her toward him, until they were just a breath apart. Heartbeat to heartbeat. He stared down into her face for a long, burning moment, tenderness in his eyes, a stain of color spreading across his sharp cheekbones. "So what do you say, Maddie? Will you marry me?"

Her gaze traveled over Rick's familiar face with wonder. He loved her! He wanted to marry her. That dear face, that fearless, full-of-life personality. In a way she couldn't explain, she sensed that God had been readying her to love Rick wholeheartedly, without reservation, with a mature, lasting love.

But how could she say yes to him . . . knowing he might not have a long life? Knowing the pain of losing him? How could she live with him without expecting every day to be their last?

She knew Rick would flip that completely around: face that fear head-on. Go ahead and assume each day was their last. Cherish every moment as if it's soon to end. But how could she live with such a conflicting tension? Life with Rick was never going to let her feel safe.

How could she do this?

How could she not?

It came down to this: God was either in control of this life . . . or he wasn't. If he was, and she trusted that was true even if her feelings didn't always line up with her beliefs, then she *was* safe. Ultimately. Eternally. This story would end well.

"I think," Maddie said, tears springing to her eyes, "that whether it's a long life or a short life or something in between, I would rather say yes to loving you than miss a single moment."

He brought her hand to his mouth and kissed her palm. His smile was so tender, so full of love, it almost hurt to look at. "So is that," he said, his voice breaking a little over the words, "a yes?"

She swallowed, breathed. "It's a yes." She reached up onto her tiptoes. "Yes, yes, yes!" And she kissed Ricky O'Shea on the lips.

Blaine's
"You'll Never Buy
Store-Bought Granola Again"

Homemade Granola

4 cups	old-fashioned rolled oats
2 cups	sweetened, shredded coconut
2 cups	sliced almonds
½ cup	vegetable oil (makes the oats get crispy)
½ cup	honey (or maple syrup)

Preheat the oven to 300 degrees. Low and slow is best.

In a large bowl, combine oats, coconut, and almonds. Pour in vegetable oil and honey and stir until everything is coated. Spread mixture evenly onto a baking sheet (one with rimmed edges so no granola goes overboard while stirring). Parchment paper helps cleanup.

Bake, stirring occasionally with a spatula, until the mixture turns a nice, even golden brown, about 30–45 minutes, depending on your oven. Remember . . . low and slow.

Remove the granola from the oven and allow to cool, stirring occasionally so it doesn't stick to pan. Add in more fruits and nuts (to your liking or what's in your pantry). Store the cooked granola in an airtight container. Can be frozen in a sealed bag for 2–3 months. (Blaine makes big batches of granola on Sunday afternoons. She divides it into daily portions and freezes it. Take care that granola, especially if there's lots of dried fruits and nuts, gets to room temperature before it's served. She served frozen granola once to the Sweetmans and won't make that mistake again.)

Optional mix-ins:

(Blaine does a lot of variations)

1 cup	raisins
1 cup	small-diced dried apricots or dried peaches or dried apples
1 cup	small-diced dried figs or dates
1 cup	dried tart cherries and/or cranberries
1 cup	roasted, unsalted pecans, walnuts, cashews, or other favorite nuts (Blaine has tried sunflower seeds, macadamia nuts, pistachios, and pepitas)
2 teaspoons	orange zest
½ teaspoon	cinnamon

Blaine plans to start selling it to campers in a cellophane bag, tied with raffia, with a Camp Kicking Moose sticker, so they can take it home or give it to friends.

Discussion Questions

1. This novel has many subthemes, but one major one: to face your deepest fears. Pastor Rick said, "I think everyone has a Jonah moment. Everyone." He meant that we all have an imagined worst-case scenario, something that could take us down. Something we don't think we could ever recover from. Do you agree or disagree with Rick's remark? And why or why not?

2. Over the last year, Maddie did a lot of work to curb her anxiety (she preferred to call it *hypervigilance*). She developed techniques to control panic attacks so they could be nipped in the bud: breathing, prayer, and meditation. And they all helped with the symptoms . . . but not the source. What was at the core of Maddie's anxiety?

3. It's not hard to see why women were drawn to Rick O'Shea. His George Clooney-ish looks, his dynamic personality, strong and fearless. As Maddie noted, he was un-

apologetically masculine. But, aside from the fact that she was the one girl he could never impress, why do you think Rick was smitten with Maddie?

4. Rick told Maddie, "A boy can get his heart broken too." Doesn't it seem as if girls and their emotions claim all the attention? It's easy to minimize boys' feelings. How would this story have changed if Maddie had realized she had broken Rick's heart?

5. Blaine is a frustrating character. So talented, so full of potential. She gets *this* close to a finish line, then drops out of the race. Why? What do you think she's looking for? And why isn't she finding it? What does her missing palate represent? If you were in Blaine's shoes, what might "go missing" for you?

6. Name a few pivotal moments in the book when Blaine calls out, though no one listens to her. Why do you think Blaine sees her family's situations in a different light? And why do you think her family ignored her advice?

7. Cam's motto: If something is worth doing, it's worth overdoing. Her energy project for the island would provide multiple benefits for everyone on the island. It's easy to see how it became a priority to her. A passion. But at what cost?

8. Cooper is a funny, complicated, endearing little boy. Cam, as his adoptive mother, seems like a total mismatch to him. While Cooper and Cam might be extreme characters,

the mismatch of personalities in a family is not such an unusual situation. Cam felt defeated by their differences. But how was Cooper so good for her? And she for him?

9. Paul Grayson turned sixty. Normally decisive, he suddenly couldn't make a decision. He lost his enthusiasm for Camp Kicking Moose. What were some of the reasons behind Paul's sagging season? What advice would you give him?

10. *Say only what is necessary.* That was the advice Paul's speech therapist gave him to avoid undue strain on his damaged vocal cords. What kind of wisdom did Paul, as a father to three daughters, discover in that advice?

11. Rick asked Maddie, "What would change if you knew you might die today? Or next month? Or next year?" How would you respond to that question?

12. Did you catch the connection between Maddie's client, Elizabeth, and the cardiologist who treated Rick at the hospital? What was their link?

Keep Reading for a

SNEAK PEEK
OF BOOK 3
in This Series!

One

It was a long way home. Blaine Grayson stood on the bow of the Never Late Ferry to fully appreciate this moment of coming home, breathing deeply of the salty ocean air, listening to the screech of the seagulls, the hum of the lobster boat engines as they came in from the day's catch. What was it about this crazy little island? Why did it always seem so far away from the rest of the world? Well, probably because it was.

Two years ago, Blaine had left Three Sisters Island to travel through Europe for a little while and find herself. Her dad thought she'd only last a few weeks, and during that entire first month in Paris, she worried he was right. The cost of living was exorbitant, even on the cheap. Broke, she'd maxed out her credit cards, had worn out her welcome at the apartment where she was couch-surfing, and had no idea what to do or where to go. But then a single magical moment occurred, and everything changed. Everything clicked into place. Meant to be.

In the blink of an eye, Blaine was enrolled as a student in the famous Le Cordon Bleu cooking school, studying French cuisine under world class chefs. She stayed there for two wonderful years, and she had actually finished something she started! Her dad and sisters were shocked. Blaine had received her diploma.

And here she was, two years later, returning to her family and the little island in Maine she had missed so terribly. Captain Ed had told her, with his usual economy of words, to expect change.

"Bah's gone."

"The sand bar? It's gone?"

He had nodded and stuck his pipe back in his mouth.

That bar, during low tide, was a link to the mainland. A lifeline. You could walk across it to Mount Desert Island, or even drive your car back and forth. If the tide was high, there was Captain Ed's ferry for passengers. If you were in a hurry, and wanted your car with you, and didn't mind a steep fee, he also had a car ferry.

As the ferry slowed to reverse its engine and ease into the slip, Blaine gazed at the little harbor, trying to assess changes. Boon Dock still looked about the same: a floating dock with fishing boats and rowboats lining the finger piers. Then she spotted another dock, fixed on piers, away from the harbor and its bar, in deeper water, with a sleek yacht tied to its piles. A *yacht*. On Three Sisters Island? And then something caught her eye and she blinked twice . . . and gasped. Far beyond the yacht, coming in from the ocean, an enormous cruise ship was slowly approaching. Her mouth dropped open. She turned to catch Captain Ed's eye—the one that wasn't in a permanent squint. He took his pipe out of his mouth and gave her a nod, as if to say, *Did I not tell you so, girlie?*

Her eyes moved toward Main Street, rising above Boon Dock, and she felt the first hitch in her gut. This was not the island she remembered. Gone was the look of an abandoned ghost town. The street—which Blaine remembered as cracked pavement, with grass growing in the middle of it—had been recently tarred. Black and shiny, with a crisp white line running down the middle. The business buildings that lined Main Street were no longer shuttered or boarded up or covered with flaking paint and rusting gutters. Tourists with big shopping bags milled up and down the sidewalk.

Her dad had kept her in the loop with changes made to Camp Kicking Moose, to the remodel of Moose Manor that absorbed most of his time. Her sister Cam told her, ad nauseum, about the self-sustaining energy that now powered the little island. Maddie told her about the growth of the church, and lots about her husband Rick, who was pastoring two more island start-up churches. Blaine had heard plenty of news from her family, but they didn't prepare her for *this* kind of change to Three Sisters Island. Prosperity.

Shouts and waves caught her attention. There on Boon Dock was Dad (so much more gray in his hair) and her nephew Cooper (so tall!) and Peg from the Lunch Counter (no change there, Blaine felt with a sweep of relief as she spotted Peg's bright purple headband), and her brothers-in-law Seth and Pastor Rick and . . . *oh my gosh*. Her two sisters!

Cam and Maddie waved and waved with one hand, the other pointing to their basketball bellies. Both! They hadn't told her *that* news, either! *Oh wow.* So much had changed, and was continuing to change. She should have realized change would come; after all, she was returning as a different person too.

As the ferry came to a stop, Blaine got choked up, bombarded by mixed feelings: joy at being home, sorrow at all she'd missed, a familiar and vague unsettledness about where she belonged in this expanding family.

But as she jumped onto the floating dock, she knew one thing for sure: she was not ever going to leave this island again. No matter what.

She stopped and turned to face the Never Late Ferry, to offer a smile. "Jean-Paul." She reached out to grasp his hand. "Take a deep breath. It's time to meet my family."

◈◈◈◈

It wasn't often that Paul Grayson felt blindsided, but his youngest daughter Blaine had a knack for it. Yes, she'd been gone two years, but the family had kept in touch with her. Regular Skypes and FaceTimes, emails and texts. Paul felt he knew Le Cordon Bleu so well that he could find his own way around the Parisian cooking school. Blaine told them all about the demanding instructors, how they liked to weed out inferior aspiring chefs with cruel tongue lashings, how often she cried after a disappointing dish.

After learning so much about Paris and the French from Blaine, Paul even felt familiar with the famous city. Each bridge over the Seine had its own personality, Blaine said, attracting a certain devotee. He knew about Blaine's quirky roommates; her internship in Zurich, Switzerland, under a crazy but brilliant chef; her weekend trips to other European cities. But he'd never heard a word about a French boyfriend. Jean-Paul something or other, a skinny fellow who looked like he needed to get outdoors more often. And she brought him all the way from Paris to Three Sisters Island to meet the family. Good grief. What did that mean?

Paul watched Blaine for a moment as she swirled Cooper around in a hug, exclaiming over how much he had changed. She was the tallest of his three girls, and Cooper had been a small boy. No longer. He was ten now, starting to spike, long limbs and a skinny middle. Blaine looked the same to him. Beautiful.

The boyfriend stood at a distance, watching Blaine twirl Cooper. One thing Paul couldn't deny, he didn't take his eyes off Blaine. Absolutely smitten.

302

"Paul Grayson?"

Paul spun around when he heard someone call his name. He tented his eyes to see an older man walk up the hill of Boon Dock. His stomach clenched as he recognized the man's gait. *Oh no. It couldn't be. Please don't tell me that's who I think it is.*

The man stopped a few yards away from the big cluster of Graysons, still absorbed in celebrating Blaine's arrival. They hadn't noticed the man. Paul separated himself from his family and walked toward him. "What brings you here?"

The man swept a hand toward the big group of Graysons. "Family. What else?"

He took his hat off and Paul could see how much he had aged. When had he seen him last? Ten years? Fifteen? Maybe longer.

"Well, son, aren't you going to introduce me to my grand-daughters?"

Acknowledgments

To Susie May Warren, who vividly described her skydiving experience to me during dinner at a book convention. Vividly.

To Laura Taggart, counselor extraordinaire, for her insights on therapy work, including the End Zone Run. Also, for my borrowing some concepts from her wonderful book, *Making Love Last*.

To Stacey Logan, one of my very favorite friends. One day, Stacey happened to meet Roger Federer. Normally, Stacey is a quiet, reserved person. But not when it comes to Roger Federer! She boldly asked him if they could be photographed together, and then whispered to him that she'd always loved him. I *love* that story. This is the danger of having a novelist as a friend! I filed Stacey's special moment away and pulled it out for Maddie Grayson and Rick O'Shea.

To Carolyn Kuemmeler, to whom belongs the port-a-potty story. Ugh. How horrifying!

To Meredith Munoz and Lindsey Ross, who read this book in chunks of chapters and gave me feedback that helped me plug holes and fix leaks. To Dylan Ross, for his help with the old, faulty underground cable that brought such spotty electricity to Three Sisters Island.

To my Revell team: Andrea Doering, Barb Barnes, Michele Misiak, Karen Steele, and so many others. Thank you for taking such care to make each book as good as it can possibly be. Andrea, I'm so grateful for your extra-special editor's touch on this one!

On a very personal note, I had worked on most of this book prior to the sudden passing of my oh-so-special sister, Wendy. With absolutely no warning, she died of a massive heart attack. Talk about a Jonah moment for me! It's astounding to think that the character of Rick O'Shea had been set on paper prior to my sister's death. His faith—truly resting in the sovereignty of God— ministered to me in a powerful way as I worked (and continue to work) through deep grief. I felt almost reluctant to finish the book and turn it in. Only the Lord could have orchestrated imagination to be used for his purposes. I am so grateful to him for doing so, and pray this book's message might minister to you too.

Suzanne Woods Fisher is an award-winning, bestselling author of more than thirty books, including *Mending Fences* and *Stitches in Time*, as well as the Nantucket Legacy, Amish Beginnings, The Bishop's Family, and The Inn at Eagle Hill series, among other novels. She is also the author of several nonfiction books about the Amish, including *Amish Peace* and *Amish Proverbs*. She lives in California. Learn more at www.suzannewoodsfisher.com and follow Suzanne on Facebook @SuzanneWoodsFisherAuthor and Twitter @suzannewfisher.

"An enduring tale of love and restoration."

—Denise Hunter, bestselling author
of *On Magnolia Lane*

When her father buys an island off the coast of Maine with the hope of breathing new life into it, Camden Grayson thinks he's lost his mind. An unexpected event sends Cam to his rescue, and she discovers the island has its own way of living and loving.

"There's just something unique and fresh about every Suzanne Woods Fisher book. Whatever the reason, I'm a fan."

—SHELLEY SHEPHARD GRAY,
New York Times and *USA Today* bestselling author

DON'T MISS ANY OF
THE BISHOP'S FAMILY

"Suzanne is an authority on the Plain folks. . . .
She always delivers a fantastic story with
interesting characters, all in a tightly woven plot."

—BETH WISEMAN, bestselling author
of the DAUGHTERS OF THE PROMISE and the LAND OF CANAAN series

Ꝗ Revell
a division of Baker Publishing Group
www.RevellBooks.com

MEET SUZANNE

www.SuzanneWoodsFisher.com